A
FATAL
RECEPTION

A
FATAL
RECEPTION

AN ELLA SHANE MYSTERY

KATHLEEN MARPLE KALB

For Edith Meininger: psychologist, wife, mother, grandmother, and generally amazing human. My husband's aunt, and my inspiration.

Praise for the Ella Shane Mysteries

"Kalb writes with vivid assurance. Her stories are well paced and well layered. Ella's matrix – the characters who surround her—are as interesting and flawed yet human as she is herself., as is the theatrical setting…This book is by a woman who knows how to tell a story."—Aunt Agatha's Mysteries on *A Fatal First Night*

"This series is truly one of my favorite cozy-mystery series! I love the mix of opera, history, romance, and mystery…and I find each book impossible to put down!"—Goodreads reviewer Ashley

"What can I say? It was fabulous! A story of love and companionship, with a soupçon of murder and a mysterious warning about weddings. Set in the early twentieth century, join Ella, Gill, Tommy, their friends and family for another mad adventure. Marple Kalb has a knack for combining humour, mystery, angst and romance in just the right proportions to keep you on the edge of your seat. In this tale, Ella, the American Opera Diva, and Gil, the British Duke, are finally heading for wedded bliss after a courtship that has been fraught with roadblocks. So you would think their final weeks before becoming man and wife would be smooth sailing. Think again. One complication after another, including a murder, demands the Diva and Duke's attention. Then, when a case of nerves hits the couple, you have to wonder if they will even make it to the altar, or will it be the wedding of the season? I couldn't put this book down. You must read this book if you enjoy a cosy mystery that will also tug at your heartstrings. Bravo, Kathleen!"—Wendy Bayne, author of the Crimes Against the Crown series

"Another wonderful addition to the Ella Shane Mysteries. A Fatal Reception follows Ella and Gil as they prepare for marriage. The story quickly immerses you in Ella's life as though you never left. As we're swept up in wedding prep a murder occurs. Is the death of Mr. Chester Lorimer all it seems or is there more to it? I loved all the characters and the addition of Gil's son, Jamie. They're like meeting up with old friends. The description is simply wonderful and I felt as though I was beside Ella and her Duke the entire story. With lots of ups and downs, this book is sure to hook you!"—Elizabeth Holland, author of the Vintage Dress Shop Romance series

"A delight! Opera diva Ella Shane is about to wed her very own wicked duke. But the nuptial plans go awry when a society matron brains a fellow patron of the arts. Written with great charm and wit, this lively, entertaining romp through Gilded Age New York will have you eagerly awaiting Ella Shane's next adventure."—Mariah Fredericks, author of *The Wharton Plot*

Chapter One

The Metropolitan Opera Welcomes Miss Ella Shane

My Metropolitan Opera debut was all that one could hope for, if one could overlook the violent end to the reception afterwards. And of an august guest.

Having signed with the Met for one production a year, and signed my marriage contract with Gilbert Saint Aubyn, Duke of Leith, ahead of our planned wedding in the middle of June, I was now well into a very busy summer. The production was *Xerxes* to open the fall season, but all sides agreed that a special gala recital night a few weeks before the wedding would be an appropriate welcome for a star of my caliber, not to mention an admirable distraction from the fluff and furbelows of nuptial preparations.

We had no idea how much distraction we would need.

The performance itself was a delight. Two of my favorite singing partners joined in: soprano Marie de l'Artois and basso Ruben Avila, back in New York for the moment after a triumphant run in Paris. Louis Abramovitz, formerly my accompanist, now making a name for himself as the composer of *The Princes in the Tower*, played piano. He did not conduct, since the Met's own conductor had rights to such a night, though Louis is better, a fact I kept to myself.

His lyricist wife Anna, who had been my costumer and dresser for years before they became a sensation with the *Princes*, had been kind enough to make me a gloriously beautiful lilac chiffon gown sprinkled with tiny sequins that made me look like a fairy princess, a major change from my usual breeches and doublets. But even a woman who sings male roles appears as her own feminine self at a recital.

It was, I suppose, a little taste of what I might expect on my wedding day, when I would wear another lovely creation from Anna, this one white, of course, not to mention a crown of orange blossoms in my hair that would be replaced by the Leith coronet after the ceremony.

Dizzying stuff when I thought about it, so I usually didn't. But yes, I, Ellen O'Shaughnessy, Irish-Jewish Lower East Side orphan, would soon accomplish every melodramatic maiden's dream and marry a Wicked Duke. Not that he was especially wicked, or even particularly ducal, most of the time. Which was why I was marrying him, after all.

That and the fact that I loved him more than I ever imagined it possible to love anyone. The intensity of my feelings terrified me. And rightly so. Even in our new century, a woman is risking everything she has accomplished in her life when she consents to marry, since she legally becomes her husband's property.

Unless, of course, she's marrying a man who doesn't want to own her and signs a contract that lets her keep her rights, as mine did. Even a New Woman has to love a man who wants to stand beside—or even occasionally behind—her.

At the moment, though, I was still, as the expression goes, a solo act. Gil, as his mother and aunts, and I address my fiancé, had just started his steamer voyage from London, having had a few estate and family matters to settle before the wedding. He sent a telegram and a bouquet of lilacs to my dressing room, and I promised myself I would wear this sweet gown for him one night soon, though he would probably be just as happy with me in a fencing outfit.

After the performance, Rosa Benedict, my lady's maid and dresser when she wasn't reading or writing, helped me quickly neaten myself a bit, trading the heavy stage makeup for my usual rose-petal lip-salve and fussing a bit with my wavy reddish blonde hair, before I went directly to the reception. Unlike a normal performance night, I had no need to greet well-wishers in my dressing room, since the debut celebration was part of the event.

Just as well, since all but a few select family members and close friends were strongly discouraged from visiting backstage after a terrible incident with an unbalanced admirer in the winter. Fortunately, everyone had escaped the theatre he had burned, and it was well into rebuilding; New York never slows. As for the madman, he was safely tucked away in a posh mental hospital upstate, and good for him, because any number of men, not all of them mine, would have been happy for his blood.

The damage was a bit greater for us.

I had a healing scar on my ribcage from the knife that had been meant for Gil's heart. And though Gil and I were indeed heading joyfully for the altar, he was still treating me like a breakable glass object. Precious and adored to be sure, but not a real woman to be *loved*. I was still nursing the admittedly unrealistic hope that a wedding ring might change that.

Dwelling on those concerns would do nothing to add to anyone's enjoyment of this debut night, however, and I resolutely turned my mind to that.

"Perfect, miss," Rosa said with a smile.

"I'll do. Anna is a true artist."

"Surely."

"The stage manager has called you a hansom, right?"

She grinned. "I have a cab and I'm going back to the house if I might."

"Of course." I returned the smile. Rosa often holed up in her little ladies' maid's workroom after a late night, because it gave her an escape from a busy flat full of siblings and parents.

"I even have a new library book."

"Lovely."

"So lovely."

"I don't want to see you working before three at least tomorrow—and only for a couple of hours, all right?"

"Thank you, miss."

"No point in sitting around waiting for me when I'm sleeping off a late night. You may as well get some rest, too."

"I might." Rosa giggled. "But Miss O'Hanlon is making divinity fudge tomorrow morning, since we both went to Saturday Mass."

"Do what you like, then."

We exchanged a happy smile. Our new cook, Mary O'Hanlon, was a confectionery artist among her other talents and young enough to be a good friend and probably partner-in-crime with Rosa. I had no need to know what capers those two sweet maidens got themselves into on their own time and hoped I never would. They usually went to the late-afternoon Mass at Holy Innocents on Saturday to allow for a bit of sleeping late on Sunday while still meeting their religious obligation and family expectations.

Tommy knocked on the door. "Time to go, Heller."

I opened the door and met my cousin's grin with my own. My coming marriage brought no change in Tommy Hurley's place as my manager and best friend; we had been looking out for each other since we were children in the tenements and always would. It's rather amazing to realize that we'd both gone from the Lower East Side to the heights of success, me as a singer, him as a boxing champion, before he decided he was both happier and safer in my world.

I took Tommy's arm, and we stepped into the hall to find his dear friend Cabot Bridgewater waiting. Cabot began as a friend to us both, but he and Tommy have grown closer in recent months, working together on reading groups for poor children at the Bridgewater family libraries. Beyond good works, they simply spend a fair amount of time together, sharing interests in books, sports, and making the world better.

Cabot and Tommy had also come very close to disaster in those terrible winter days, and even when the danger was over, it was not at all clear that they would remain friends. At one point, Tommy believed that Cabot was the only person who might have had a chance to stop the madman, though it was an entirely unfair view, considering Cabot's danger had been at least as grave as mine.

But Tommy and I are precious to each other, and he initially blamed Cabot for his brush with losing me. The very fact that they did manage to stay friends tells me how important they are to each other. I'm glad of that, especially since I spend so much time with Gil when he's about.

Tommy isn't the marrying kind, but that does not mean he should be lonely.

"Lovelier than ever, Miss Ella," Cabot said as he bowed.

They were quite nice to look at themselves: both tall and elegant in black tie, Tommy with the muscles and dangerous air that lingered from his fighting years, his sharp Celtic features set off by dark-auburn hair; Cabot the classic blond, blue-eyed Knickerbocker, with an appealing boyish smile.

"You'll do, Heller." Tommy teased. "You might want to wear that one for the Barrister."

He, and most of our friends, generally refer to Gil by the profession he chose and trained for, not the title he acceded to, and Gil much prefers it, for any number of good reasons. Chief among them the fact that he's an unpretentious North-of-England man with little love for aristocratic fripperies.

"I planned to."

"When does your beloved arrive?" Cabot asked.

"His steamer—the *Atlantic Star*—left a few days ago…so likely Monday or Tuesday."

"I'll be delighted to see him. Perhaps you two and his mother, of course, if she likes, would join Tom in coming to a small dinner party at my home before the wedding?"

"We would love that." A small dinner party at Cabot's meant close to two dozen people around a giant table, but it was good training for a future duchess. Tommy would tolerate it for Cabot's sake.

"And my great-aunt wants to host you for tea after the honeymoon." Cabot shook his head. "You know the matriarchs."

"Oh, yes." I merely nodded. I surely did know the matriarchs, though Great-Aunt Cecily Bridgewater was apparently an order of magnitude more so, being a good twenty years older and correspondingly ornerier than the feisty dowagers of my acquaintance.

Tommy's eyes took on a teasing gleam. "Go ahead, tell him about the honeymoon."

I blushed. "Niagara Falls."

Cabot shook his head. "No."

"Gil- His Grace thinks it would be amusing to observe the scene and rather awe-inspiring to see the falls."

"The Barrister has a finely tuned sense of irony," Tommy said. "And I'm told the scenery really is magnificent."

We all smiled at that.

"I shall at least get a few new pieces for my postcard collection," I said, attempting to pull the conversation away from romantic matters.

"My darlings! How wonderful you were, Ella!" Speaking of matriarchs. Flora, Dowager Countess of Blyth, and soon to be my mother-in-law, descended upon us in a flutter of pearl-gray silk gauze, crystal beads, and plumes as we moved toward the stage door.

She had rather firmly taken charge of wedding planning, with welcome assistance from my Aunt Ellen, Tommy's mother, and was happily stage-managing the event...and our lives in general in the run-up to it. Thankfully, her two sisters had decided they had too many family matters to consider at home to return for the ceremony, not to mention being at least mildly unwelcome in New York in the aftermath of an unpleasant incident at the Waverly Place Hotel.

The Dowager Countess, however, had no interest whatsoever in whether the local authorities welcomed her presence. No power on Earth would prevent her from seeing her son properly and joyfully wed.

While everyone favored a simple and private ceremony to a society splash, it was still the wedding of a duke and a diva, and inevitably rather a thing. And of course, there was also the trousseau, since a duchess required somewhat different costuming. The countess had thrown herself into all of it with glee, consulting with Anna on outfits, plotting refreshments with Miss O'Hanlon, and tutting with my Aunt Ellen over where to place everyone during the ceremony at the Washington Square townhouse.

Many might find Countess Flora's affectionate interference annoying, but having buried my mother as a child, and being a rather mature bride, I was able to brush off the worst of it and thoroughly enjoy the love and caring that drove her efforts. We got along just fine.

The Dowager Countess soundly hugged us each in turn; since the engagement, she had happily adopted me as another daughter, and just as naturally added Tommy and Cabot to her nest as additional chicks deserving of affection and concern. Aunt Ellen, Tommy's mother, finds this adorable because the countess has also thoroughly embraced her; they gossip about all of us and our various doings over tea as if we were misbehaving seven-year-olds.

Perhaps to them, we are.

"Come along, children," urged the Countess. "It doesn't do to be tardy, even if you are the guest of honor."

Soon enough, we would all wish we'd had other plans that night.

Chapter Two

Frivolity and Fatality

The cab ride was quick and convivial as we discussed the finer points of the evening's performances. The orchestra and my partners had, of course, been brilliant. My reviews were mostly good, too, though the Countess pointed out that I had slightly rushed an embellishment in one aria and suggested I work on it with Louis at our next session. Tommy and Cabot swallowed their grins, and so did I. Those she loves, the Countess "encourages."

We had little time for encouragement just then, because before I knew it, we were at the reception. And an astonishing surprise. In a career spanning the better part of two decades, I had received my fair share of acclaim, but I had never entered a party to applause as I did that night.

Humbling for a poor girl made good, and I suspect not nearly as much for me as for what I would soon be. Our title-mad society would not want to miss the opportunity to curry favor with a future duchess.

Even if the duke in question was a Northerner who would rather spend his time on criminology and legal arguments than waltzes and ices, he was still near the top of the aristocratic heap. Meaning, as was beginning to dawn on me in these social engagements ahead of the wedding, that I was no longer merely a performer dependent on the goodwill of patrons. I, of course, would never give an audience less than my best. But in my new social position, I would be well beyond the snobbish matrons who had so enjoyed looking down on me.

I thought of this as I greeted the glittering patronesses of the Met and their men.

More than greeting the patronesses, though, I was glad to enjoy the evening with my friends and family. Once I had made the circle, accepting good wishes and exchanging vacuous pleasantries as one must, I happily adjourned to the performers' corner near the door to the garden. One of the large glass-paned doors was open, allowing a refreshing night breeze into the warm room. My crowd, however, had not chosen the space for comfort nearly as much as refuge from the glitter and condescension.

We made a happy and unpretentious island in that sea of plumes, jewels, and archly deployed bad French.

The Countess was still doing the circle and appeared to be taking a fair amount of pleasure in it. Or at least in studying the customs of the robber barons and their ladies, which were so much more precious than her own genuinely aristocratic milieu. As best I could tell, Gil and his clan were far more like Cabot and a few old Boston families I had met over the years: almost entirely unconcerned with status and possessions (because they had more than sufficient quantities of both) and very concerned indeed with character and "knowing how to behave."

That last had little to do with the correct fork, or how to address a marchioness, incidentally, and everything to do with maintaining a certain graceful demeanor at all times, no matter how trying. Much like what a good diva is trained to do.

The Countess appeared to be greatly enjoying her education in the pretensions of the Colonies. She shot me a deeply amused glance as a beer heiress who had always been rude to me dropped an entirely unnecessary curtsy and wrongly called her "Your Grace."

I, soon to be an actual Grace, was more than happy to hide with my fellows for a time. Especially since so many of my favorites were here tonight. The Met patrons had been unusually generous with company tickets and reception invites, and our friends had taken advantage, not because they wanted a fancy night out, but because we all enjoyed being together.

Preston Dare, dean of the sports writing corps and informal uncle to Tommy and me, had brought his wife of a few months, Greta, a vision in peachy-pink crepe. It was not their first major social outing together, but they still had that adorable newlywed solicitousness, carefully tending to each other and exchanging loving glances.

My partner in the *Princes*, Marie de l'Artois, and her husband, lawyer and newly appointed civil court judge Paul Winslow, were long wed and parents to three wee ones, but they still shared the loving glances. By now, though, Paul knew exactly which chair and drink she would favor, and he relaxed behind her with his own glass. They were a most handsome couple, she small, and silvery-blonde with a magical smile, he tall, dark, and serious. Tonight, she was fairy-princess lovely in soft pale-blue charmeuse trimmed with tiny iridescent beads, reflecting light with her every move.

Ruben was with his mother, Susanna Avila, regal in a simple but elegant garnet silk that could only have come from their Paris stand. It was easy to tell where he'd gotten his darkly handsome looks. Also, his good manners, as he stood by her chair, settling her in with a plate and punch glass.

The punch and the buffet, as I had discovered on my way to my dear friends, were nowhere near the standard Greta Grazich, now Dare, had set and Mary O'Hanlon did her best to meet at our home, but they were not the point, after all.

After taking a moment to hug and greet Mrs. Avila, whom I hadn't seen since the New York run of the *Princes*, I settled in between Marie and Greta, taking a sip of the very pink punch, which had a faintly floral aroma and a strangely sour taste.

They both laughed at my expression.

"I do not know what the recipe is," Greta noted, "but I do not approve."

"The missus here is thinking about launching a catering business," Preston said. "So she's critiquing everyone else's efforts."

"Well, there's much to critique here," Marie agreed, casting a rather mournful eye on her plate of canapes.

"I believe I might do far better for a few select clients on occasion." Greta gave Preston a shy smile. "I dearly love cooking for my man, of course."

"But he doesn't expect you to sit patiently at home all day and night waiting for his return." Preston returned the smile. "A small business, for a few select clients, might be precisely the right balance."

"A woman needs something of her own," Mrs. Avila said it quietly, but with force.

"We'll keep you busy," I said, looking to Marie, whose social calendar was expanding along with Paul's elevation to the bench.

"We surely will. My Coralie would thank God fasting if I could spare her from another reception for the bar."

I joined in. "I was concerned about overwhelming our new Miss O'Hanlon with a celebration when we return from the honeymoon..."

"Oh, all right, ladies." Greta blushed a bit and smiled. "I will practice on you this summer. If my husband approves."

"As long as you test out all of the treats with me first."

They exchanged happy grins.

"To your new business, then." I raised my glass.

Tommy and Cabot had been greeting Ruben and turned to us just then.

"What are we celebrating?" Toms asked, even as he lifted his glass.

"Greta here is starting a small catering business," Preston said, bowing a bit to his radiant spouse.

Cabot beamed. "Oh, that is truly wonderful news. May I call you about a dinner party soon?"

"Certainly."

"Excellent." He joined the toast, and we all drank, Ruben and his mother adding their congratulations.

We had just returned to amiable conversation, catching up on our various busy lives, when we heard the scream from the garden.

"Help!" A truly bloodcurdling wail. "Help! Oh, help me!"

Swashbuckler that I am, even in my elegant evening attire, I was faster than the rest, and I ran out with the men on my heels, all of them trying to slow me down or get in front of me. I knew they were afraid I would be hurt again, and I did moderate my pace enough that Tommy and Cabot were within arm's length before we reached the scene of the yelling. I, too, had no desire to repeat the horrors of February.

This time, however, none of *us* was in danger.

The same could not be said for the formerly magisterial gentleman sprawled on the ground, blood pouring from his forehead onto the buff brick of the path. He was clearly insensible, in a limp, strangely-angled heap, apparently in the place where he fell, a fine gold-headed ebony cane a few inches from his hand.

It certainly looked as if he'd landed at the feet of the woman who'd sent him there. Aline Corbyn, society matron *par excellence*, stood over him, plump face grayish in the moonlight, golden hair mussed, her gown, an extravaganza of *eau de nil* charmeuse, lace and crystals, badly ripped. I'd admired it earlier, taking note of the lovely crystal embroidery on the lace flowing from the shoulders down the *décolleté* like a waterfall. Now, the frill from the left shoulder was ripped loose, hanging in the froth at the front like an extra wave.

If we were not entirely clear on what happened, the bloody rock in her right hand might have offered a clue.

When she saw us, she stopped screaming, dropped the rock, and abruptly began sobbing, almost as if she were changing the setting on a metronome.

"He—" she gasped. "He—was trying to—"

She fluttered her hands for a moment and flung herself into my arms.

It was one of the least welcome embraces I have ever received.

It was also the second time in recent months that an apparent killer had thrown themselves at me for consolation. I wondered if there was something about me that suggested I would offer appropriate comfort after homicide.

In any case, she was now in my charge, so I patted her back and muttered something soothing but neutral, even as I sent an imploring glance to Tommy over her head.

"I'll go call the police," Ruben offered. "I imagine you gents would like to stay with Miss Ella."

Miss Ella would have been happy to stay anywhere else.

Chapter Three

Another Shocking Turn

Within perhaps five minutes, the first uniformed officers had arrived. It took some time longer for the arrival of the detectives and the matron required for Mrs. Corbyn.

By that time, I was well out of the play.

As the garden filled with distressed spectators, the Countess swept in, took one look at me and Mrs. Corbyn, and snapped:

"Let go of dear Ella at once!"

Stunned by the command tone, Mrs. Corbyn backed off and stood there staring at her for a measure or two, her ample and bejeweled bosom still heaving, her hands flapping once more.

"But I—I—"

"Stop that whingeing, now," continued my dragon protector. "You are not helping anyone, least of all yourself."

"It's all right," I started soothingly. "She's quite distraught…"

"As well she should be," conceded the Countess. "That does not mean she has the right to cause you an upset after all you've suffered in recent months."

She very calmly took my arm and motioned to our men. "Dear Ella will be indoors having a medicinal sherry. I suggest we all do the same."

We had our orders, and so our entire company returned to our pleasant corner by the window. Most of us were more or less versed in the ways of law enforcement and well aware that we would be forced to stay here until we talked to the police. But at least we had good company whilst waiting to be interrogated.

The sherry was mediocre, but the conversation, as it always is among our circle, was superlative. First, we established the identity of the unfortunate victim: Mr. Chester Lorimer, a dry-goods magnate who had made his fortune just after the Civil War.

I knew him slightly from various society musicales and considered him somewhat kinder and more polite than many of men who attended such things; he had never looked at me with anything other than respect, nor even attempted any of the "accidental" grabbings that some alleged gentlemen considered their right. Our society expert, the Knickerbocker Cabot, was able to contribute that he had been widowed for years, with two sons, both grown, one married.

Which did indeed bring us to Mrs. Corbyn. I vaguely remembered that one of her three daughters, but not the youngest she had thrown at Gil's head early in our acquaintance, had married into the Lorimer clan. Cabot confirmed that, only adding to our confusion. Why on earth would one brain an in-law at an opera reception? Or make an outrageous advance to get oneself brained?

Surely, it would make more sense to attack one's family at home.

At least, that was how it was done in our part of town. Perhaps not in the mansions of Fifth Avenue.

Having established the players and found no obvious answers by doing so, we moved on to more pleasurable topics...of course, in suitably subdued tones. The countess asked Preston about a column he'd written on the latest controversy in the boxing world, sparking a quietly animated dialogue that would have kept us going until morning. Unfortunately, we were not left to enjoy it.

"Miss Ella, a word?"

Before us stood Grover Duquesne, Captain of Industry, until the theatre fire, the worst of my stage-door Lotharios, a ranking sadly re-evaluated in the wake of our brush with disaster.

The gentlemen all tensed protectively, even Ruben, who had no reason to consider himself my defender. The countess narrowed her eyes and sat a bit straighter, now at least as terrifying as the men.

"I mean no insult. I was terribly sad to hear what happened to you all in February, and I'm sorry I didn't see how unbalanced that fellow had become."

My eyes widened a little. The Captain of Industry, who'd waged a years-long campaign to make me his mistress, repeatedly insulted me in the presence of the man I intended to marry and finally stormed away in a fury, was *apologizing*?

"He clearly didn't understand the difference between flirting and good fun and something more serious. Terrible thing."

I would never have described the Captain of Industry's treatment of me as good fun, but perhaps he saw it differently. Perhaps if one were stone blind, deaf as the dead, and completely lacking in sensibilities.

"Um, yes," I said finally. "Terrible."

"In any case, perhaps you and your friends in law enforcement might take an interest in tonight's matter?"

"Why?" Tommy asked.

"I'm quite certain Chester would never have attempted to assault Mrs. Corbyn."

"Oh?" Tommy was not moved.

"He, well, couldn't." The Captain of Industry's face turned red, and he glanced at me, then leaned over to Tommy, trying for a whisper and failing rather impressively. "Old war wound."

All of the men winced as one. The Countess simply pursed her lips. Greta and Susanna Avila pretended they had heard nothing, making them far better actresses than the actual lady performers among us. Marie and I stared, and I found myself fighting a terribly inappropriate giggle. Though a properly brought-up Irish-Jewish maiden lady, I am also a woman who plays roles once originated by castrati, so I had a rough idea of what he was getting at, even if not the precise details.

"So sorry, Miss Ella, ladies."

All right, he had changed a bit.

The four men gave grim little nods, almost in unison, accepting his appropriate embarrassment in the presence of respectable females.

"Happened in the last months before Appomattox," Duquesne said in a quiet tone I'd never heard before. "He never spoke of it—I only know because we were mustered out together."

Preston, who had been a drummer boy at Gettysburg, held his gaze. "Terrible time."

"Terrible."

They nodded together, men who'd seen horrors the rest of us could only imagine.

"So," I interposed, carefully giving them a subject change I suspected they dearly wanted, "that just might make one wonder what really happened here tonight."

"Precisely, Miss Ella."

Which is how we ended up being drawn into yet another misadventure just weeks before my long-awaited wedding.

What we could not know then was how glad we would be for it.

Chapter Four

A Grim Message

The next morning, I wandered downstairs well after breakfast, as is my habit on the day after a performance. Any show is exhausting, but such a night as we'd just endured was even more so. I had no compunction about sleeping well into the forenoon.

Especially since I expected no relaxation once awake.

In view of the previous night's events, I fully expected to find some representative of law enforcement in the parlor, so I put on a simple lilac shadow-stripe cotton house dress and pinned up my hair. I was not disappointed.

I was, however, rather surprised to discover that Cousin Andrew the Detective was the emissary from the constabulary. On two counts: he was from our local precinct, rather than that of the reception, and he was newly married. *Very* newly married.

Father Michael, Tommy's best friend and the lawman's cousin, hence the nickname by which everyone called Detective Riley, had united him and Miss Katie McTeer in holy matrimony just last week in a ceremony marked by great joy, much dancing, and wicked headaches among the gents the next morning. The good father was in the parlor along with Tommy and Cousin Andrew, the three of them enjoying cookies and coffee and laughing at some masculine jest.

I knew it was not suitable for the ladies by the way all three of them went quiet and scrambled to their feet the moment they saw me, looking like guilty little boys. Cousin Andrew certainly seemed almost small enough to be a boy, standing next to his cousin and mine, both of whom were well north of six feet, sturdy and powerful, in contrast to the slight, redheaded detective.

"Miss Ella!" Cousin Andrew recovered his demeanor and walked to the door to meet me. "Good to see you."

"And you." We shook hands. "Marriage certainly agrees with you."

"Thank you." He blushed, but his eyes were sharp. "I'm sure it will agree with you and your duke soon, too."

"Thank *you*." I returned his discerning look with one of my own. "You're not just here to wish us well, though, are you?"

"Sadly, no. I've been keeping Tom and Mike from their checkers match because I wanted to speak with you about the Lorimer matter."

"Certainly," I said. "Miss O'Hanlon has provided well for us, I see."

"My wife keeps me in cookies," the detective agreed, smiling at the new subject of his sentence, "but a copper always needs coffee."

"Don't we all." I sat on the settee and poured myself a cup, then turned to the priest as he sat beside me. "Good to see you."

"And you." Father Michael's blue eyes sparkled as he grinned and picked up a snickerdoodle. "No one at the rectory makes it their mission to keep *me* in cookies."

"Well, fortunately, you have us." We shared a smile.

"Very true."

The detective pulled us back to business. "So, as much as I would like to dwell on my marital felicity and congratulate you on your impending joy—I've been asked to handle some of the inquiries in the Lorimer case."

"Really?" Tommy asked.

"Apparently, I have a certain expertise with the opera and theatre community, so described, and my captain asked me to take a look." Cousin Andrew colored a bit. "I'm happy to do his bidding anytime, of course, but anything I can do to increase my chances of promotion these days..."

Smiles around the room. A promotion, of course, would be most welcome for a man who hoped to have a family soon.

"Well, what can we do, Andrew?" Tommy took another cookie and settled in, preparing for a long talk.

"You know many of the players, do you not?"

"I know only a little about Mr. Lorimer," I admitted. "But I'm rather familiar with Mrs. Corbyn and her ambitions."

"There are other folks who can help with Lorimer. I was hoping for insight into the woman and some of the other players on hand last night."

I took the pot and topped up everyone's cups. "Well, then, let's start with Mrs. Corbyn."

"Society matron?" Cousin Andrew asked.

"And how!" Tommy shook his head. "Heller has had a few run-ins over the years."

"How so?"

"I sang at her musicales occasionally, same as I do with plenty of other ladies."

"Done with that now, right?" The detective smiled.

"Mostly," I agreed. This was one concession to my new position I was happy to make; a duchess really could not be expected to serve as the entertainment at another hostess' home, and I'd always hated singing for my lukewarm tea at those pretentious little functions anyhow. "And glad for it."

Tommy's brow quirked.

Cousin Andrew knew what that meant. "Was she mean to you?"

"Not mean, exactly. A bit less than the usual condescension, actually, most of the time."

"Until," Tommy cut in darkly, "the Barrister came to town."

Father Michael did not know this part of the story either and his gaze sharpened on me, exactly as his cousin's did.

I took a sip of coffee. "Well, it was meant to be the standard Dollar Princess saga. Mrs. Corbyn had one more, nicely-dowered daughter left and she hoped His Grace might be taken with her."

"Except, of course, that Heller had already won him." Tommy grinned.

"Well, we had certainly made a congenial acquaintance by that point," I admitted. "And she attempted to convince me that His Grace could not possibly have honorable intentions toward me."

Tommy scowled. "More than that. She was poison mean to Heller and even dropped a gossip item in the papers suggesting that the Barrister was in town courting her daughter."

"Sounds like an unpleasant lady."

"Not always," I shook my head. "We've essentially mended fences since my engagement. I doubt my opinion of her matters anyway."

"We don't know what matters yet." The detective shrugged. "Just trying to get a sense of the woman. Can you trust her word? Would she have any reason to attack Lorimer?"

"What, you don't believe she's a poor, outraged victim?" Tommy asked, his sharp tone drawing a glare from the priest.

"Certainly, it looks that way," Cousin Andrew said coolly.

And certainly, we all knew the detective did not readily accept what he saw…without plenty of proof.

"You're right to be suspicious, Andrew." Tommy's tone was still steely. "In general, I really don't believe women make up accusations like that."

I nodded. "It's so difficult to talk about these matters at all, and harder still to get any justice."

"Exactly." The priest shook his head. "And women know that if they lie, it will be harder for the next woman to be believed…which most would not wish on anyone."

We were all quiet, grim, for a moment.

"But," Tommy continued, "Mrs. Corbyn is exactly the sort of woman who might not care about what she's doing to her sisters by making up an accusation to save her neck."

"And there's also what Mr. Duquesne told us," I added, looking to Tommy.

Cousin Andrew looked to me.

A huge and terrible blush crept over my face as I realized that I could not possibly repeat what the Captain of Industry had said to a man. It was quite bad enough that I had *heard* it in mixed company.

Even worse, that I had foolishly brought it up. Oh, dear.

"Well, Andrew," Tommy said, clearing his throat. "I'll tell you when I walk you out. It's a rather delicate thing."

The priest glanced between us all. "Delicate?"

"Yes," I said, clearing my throat and recovering some level of demeanor. "Better discussed among men."

"Well, all right." Cousin Andrew's eyes widened at the thought that I, New Woman I am, believed there was anything so sensitive as to be a male-only matter. "What else can you tell me about Mrs. Corbyn?"

"Very ambitious," I said, taking another sip of my coffee as my blush receded. "And the whole thing is really quite odd, since they're in-laws."

"In-laws?" the detective asked. "I was told they were related—but I didn't realize so closely."

I nodded. "Her daughter is married to his son. I don't know much more than that."

"I think I'd best find out."

I picked up the plate of cookies. "Have another snickerdoodle first, and tell us how Mrs. Riley is doing."

Our copper's serious face gave way to a boyish, joyful smile. "Marriage is wonderful. I know men go on about having an angel in the house and all that, but I really do feel like I'm coming home to my own personal heaven when I walk in and find her there."

"She's happy too, I assume." Tommy took a cookie, too.

"I saw her at Mass Sunday," Father Michael put in, taking his cookie. "At least as joyful as the detective here."

"Exactly what we like to hear." I decided against a cookie, since I had to fit into that lovely white gown very soon.

I was adding a bit more to my coffee cup when a worried and uncomfortable Sophia ran in from the foyer. "Miss! A visitor."

I wondered what imposing arrival could cause such concern and nearly laughed when I saw who it was: just one of the young copyboys from the *Beacon*. But he did look nervous, and I wondered if Sophia had taken her cue from him.

"What's wrong, son?" Tommy asked in a kind tone intended to set the boy at ease.

"Mr. Dare sent me. Said he didn't think Miss Shane should find out from the special edition."

"Special edition?" I asked, feeling the edges of the world start to slip under me.

"Find out what?" Tommy's gaze sharpened.

"There's been an accident at sea, miss. A freighter and a steamer."

"What steamer?" the priest asked.

"One from England. The *Atlantic Star.*"

"Any word on-" I started, trying to keep my voice and the rest of myself steady.

"No word on casualties, miss. Too early to know."

"Thank you." I managed to say it carefully to the young man and nod to Tommy, who gave him a generous tip, before I walked through the pocket doors into the quiet drawing room.

Tommy and the others followed me.

"Heller?"

"Someone—someone needs to tell the Countess." I took a breath. "I will."

"Heller-"

"It's all right." My voice was shockingly calm. "We don't know anything yet. I will talk to the Countess, and then we'll get back to our conversation about Chester Lorimer."

Father Michael and Tommy exchanged glances.

"It will hold, Miss Ella." Cousin Andrew patted my arm awkwardly. "I'll see you all later."

"I'll be back in a few minutes," I said, grateful to have a few seconds to myself on the stairs.

The Countess, who had been reading in her window seat, was every bit as calm as I was, absorbing the news with the same careful, quiet replies as I did. So, I knew exactly what it meant. She felt the same as I did...only far worse. It was, after all, only my fiancé. It was her son.

Unimaginable.

For a measure or so, we stared at each other in silence.

Then she set her book down. "Well, my dear, we are not going to know anything for some time. We had best find something to occupy ourselves."

"True."

"Could I interest you in a trip to the Natural History Museum? I believe a good look at the giant preserved millipedes might be just the thing."

"Millipedes?" I asked weakly.

She nodded. "When one is exercised in mind, it is helpful to contemplate something amazingly disturbing and entirely foreign. During my husband's last illness, I spent an inordinate amount of time at the Zoological Garden observing the dragon lizards."

Dragon lizards and giant millipedes?

An entirely different kind of unimaginable.

I shrugged. I certainly had no better idea for filling the hours until we got word…and there was just the chance that the giant millipedes might help. Or at least give me different nightmares than the ones I had been anticipating.

That was enough for me.

Chapter Five

In Which We Find Unexpected Consolation

During those awful days of waiting, the house was full most of the time, with friends and family coming to offer whatever comfort or distraction they could. By the time Tommy, the Countess, and I returned from the Museum (Father Michael could not be convinced to look at giant millipedes, even for the sake of our peace of mind), the visitations and offerings had already commenced.

So had the first reports from the sea, with word of two crewmen lost in the collision. Nothing was said of passengers, and we clung to that, because surely if they knew crewmen were lost, they would know about passengers.

In the meantime, we had visitors.

The earliest were the dearest and most welcome.

Greta Dare brought a huge plate of meringue kisses and made excellent tea as only she knew how. Her husband gave me a pat on the arm, a kiss on the forehead and the first of what would be hundreds of promises of "It will be all right, kid," only to blast right back out the door.

Preston had decided the best thing he could do was camp out at the *Beacon's* wires, and this he did, calling when there was even a scrap of new information. By afternoon, our poor phone had seen more use than it had since we got it.

Aunt Ellen dropped off a sizable pot of barley vegetable soup "to keep our strength up" and swept away to make a novena with Aunt MaryKat, who fortunately sent only her good wishes and not her terrifying soda bread. Aunt Ellen also assured me that the second sight had told her Gil was safe.

I did not believe, but I hoped.

I remember very little of that first night other than Tommy and the Countess handing me a generous glass of brandy sometime around midnight and pushing me up the stairs.

By the next morning, the visitations proceeded apace. Mack McTeer, my little protegee and not incidentally younger sister of Cousin Andrew's new wife Katie, brought bread from the McTeer family bakery and a scientific magazine with an article about women chemists she thought I would enjoy. I didn't have the concentration to read the article, and I certainly wasn't hungry, but I was warmed by her sweet concern, and more by her cheerful presence.

Cabot appeared as Mack was leaving, still only about ten o'clock, insanely early for him, with flowers and a picture book on Niagara Falls, confidently assuring me that Gil and I would soon see it together in person.

I seconded that, welcomed, thanked, and refreshed all our well-meaning visitors, answered notes and telegrams, even the ones that expressed oblivious good wishes for the impending (still impending, please God!) wedding, and generally occupied myself playing the good hostess. It gave me something to do, and the whirl kept me so busy I was unable to answer anyone's well-meaning questions.

Hetty MacNaughten, crack investigative reporter for the *Beacon* and my best friend outside the opera world, came over on her way to work that second day.

"Honestly, doesn't that man understand that he's supposed to stay out of trouble until the wedding?"

"Clearly not." I managed a chuckle as we embraced.

Hetty, at least, was looking better than ever, her usual simple gray serge suit finished with a soft and frilly shirtwaist in a pale peachy tint that set off her creamy skin and copper hair. The color and the embellishment were a definite step away from her usual simple and severe white broadcloth, and a declaration to anyone who knew...and I did.

"You're looking quite well."

My comment was an observation of fact, not an arch comment on her private life, but she blushed nonetheless. "Well, I didn't think Rowan should get the plain reporter at our coffee this morning…"

"Coffee?" I was of course happy for her, and the distraction as well. Her beau, Rowan Alteiss, is a top defense lawyer. She was briefly his client, during the misadventure involving Gil's mother and aunts, and they've since begun a much happier connection.

"He had an hour or so before court, so we managed a little chat at the coffee shop."

I smiled at her joyful face. Rowan had spent most of his adult life concentrating on his work, whether studying hard to win scholarships for college and law, or later working long hours on difficult cases, and he had apparently never found a woman he wanted to court. Until Hetty. And he was simply head-over-heels.

If anyone deserved an adoring swain, it was Hetty. One of exactly two women reporters at the *Beacon*, she was often relegated to hats and handbags despite impressive investigative skills and a wickedly good sense for a crime story. Her love of her work had put off one colleague who might possibly have made a good companion, sports writer Yardley Stern, who could not bend on his demand for an Angel in the House.

Fortunately, the defender discovered far more than professional feelings for his client right about then. Unfortunately, Hetty had a few other things to do. After a few brief and sweet walks in the park, Rowan spent most of the spring mooning about the post office and newsstand, following every development in her latest reporting stunt: driving from New York to Chicago in a motorcar. I'd been in London for the run of the *Princes* while she was on the road, so I had kept up the same way: colorful letters and her wonderful stories in the paper.

Now, everyone was home. Hetty was off hats and onto what her editor called "Improving and Interesting Women's Stories" and in the midst of a real courtship with Rowan. Not to mention that she and I were back to our regular velocipede rides in the park.

"You two are well matched," I said as we sat.

"Better even than you know."

"How so?"

"A lawyer, you will know, always likes to have a friend in the papers. And a good reporter is pleased to know a lawyer who can put her in contact with clients who might wish to talk."

"Well, then. Which case is it this time?" I checked the watch on my charm bracelet. It was only about two o'clock, too late for luncheon and perhaps too early for tea, even if one hadn't already had coffee. Still, a good hostess makes the offer. "Would you like a cup of tea?"

"Not really. You go ahead if you like."

"Ugh, no. I haven't much appetite right now."

Hetty's eyes lingered on my face for a long moment. "No doubt."

"Anyway, the client?"

"Aline Corbyn."

"He's defending her?" Of course, it made sense. She was a woman in very serious, very public trouble, exactly the sort of client Rowan Alteiss would like.

"Yes. I think she's a nasty piece of work, but she's entitled to a defense."

"As is everyone." I nodded. "And no doubt she'll pay well for the privilege."

Hetty's eyes gleamed with pride. "Rowan says the society cases pay for the *pro bono* work."

"Exactly the sort of thing he would say." Alteiss shared her strong ethics and determination to improve the world, another way they were well matched. "So when do you sit down with her?"

"Later in the week, likely. You know her, don't you?"

"A bit. I've sung at her musicals."

"Oh, she's the mean one who tried to throw her daughter at the Barrister."

"Yes." I realized I was twisting the band of tiny, jeweled flowers on my little finger Gil had given me when I accepted his proposal. Originally his mother's, it was not a conventional engagement ring, but it was the one he had put on my hand, and so the one I would keep forever.

Hetty caught the gesture but didn't acknowledge it. "What do you think about this latest incident?"

"I don't know. But I've heard hints that she may be lying about the attempted outrage." I saw Hetty's stunned look and quickly continued. "Making it up to give herself a motive for self-defense."

"That's awful—even for someone like her."

"I know, which is why I am having a hard time believing it." I decided to leave it at that, partly because I had no desire to discuss the grisly details of Mr. Lorimer's alleged condition and partly because I did not want to unfairly prejudice Hetty against her subject. "You will learn much more in that interview."

"It will be fascinating."

"Probably more than that."

"A nice gift from my man." She grinned. "Better than flowers or candy."

"Not that you don't love those, too." An easy and pleasant change of subject.

Hetty blushed again. "I didn't realize how much I would enjoy all of those little tokens and things. He left a card at my house the other afternoon on his way to a deposition, and it's still in my jacket pocket."

"I still have the first card Gil ever left at the house," I admitted. "I use it as a bookmark, but-"

For a moment, we just stopped as I realized how precious a memento that card might become.

Hetty quickly patted my arm. "He'll be back. Those smaller steamers are safer than the big Cunarders. Less fuss and more speed. And plenty of lifeboats. He's fine."

I nodded. "I know. We just have to get through the next few days."

"Precisely."

We returned to aimless—and distracting—talk of news office life and minor City scandals for a few more minutes until she left for work.

After Hetty left, I was actually alone for a short while.

It gave me time to wonder how long a person might survive in the water of the North Atlantic. And if one would somehow know if one's beloved were no longer among the living.

I do not share Aunt Ellen's belief in the second sight, but I do believe that our modern science has not solved all the mysteries of the human mind and brain, and people may sometimes sense things. Given the deep connection between Gil and me, I had to believe I would know—*something*.

Parsing these dark thoughts, I picked up the same book I had been reading without comprehension for more than a day, just as the doorbell rang yet again.

These footsteps were quiet, cautious, as Sophia trod slowly behind them. "Mr. Coughlan, miss."

Connor Coughlan was, if not the ruler of the Five Points underworld, certainly one of its ranking members. In his day suit, his Black-Irish brown hair slicked back, his carriage carefully calibrated to dilute the menace from his tall, muscular form, he seemed almost like any other well-off gentleman.

But one look in his shamrock-green eyes was enough to disabuse one of that notion. Even when he was trying to seem harmless, something terrifyingly cold remained in the depths of his gaze, a reminder that it was the last sight of the world for any number of people who had crossed him.

At the sight of me, though, the eyes warmed, and the hard lines of his face softened. "Ellen."

"Connor." He grew up on the same Lower East-Side street as Tommy and me—I'd once even jumped on his back and pulled out a handful of his hair when I threw in with Toms in a scrap over some long forgotten but desperately important slight.

More recently, I'd done exactly the same thing to a killer who was choking Connor backstage at the *Princes* during the New York run. Connor had always kept a loose acquaintanceship with Tommy and me, and he and Gil had discovered a shared interest in an earlier murder in Britain, leading to his presence in the theatre on that fateful night.

Officially, Connor now claimed the right to protect me and assure my safety and happiness because I had saved his life. Unofficially, and unsaid, since that night in the dressing room was far more.

I had not seen Connor since the theatre fire and stabbing, but I knew, from the note he'd sent with a large bouquet of white roses, he blamed himself for it. He did not take so much responsibility, though, that he did not also make it clear the actual culprit's life would be short and ugly if he ever set foot outside his fancy mental hospital.

Now, I held out my hands, and he took them, staying at an entirely respectful distance, but looking me over, with a gentle care and concern I was sure no one else ever saw.

"How are you?"

"I'm holding up."

A faint smile tugged at the edges of his mouth. "All healed?"

"Very nicely. A small scar no one will ever see."

"Good. You're too brave, Ellen."

"Probably."

He let go of my hands, and I motioned him to a chair.

"Tea?"

"No, no. I just came to see that you're properly taken care of." He shrugged like an uncomfortable little boy. "I can't do anything about the shipwreck, of course, but if you need anything..."

It was almost sweet, if a murderous gangster could be so described.

"Thank you, Connor. I appreciate it."

He nodded. "Just making sure you're all right. I failed you once, Ellen. I won't again."

"You know that nobody could have stopped him. Even his own family didn't realize-"

"And you know that if I'd had the sense to have someone watching over you, you and Tom would have had an extra pair of hands when you needed it."

No point reminding him the only hands that had mattered were the ones I used to punch the madman and the one in which he held the knife, in the minuscule grace-note of time I had before he drove that weapon into Gil's heart. Connor would see things as he wished.

Had I been my normal, controlled, and balanced self, the discussion of the incident would likely have ended there. But, of course, I wasn't, and under Connor's searching gaze, I found myself making an admission I'd never intended to make to anyone.

"It was my fault."

"What?" Connor's jaw tightened, and his eyes burned. "You, of all people, can't blame yourself for the evil in a man's mind."

"No, no." I shook my head. I hadn't wanted to talk about this, but Connor was probably the only person in the world who might understand, considering what he did for a living. "In the fight. I made a mistake."

"How's that?"

"I didn't know where the knife was for a moment, and that's when he got me."

Connor nodded very seriously, but his face relaxed a little. "That's very true—and very wise."

"I thought you might understand."

"More than I'll ever tell you." A faint smile before his expression sharpened into a careful, protective gaze, much like Tommy's. "You aren't ever going to be knife-fighting again, right?"

"Your lips to God's ears."

"Good." He nodded, taking it as a promise, even though I hadn't intended it as such. "But you're right. In a knife fight, you have to always know where the blade is…or else."

"And I didn't."

"Well, it was your first knife fight, wasn't it?"

"Yes. Toms and I always somehow managed to stay away from the really bad stuff."

"Then consider yourself a winner. You survived, and the other fellow's out of the game."

Connor's faint smile turned into a grin.

"We do know he won't hurt anyone again," I agreed.

"He definitely will not."

Something cold, resolved, and feral crept into his expression, and I suspected if Connor ever got ahold of the madman, his last sight of the world would be very much like that grin.

I did not need to think of Connor in that way.

"How are you?" I asked for a rather desperate change of subject.

"Very well, as always." He gave me a cagey smile, acknowledging he could hardly give me a cheerful round-robin on the rackets and leg-breaking. But then his aspect changed to something sharper. "You may be able to help me with a bit of information, at that."

"Absolutely, if I can."

"I know you two are planning a simple wedding here at the house, but I'm hearing talk of a big society affair around the same time."

"Not just one. June is the wedding month, after all. There are at least three society ceremonies."

"All in the same week or so as yours?"

"Yes. One even on the same day. The Four Hundred and their jewels will be working overtime."

"Jewels, yes." Connor nodded. "I'm assuming everyone gets all decked out for these society to-do's?"

I laughed. "This gang is not known for restrained elegance."

He laughed. "You are."

"I am a working artist marrying an unpretentious Northerner," I reminded him. "Neither of us feels the need to cover ourselves in rocks and minerals to show our importance."

"True. It will likely be a very different scene at the other ceremonies."

"Oh, such a different scene. I was never good enough to invite to these things, you understand-"

"Bas-" Connor muttered and caught himself.

I shook my head. "The world is what it is."

"But don't tell me it's not a little bit of fun seeing those fancy folk bow and scrape now that you're going to be a duchess."

"Oh, a little." I *hoped* I was going to be. "The thing here is that people will be at those other weddings to show all of the expensive things they have and how important they are."

"Instead of wishing the happy couple well?"

"Exactly. And, of course, the happy couple will be the most done-up of all. I've heard of aristocratic brides who could barely hold up their heads for the tiara and earrings."

32

"Well, now it makes sense."

"What does?"

"Can't tell you much, Ellen." He leaned back in his chair with a contemplative expression. "Someone may be up to something interesting...and I may be able to turn it to my advantage."

I watched his expression, just absorbing this unexpected view of him. He was much like Gil when he was parsing a case, though, of course, from an entirely different direction.

"You and yours aren't involved in any of the other weddings?" His tone and gaze were deadly serious for a moment.

It was better not to speculate why it was so important to him. At least I could reassure him on that score. "Not at all. Far too fancy for us."

Connor laughed. "Ellen, you are marrying a duke. Even I know he's at the top of the social tree."

"Technically. He's half-Scots, and, as you know, has no love for fripperies."

"Best thing about him."

"So true. But the other weddings involve a robber baron, a French *Vicomte,* and a Polish Prince. Dollar princesses and rich widows, naturally. At least one of those grooms is probably a fraud."

A grin from Connor. "Which probably means the fanciest wedding of all."

"Precisely." I joined the grin. "I won't ask you to tell me how it all turns out..."

"Oh, you'll know."

"I probably will, at that."

"I should go." Connor rose, and I heard Sophia let out a little squeak as he smiled and nodded to her.

"I'll walk you to the door."

In the foyer, he took my hands again, with that surprisingly gentle expression he seems to save only for me. "Next time I see you, I'll be congratulating a married woman."

"Please, God."

"I don't put much on God these days, but I know that man of yours would walk through the fires of Hell for you. A little water won't stop him."

33

"Thank you." Suddenly, embarrassingly, my eyes filled.

Connor pulled his hands together, enfolding both of mine between his, warm and reassuring and entirely unexpected. "Ellen, *acushla*."

For a measure, I felt almost as safe and protected as I did with Gil.

"I'm sorry, I-" I pulled away quickly, clasping my hands behind my back, the same as Connor was doing.

"For all that God listens to me, Ellen, I'm praying for your man."

"Thank you."

When the door closed behind him, I sat down on the stairs and gave way to tears for the first time that day.

It would not be the last.

Chapter Six

A Shocking Question

That second day, I tried for some minimal level of normalcy. I called my fencing instructor, the *Comte du Bois*, otherwise known as Mr. Mark Woods of the Bronx, for an afternoon lesson to burn off some of the blue devils from the waiting.

Though we sensible artists do not believe in Aunt Ellen's second sight or other psychic vibrations, we do clearly share some habits, including the need to stay busy at bad times. So, I was not entirely surprised when Marie and Louis invited themselves over for a good vocalization session later.

Afterward, over tea with Tommy, we decided that a benefit for the families of the two lost crewmen was a very good and necessary idea. Not to mention giving us a valuable distraction while waiting to hear about the fate of the rest of the souls on board. We resolved to put out the word among our acquaintances and see what we might assemble for the unfortunates.

Over those terrible few days, I played with countless cups of tea, passed innumerable plates of treats, and made sure the sideboard was full of good, healthful dishes at mealtimes. Just about everyone who came to offer consolation, carefully *not* condolence, brought some kind of soothing dish or sweet, and all had to be appreciated and shared with the visitors of the moment.

Not that I was eating. Though I cultivated a calm and hopeful air, I had been unable to swallow much more than a few sips of tea or coffee since we got the word. An incredible thing for me, after my impoverished girlhood, to be surrounded by food and utterly unable to eat it.

I knew that Tommy and the Countess were becoming very worried by this, and I made a pretense of taking a plate at most meals and toyed with a few bites of something, though I hated wasting the food. They were not fooled.

The first two days passed in this strange slow spin, time seeming to crawl, though I was vaguely aware in a corner of my mind that I would wish I was back to waiting and hoping if the worst news came.

Resolute hopefulness was possible in the morning and throughout the day, but as evening came in, it was sometimes difficult to maintain, and it no doubt preyed upon all our minds.

This is the only reasonable explanation for my extraordinary conversation with the Countess that second night. Tommy had gone to the *Beacon* again, hoping the news office might have early word and likely for some support and companionship with Preston and the sports writers.

Soon after the door closed, she poured us both a brandy and motioned to me to join her on the settee. "Please understand I mean no insult by this question."

I blinked at her, puzzled.

"I ask not in the interest of judging, but of hope. For me, and especially for you."

"I'm sorry, I don't know…"

"Forgive my plain words, but I'm still a blunt Scotswoman no matter how many tiaras I wear." She took a breath. "Is there any possibility of a baby?"

"A baby? For whom?"

"My dear, you haven't been eating, and you're so pale…"

She blushed furiously, and so did I as the realization dawned. For a moment, we stared at each other in absolute shock and embarrassment at the conversation.

"I had it all worked out, you see," the Countess continued in a rush. "I was going to tell everyone you had a private ceremony before you left London, and of course, no one could say you hadn't."

36

"But he would never—I would not—" I sputtered, unsure whose honor it was more important to defend.

"I'm so sorry, dear." She took my hands, her eyes filling. "I know the two of you are honorable and good. But you are also healthy adults who are very much in love and who have a signed marriage contract. Things do happen…"

I shook my head. I wasn't sure whether to laugh or cry or throw things. Even though I hadn't yet had my very frank premarital conversation with Dr. Silver, I was quite certain the few kisses Gil and I had shared, so cautious and restrained in recent weeks, would be no cause for the Countess' hopes.

A wave of embarrassment and regret and who knew what other difficult feelings washed over me, and I started crying, which I simply *never* do unless alone. Then the Countess began weeping too, and we collapsed in each other's arms, both sobbing like lost children.

"I didn't mean to insult you," she choked.

"I wish there *were* a chance." The shock of hearing the words come from my mouth and the realization that they were absolutely true just made me cry harder. I had been taking the good Irish girl's pride in bringing my innocence to the altar, and now it could all be for naught and, in fact, deprive me of the one consolation I could have had: Gil's baby.

She pulled back from me a little and put her hands on either side of my face. "You are such a good girl."

"I should not have been so good."

The Countess smiled just faintly. "It's who you are, just as it's who he is. No use crying over it now."

"True." I took a ragged breath.

"It's poor consolation, I suppose," she began, stroking my arm as if I were an upset child. "But I should like to think, whatever happens, you and I will stay as mother and daughter."

"Oh, yes." More tears oozed out of my eyes as I nodded. "Not poor consolation at all."

"We are borrowing trouble, as the crofters used to say. Gilbert will be back and scolding us for worrying before we know it."

Her tone brooked no argument, and I joined her firm nod. "He absolutely will."

She suddenly gave me a rather uncertain look. "Please don't tell him what I asked you, at least not right away."

"Of course not."

The tentative expression gave way to a smile. "You wouldn't. It's quite all right to tell him later, once you're wed and working on that baby."

The phrasing, and my admittedly vague idea of the manner in which one might work on the said baby made me blush, and, probably from all of the strong emotions we'd just been sharing, giggle like a schoolgirl.

The Countess studied me in a sharp and canny way for a moment. "Why, you really *are* innocent, aren't you?"

"Um,"

"I had simply assumed that given your age and playing men as you do, that you had some understanding of—"

"I am having a very frank conversation with my doctor before the wedding," I said with as much dignity as I could manage. "And Madame Marie has promised me a whiskey and a good talk."

The Countess grinned. "Excellent. We really do a shameful job of educating young ladies…but I made sure my daughter knew what she needed to know before she walked down that aisle."

I nodded. As a matter of principle, I believe the same. As a practical matter in my own life, I was utterly confounded. Not to mention horrified by the thought of having such an intimate conversation with the Countess. Difficult enough to discuss private matters with Marie, as dear and close as she is.

"I'm just surprised, dear. You've educated yourself so well on everything else."

"I haven't needed to know, so I haven't -" The thought that I might now never need to know such things occurred, and I started crying again. What a mess I am.

The Countess pulled me in for a motherly embrace. "There, there, dear. You poor thing. You waited so long for your proper man, and you're finally ready to give yourself to him, and he goes and gets himself in danger on the sea. I am going to have a few sharp words for Gilbert when he returns."

"Me too." I took a breath and composed myself again. "I think we need to find a way to distract ourselves."

"I know you have an excellent command of elevated music, but how are you with drinking songs?"

"Better than you might think. Tommy and the sports writers have taught me a few."

She grinned. "I had four brothers who made sure I could hold my own. I'll teach you a few old Scots airs you probably haven't heard."

"Montezuma will want to join us."

"The more the merrier."

And so it was, when Tommy returned well after midnight with word the steamer had sunk slowly enough after broadsiding the Danish freighter that most—and quite likely all—of its passengers had been picked up by a passing Cunarder, he found the three of us at the drawing-room piano singing an at least slightly off-color Gaelic ditty.

There was no definitive word, but that initial report made no mention of any further souls lost, and so we had hope. We just had to wait for that Cunarder to return.

Chapter Seven

In Which Dr. Silver Offers Insight

On the third day, as radio messages began to filter in from the incoming Cunarder, but so far none for us, we rode a terrifying whiplash of hope and terror. While the two members of the *Atlantic Star* crew were confirmed lost, there was still no indication any patrons were missing. Still, the admittedly incomplete passenger lists that were coming through did not include Gil's name. Preston staked out the *Beacon's* telegraph and called us with every scrap of new information.

There were also unconfirmed reports that some male passengers who had helped the last of the women and children to the lifeboats might have stayed with the freighter that the *Atlantic Star* hit. It had apparently suffered very little damage and was steaming for New York and repairs at a decent speed. But since the freighter and its radio man were both Danish, it was proving very difficult to get any answers from that direction.

The best thing we could do for ourselves, we concluded, was to continue keeping busy. Fortunately, the affair of Chester Lorimer and a house full of visitors were very helpful in that regard.

Dr. Silver came over early in the day, partly because she was looking in on a new mother on MacDougal Street, and partly because of a concerned call from Tommy.

"Tom says you are not eating, and he is beginning to worry," she said, fixing her usually gentle hazel eyes on me with a sharp glare as I poured her coffee and offered the plate of Miss O'Hanlon's latest batch of cinnamon rolls.

"There's nothing to worry about. Any reasonable person would be a bit off her feed, after all. And quite literally, everyone is trying to make me eat."

She chuckled. "They probably are, because it's all they can do."

"I suppose."

"Well, at least stop playing with your aunt's soup and start eating it, all right? We don't need you fainting."

"That's fair," I agreed, sipping a little of my own coffee. "While you're here, perhaps you could provide a bit of medical insight?"

"On the Chester Lorimer matter?"

"Yes. We've been keeping an eye on that, at least partly as a distraction."

She nodded. "Well, if the head injury is as bad as they say, Lorimer is not likely to survive for long. There is only so much medical science can do in terms of keeping alive a person who cannot eat or drink for himself."

"That's true. I understand the family is still hoping he will recover."

"Faint hope at best by now, I'm afraid." She took a thoughtful bite of cinnamon roll. "We do not understand the brain very well, but it's quite clear that very few people return to themselves after being insensible for three days."

I nodded. "Have you heard Mrs. Corbyn's defense?"

"That he was attempting an outrage?" Her mouth tightened. "If true, she was certainly within her rights to fight him off."

"No question."

The doctor studied me for a moment. "But?"

"But I have been told that Mr. Lorimer might not be capable of perpetrating such a thing."

Her clear hazel eyes widened. "Really."

"A—gentleman—who knows him well claims that he had an old war wound...and he was unable to, um..." I trailed off, casting about for an appropriate verb and finding none.

"Hmm." Dr. Silver contemplated her coffee cup, considering the matter with cool professionalism. "Civil War, right?"

"Exactly."

"Many men were maimed in the most horrible ways and were lucky to survive. Some men, of course, might not consider themselves lucky to live after such a wound."

I nodded.

She gave me a tiny smile. "When you're married, dear, you'll understand. Men define themselves in very specific ways, and anatomy has a great deal to do with it—for some men."

"I suppose that makes sense."

"More sense than you can imagine right now." The doctor sighed before continuing. "Was poor Mr. Lorimer married?"

"Before the war. His wife bore him two sons before he enlisted. She died a long time ago—at least twenty years, I think."

"Never re-married, and no female companions?"

"Not that we know of."

"That certainly points in the direction, but it means nothing. Plenty of couples get and stay married without having marital relations, of course."

I managed what I hoped was a sophisticated nod.

"Don't worry. You and your duke won't be one of them." She allowed herself a little grin.

I shook my head. Marital matters could wait for our frank talk before the wedding, which, please God, please God, I was still going to need. "So?"

"Well, there's no reason that a man who is incapable of completing an outrage in the conventional sense would not try some sort of attack...but it certainly lowers the probability."

"I would think so."

"Depending on the wound, he might not have had the usual masculine drives at all."

"You mean like a castrato?"

Dr. Silver smiled. "Yes. Exactly like a castrato. I forget that even though you're an innocent Irish girl, you've spent much of your life singing roles once played by those poor mutilated men."

I blushed. "I know a bit about the anatomy, of course. I haven't the faintest idea what one's supposed to do with it...or what all the fuss is about."

Dr. Silver swallowed a laugh and put down her coffee cup. "That, dear, will wait for another day."

"Please God."

"My dear, I've seen him, and I've heard the way he says your name. If he has to swim across the North Atlantic, he will return to you."

"Your lips to God's ears."

"Never mind *my* lips. My Aunt Myriam is praying for 'the poor people on that boat,' as she puts it."

"So are my Aunts, Ellen and MaryKat."

"Then they are all as good as home."

I did my best to match her determined smile with my own, knowing nothing else would do. And, once she moved on to her next house call, I forced myself to think about Chester Lorimer.

Mrs. Corbyn, then, had at least a possible reason to want him dead—her daughter's advancement—and a more than slightly questionable self-defense claim. More, if the Captain of Industry were truthful, she would have had no way to know he was the one man who would have a strong defense against that usually difficult allegation. Ultimately, it was the man's word against the woman's...and while far too often, society believes the man, a powerful and determined woman might well make herself believed.

As I turned away from the door, I caught a glimpse of myself in the hall mirror. I barely recognized the bony-faced, scraggly-haired thing I had become, in just three days of neglecting myself. The simple gray and lavender printed cotton dress that had felt easy and comfortable a few hours ago now seemed like half-mourning, and my skin nearly matched it. The less said about my hair, the better.

No wonder everyone was trying to feed me. I frightened myself.

This could not continue. My mentor, Madame Lentini, taught me a diva must maintain a certain standard, no matter what, and so I must.

I had just started smoothing my hair and pinching my cheeks when Tommy walked in.

He didn't have to speak. The expression on his face told the story. I grabbed the banister as my knees turned to water.

"The Cunarder is coming in right now," Tommy said slowly. "He's not on it, Heller."

I nodded, took a breath, and tried to pull myself into form.

"There's still the Danish freighter. People on the Cunarder saw some men stay with it after they were safe. There's still hope."

"Hope for what?" The countess was just coming down.

"The Cunarder is in," I said, shaking my head, and then watching something break in her eyes, the same as I knew it must have broken in mine.

"We don't know about the freighter. There's a very good possibility that he's on it," Tommy said decidedly. "After all, there is no word of any passengers lost. The two crewmen are the only ones who did not survive."

"Neither did Chester Lorimer."

We all turned to see Preston walking in, carrying a late edition. "Died three hours ago without ever opening his eyes."

"Well, then, children," the Countess said with a calm determination none of us felt. "It appears we have a murder to solve."

Chapter Eight

Murder Most Distracting

When in doubt, do something constructive. It had been my mother's maxim when we were scraping by in our cold tenement room, and I later realized she must have learned it from my father, because his sister, my Aunt Ellen, lived by the same rule. For my mother and me, it had usually taken the form of redoubling our efforts at the piecework that kept us (barely) alive after some bit of sadness or bad news.

For Aunt Ellen, it meant that one was expected to keep busy no matter how upset one might be about minor rubs or reversals. Anything short of an actual death meant a few minutes to cry, a pat on the head, and a gentle, but firm shove toward the books or the broom.

We no longer handled our own brooms, of course, and no one was in the mood for quiet reading, but we could certainly help with the Lorimer inquiry. It being a Tuesday, the countess decided she would take advantage of society ladies' "at-home" hours and her own high cachet to gather a little information from the parlors of Fifth Avenue.

Preston, after giving me a kiss on the forehead and what must have been the one-thousandth "It will be all right, kid" of the last three days, offered to search the newspaper morgue for Lorimer's business dealings and any other matters of interest.

And Tommy and I decided our best play was to ply Cousin Andrew with baked goods and offer my (carefully phrased) insight from Dr. Silver and Tommy's from our talent agent Henry Gosling, who had visited earlier in the day. Henry was known to send rising young talents to Mrs. Corbyn's musicales, though he shared the general opinion that she was not especially honest or kind, warning the singers to be sure she paid up front if she asked them to entertain at a later event.

Those horrid group musicales, hosted by many society ladies, are a required way to get one's name known in the world, and singers understand they are giving away those performances to help build a career. But if the matron then books one for a small concert or other event at her home, *she* is aware she is expected to pay the same as any other theatre manager would. Or she should be. Mrs. Corbyn, it was said, had been known to "forget" to pay, and more than one new singer had gone away empty-handed and uncertain what to do about it.

The fact that she would coolly cheat a hungry young artist did not mean that she would lie about being attacked, of course. But it certainly spoke to the sort of person she was.

I went downstairs to get a basket to pack up some of the choicest cookies and confections from the sideboard and was welcomed with the blessed sound of girlish giggles.

When we hired Mary O'Hanlon, she'd been scared, starved, and exhausted, a pale little creature who looked more like twelve than the nineteen she actually was. A few months of safety, decent pay and food, and good friends had worked magic. These days, she was a Black-Irish stunner, with sparkling changeable deep green-gray eyes, silky dark curls and creamy skin, all lit by a radiant smile.

Rosa Benedict (the name was di Benedetti before Immigration), my lady's maid, dresser, and hopefully someday famous novelist, was a perfect foil for her. As lovely as Miss O'Hanlon, in a warmer-skinned, brown-eyed Italian way, and a couple of years younger, she used the perks of her job to keep herself and her friend in the latest modes on their off hours. Even in uniform, as they were now, they seemed much more stylish and individual than the usual servants, thanks to the smooth and perfect fit of their dresses, a little girlish embellishment of crochet lace at the collars, and a saucy tilt to their caps, all of which was just fine by me.

When I walked in, they stopped giggling and looked up.

"Oh, miss!"

The abrupt end to giggles had everything to do with the current situation and nothing with fear of me. Under normal circumstances, they might well have brought me into the joke, but everyone had been walking terribly carefully in my presence during these awful waiting days.

"It's all right, girls. I'm glad to hear laughter. Anything you'd like to tell me?"

"Only that we're going walking out on our half-day." Rosa grinned. "Both of us."

"How's that?"

"We were out doing the marketing this morning, Miss Ella, and ran into two very nice printers who were coming out of the daily Mass at Holy Innocents."

"Did you, now?"

They giggled.

"I doubt anything will come of it," Rosa said quite seriously. "But it's awfully sweet to be asked."

Miss O'Hanlon smiled. "They're both rather nice to look at. Cousins. One blond and one dark."

"Jim and Tim," Rosa added. "They go to Mass most days, they say."

"Well, good on them. Why not bring them by to meet Mr. Tommy before you go out for your walk Saturday?"

The girls nodded. Miss O'Hanlon's parents were gone, and she lived with an aged aunt, while Rosa of course had the whole Benedict clan to look out for her. But Tommy and I, as their employers, were their first protectors, and Tommy would absolutely expect to shake the boys' hands before allowing them to squire our young ladies in the park.

"We'll bring them by," promised Miss O'Hanlon solemnly.

"It'll be fun to see what Mr. Tommy thinks." Rosa grinned.

I picked up a basket from a shelf near the door.

"Do you need me to pack something, miss?" the cook asked.

"No, no. I'm taking some of the treats from upstairs while we go visit Detective Riley."

"Oh. Of course." She and Rosa looked troubled.

"Nothing serious," I assured them both. "Just looking for a distraction while we wait."

"Of course."

Both were silent for a moment, then, as I turned for the door, Rosa touched my arm.

"You know we're praying, too, miss."

"I had no doubt. Thank you." My voice was thick, and my eyes damp as I stepped out. I did not need to cry anymore, and I surely did not need those two happy girls to see it.

The rest of the afternoon and evening passed in a most constructive fashion. The detective was happy for the assorted baked goods and Dr. Silver's insight, delivered mostly by Tommy in a very oblique fashion. And we all reconvened at dinner to discuss what we had learned about Mrs. Corbyn and her family.

It would have been even more constructive if I'd remembered any of it.

Chapter Nine

Those in Peril on the Sea

During those terrible days, I'd taken to sneaking back downstairs after everyone else had gone to bed and just sitting by the remnants of the fire, reading if I could, often the same page several times, or steaming through entire chapters without absorbing a word. It was better than lying awake in my bed, surrounded by the growing pile of boxes for the trousseau and other accouterments I might never need.

That night after the Cunarder came in without Gil on it, I did the same. There was simply no hope of sleep, even though we had spent a very, long time discussing matters at the table, and the countess and I forced Tommy to squire us on a long walk in the park after Preston went home to Greta.

We reminded ourselves we still had the hope of the freighter, and I clung desperately to the same routine as before. Tommy and the countess finally went to bed with medicinal beverages around midnight, and I did the same, holding up the pretense that I was all right.

Within less than an hour, I was up again, keeping watch as I'd been. It was the only way I could stay sane.

I knew I would not die if he did not come back. But I also knew I would not love again and certainly not marry. Gilbert Saint Aubyn, for all his faults, was the only man for me, and there would not be another.

That night, like the others, I was on the settee, bundled in my lilac sateen summer wrapper and an afghan, crocheted by Aunt Ellen, reading and not comprehending and hoping vaguely that perhaps I would soon finally be tired enough to sleep.

Which is when I heard the knock.

It was far too late for anything good. No one would send a messenger with happy news in the dead of night. All right. Better to get the word alone, with time to collect myself before I had to face anyone else. Especially the countess.

Yes, it was my fiancé, the love of my life. But it was her son. Her little boy.

I would never have a little boy, or girl, now.

I pulled myself up and took a breath. The least I could do was take it like the Duchess I would never be.

Tommy would have strangled me for what I did next, just opening the door and looking out. Dangerous and foolish, even if I was expecting or dreading a messenger.

But it was no messenger.

For an instant, I thought it was exactly the sort of mad ruffian attacker I had invited by my foolishness. Then I realized that despite the less-than-elegant attire and somewhat disheveled appearance, it was the only person on earth I wanted to see.

Gilbert Saint Aubyn stood on my doorstep, smiling a little sheepishly.

I must have pulled him inside. Someone must have closed the door. I don't remember any of that.

One instant, our eyes met as he stood there on the step in the weak glow of the gaslights, and the next, we were in the foyer, tangled together in an embrace that was like nothing any properly brought-up Irish woman would have entertained, even with her wedded husband. The strange reserve of the previous months was gone, and he pulled me to him like he couldn't hold me tightly enough, kissing me with a desperate intensity that would likely have terrified me under any other circumstances.

As it was, I met his passion with my own, any concern for respectable behavior now far beside the point as I wrapped my arms around him, hanging on for dear life.

I don't know how long it went on, but it wasn't long enough. Finally, he pulled back for a second to catch his breath and put his hands on either side of my face.

"Dear God, I love you," he said, his voice low and raspy, the Northern accent pronounced.

"I love you." My hands were still on his arms; I couldn't let go of him, digging my fingers into the scratchy wool of his jacket. "I thought I might never see you again."

"I'm here, *mo chridhe*."

Talk, beyond that was a waste of time as far as I was concerned. I got on tiptoe and kissed him again, and once more, he pulled me close, right back to where we'd been. It was like being swept up by a hurricane, only in the best possible way. I was quite sure respectable ladies did not do this with their fiancés, and equally certain I didn't care in the least.

A lifetime of reading had not supplied me with any words to fully describe the amazing feeling of being wrapped in his embrace, his mouth hot on mine, the closeness of his muscular body — the affection and connection between us transforming into some kind of entirely new quicksilver lightning thing.

All I knew was that nothing in my life had ever felt so good...and that I did not want it to end.

"*Mo laochain!* Gil!"

Countess Flora's joyful cry and the sound of her footsteps blasting down the stairs stopped us like a dash of cold water, and we instantly broke apart, shy and guilty. The Countess flew at her son and embraced him, throwing herself into his arms without the least concern for protocol.

"Mother."

I started to turn away to give them their moment, but a hand on my sleeve pulled me back, as first Gil, and then his mother, brought me into the circle.

For a little while, we all just clung together in joy and relief, the Countess openly sobbing and Gil and I just holding and reassuring her. Eventually, the storm subsided a bit, and she managed to back away from him enough to take a good look at him, though she was still clinging to his sleeve and gave every impression that she would not let go any time soon.

I understood completely and didn't begrudge it in the least.

"Well, you scared us all badly enough, Gilbert."

"Terribly sorry, Mother. Steamer travel is normally mundane and reliable...until it isn't."

"Just so." She leaned her head on his shoulder and pulled me closer, too. "What a relief, children."

Only then did she look up at Gil and me with a twinkly smile. "I believe I interrupted a happy reunion."

I had not realized until that exact second we could blush simultaneously.

"Well, really, children." The Countess laughed. "You're both healthy adults, and you're just days from the altar. Even before the shipwreck, no one would blame you for enjoying the privileges."

"Mother," Gil growled.

"Of engagement, naturally." She winked at me before glaring at her son. "I would never suggest that either you or dear Ella would so forget yourselves—"

Had the Countess not appeared when she did, we might well have forgotten everything except the incredible pleasure of that happy reunion, and all three of us knew it.

It was only then she noticed his attire.

"*Mo laochain*, you look perfectly awful. What on earth happened to you?"

"Well, Mother, you know I travel incognito."

"That's rather more than incognito."

"Well, one likes to be unobtrusive."

I heard something in his voice. I wasn't sure what, and I surely did not have the energy to care just then, but I marked it.

"My large trunk came with you, did it not?" he asked her.

"Of course." She smiled. "It's still here, so you can assemble yourself properly in the morning, before you move over to the hotel."

"Good." He doffed the shapeless grayish wool jacket he'd been wearing, then revealing a rather unedifying dull plaid waistcoat and shirt much coarser than his usual fine cotton weave.

Even with the awful clothes, a shadow of a beard, and deep purple smudges under his eyes, he was still the most beautiful sight I'd ever seen. I'm sure for his mother, too.

Though I'm sure she was not observing the fit of that waistcoat and shirt with the appreciation I was. Those sinewy arms that had just been holding me close…and I hoped would be again soon. *Oh, dear.*

I realized the best possible word to describe what had just happened between us was lust. I wasn't entirely certain what I was supposed to do about it, but there was no question that I had undoubtedly been lusting after my future husband.

One was supposed to, wasn't one?

"*Mo laochain*, you're exhausted," cut in the Countess, reverting to her usual cool demeanor since all was now well and settled. "Why don't we have a medicinal brandy, and you can tell us what happened?"

I poured three generous portions, and we sat down together on the settee by the fire, none of us yet willing to break the physical contact for long.

Gil took a few sips of his drink while his mother and I settled in on either side of him. He wrapped an arm around each of us, and I put my head on his shoulder, enjoying the simple fact of his presence.

And yes, once again being so close.

"Well, it's all quite simple if rather upsetting," he began. "Our steamer collided with a freighter in all of that North Atlantic fog, and it would have been very bad indeed if the other boat had not been quite sturdy and the Cunarder had not been only a few hours away. The two crewmen fell overboard in the collision, and they could not rescue them in time."

The Countess and I shuddered, and Gil drew us closer. "It's all right. No other souls were lost."

"I'm sorry, *mo laochain*, but only one other soul matters to me."

"I sent word that I was safe." He looked sharply at us.

"We did not get it," I said, carefully keeping my voice steady.

"I left a message with the mate on the Cunarder and went to the radio room on the freighter—twice." Gil's jaw tightened as he realized what we must have been through in the last day. "Well, my Danish *is* awful, and the Cunarder was likely swamped in society prattle. I am terribly sorry."

The Countess and I both shook our heads, unable to form a response, not to mention unwilling to distress him with what we might have been able to say.

"I will have a word with someone at Cunard. And with the Danes, if I can figure out which word it should be. But," he smiled a bit, "all's well that ends well."

"Easy for Mr. Shakespeare to say," I grumbled as I burrowed closer to him.

"We are all here and safe now." Gil pulled us both in a bit more, and there was really no need to talk for a while, the three of us just huddling together, utterly relieved and exhausted. It probably violated any number of proprieties, especially considering my intense new feelings. But with a signed marriage contract and just under two weeks to the wedding, not to mention his mother on the other side, and the simple fact that I'd come so close to never seeing him again, I did not especially care.

Tommy found us all asleep on the settee a couple of hours later when he came down for his own medicinal drink. "Well, aren't you a sight for sore eyes."

I woke first at the sound of his voice, carefully lifting my head from Gil's shoulder and loosening my hand from the Countess's. She and I had wrapped him in a protective circle, even as he embraced us. It was a rather happy family moment, even if I had a nasty cramp in my arm. "Toms."

"See?" He grinned. "I told you he'd come back. So did Mother."

I laughed lightly, and the sound and movement woke Gil. For a second, he blinked at Tommy and me in confusion, and then he smiled. "Shane. Tom."

Gil very carefully sat up a little, trying not to wake his mother. She stirred a bit, but that was all.

"Glad to see you again, Barrister." Tommy tried for a stern face. "But I'm going to have to insist you marry Heller."

Gil laughed. "I suspect she'll insist as well."

"Well, now that I've bought my dress and all…"

He reached for my hand with his free one and pulled it to his lips. "And you did sign the contract, after all."

"You've been quite decently chaperoned, children," the Countess put in with a sleepy smile. "But we should all find our way to a proper bed now."

Gil's fingers tightened around my hand, and his eyes burned into mine. Until that exact moment, the fact we would very soon be sharing a bed still seemed an entirely theoretical matter, something other people or possibly characters in books did. Not really anything *we* might actually do, and just a few days from now at that. Even after my dramatic discussion with the Countess, I had sent the entire matter to a far corner of my mind, since I had no need to entertain such thoughts just then—and I had feared, quite possibly ever.

I'd best start thinking about it now.

And all of those amazing feelings…what did one do with them behind a closed bedroom door? When there was no one to walk in and tell you to behave?

I wasn't the only one stunned by the thought. After that first scorching instant, Gil's face changed, and he stared at me with an expression more suggestive of fear than anticipation. But aren't men supposed to want a willing wife in their bed for their "demands," whatever those might be? And willing, I certainly was.

My blush must have been truly volcanic, because the Countess actually giggled.

"Our respective beds, children. No one will be anticipating their marriage vows in this house."

Tommy nodded with a stern face given away by his sparkly eyes.

"Of course not, Mother." Gil coughed and let go of my hand, but I knew he was remembering our embrace when he returned, just as I was. If we had not anticipated the vows, in fact, we surely had in spirit.

And if there was more of the same to come—which I had to believe there was—how on earth did married people manage to get themselves out of bed and think about anything at all?

Marie was quite right about not making breakfast plans for the day after the wedding. For my money, if embraces like that were on offer, why would anyone trouble with Eggs Benedict?

"You can stay in the open guest room next to me tonight, Barrister," Tommy said, the cool host's words barely covering a chuckle. "Your mother is staying a floor above with Heller."

"Still no hotel, Mother?"

"Why bring back unpleasant memories when dear Ella's home is so cozy?"

"Just so," I agreed, finding some thread of a voice and standing.

Tommy offered the Countess a hand, and she happily took his arm, and then the two of them unobtrusively but very firmly shepherded Gil and me toward the stairs.

"There will be plenty of time for sparking tomorrow, children." She grinned. "It's entirely possible that you might even be left alone for a while..."

"Or not." Tommy and the Countess shared a smile, most definitely at Gil's and my expense.

At Tommy's landing, we all paused for a moment, and the Countess gave her son another kiss and embrace, the last clutch of her fingers on his sleeve betraying her emotion. "Good night, *mo laochain*."

"Good night, Mother."

She started up the stairs, and Tommy turned to open the guest room door, giving Gil and me our moment.

"Good night, *mo chridhe*." He pulled me into his arms and just held me close for a breath or two.

"Good night." I rested my head on his shoulder. "I love you."

"I love you." He kissed my hair, still in its night braid despite a few loose curls. "I-"

He broke off, his voice thick with emotion, just burying his face in my hair for a moment. I clung to him, neither of us able to speak. This had nothing to do with the fiery emotions of earlier in the night and everything to do with the deep and caring bond between us.

Bashert. My mother's Hebrew word. Meant, fated...belonging together.

"Plenty of time for pretty scenes in the morning," Tommy said with a carefully teasing tone, smacking my arm. "Let's all get some sleep."

Chapter Ten

A Bright Day and Dark Questions

N ext morning, everyone was back to some minimal level of decorum, though Gil's mother did not let him out of her sight, and he took full advantage of the fiancé's privilege of sitting beside me at our late breakfast.

When he walked into the sunlit dining room, I took the fiancée's privilege of admiring my man, once more clean-shaven and dapper in his usual style, today a simple light-gray suit with a pearl-gray tie, emphasizing his dark hair and ice-blue eyes.

"A vast improvement, Gilbert," his mother observed. "Last night, you looked like the barber's cat."

"The *what?*"

Gil said it, but we all stared at the Countess, surprised by the unusual expression. From his reaction, I was certain it was not Scots.

"A peculiar way of saying that one looks dreadful, I heard from Pearl Lally's fiancé when I was visiting yesterday."

"Peculiar indeed," Tommy said. "But it sounds oddly familiar."

"Do you know many Poles, darling?" asked the Countess. "He's a prince from Warsaw."

"Is he now?" I rather doubted he was, but Pearl Lally, widow of a rail magnate, was eager to accept Prince Jerzy Mrzawzy at face value, and the rest was none of my business.

"So he says." She met Tommy's canny gaze before adding another bit of intrigue. "He was on the *Atlantic Star*, as it happens…had just come in on the Cunarder."

"How astonishing," I said. Better her than me; I'm not at all sure I could have calmly sipped tea with a man who was safe from the same disaster that might have claimed my own while still waiting for word.

The Countess is a woman of many layers. And many of those layers are steel.

"Indeed. I was stunned to see him just sitting in the parlor drinking tea." She reflected on the moment. "He *was* a bit the worse for wear and used that rather extraordinary expression to describe himself. It was practically the only thing he said."

"On the *Atlantic Star*, really?" Tommy asked. "Remember any Polish princes, Barrister?"

"My attention was otherwise occupied." Gil's oblique reply meant something, and I marked it, but that was all at the moment. "It was not a particularly social voyage, and of course, at the end, I had other matters in mind."

"Of course." I nodded but said no more.

During one of Preston's many calls from the *Beacon's* wire room, he had told me several passengers on the Cunarder remembered a very tall, dark-haired man, British from his accent, helping shepherd a group of women and small children from second or third class to the lifeboats…and even grabbing a panicked toddler by the back of his jacket as the wee one almost ran away from his family in the crush. My modest beloved would never tell that tale if he could avoid it.

The Countess, who had taken the same comfort in the story as I, gave her boy an indulgent smile. "Prince or no, he is presentable enough and makes the occasional intriguing remark, neither of which can be said for Mrs. Lally."

"Is that so?" Gil asked with the sharpness around his eyes that means he's observing for a reason.

"Another time, *mo laochain*." She shook her head. "At the moment, I find breakfast far more worthy of discussion."

The dollar princess dismissed, we took up our convivial meal. As Gil sat beside me, I took a moment to carefully study him, admiring him long enough he gave me a rather puzzled face.

"You are looking quite lovely in your clothes," I said.

He grinned at the reference to a private joke between us. We met when I was in fencing gear, and he did not recognize me the first time he saw me in women's dress, then observing quite innocently, if inappropriately, that he did not know me in my clothes. "As are you."

"Was that outfit last night your standard travel attire?"

Gil shrugged. "Sometimes I travel *very* incognito, sweetheart."

"Ah." I nodded. The tone meant this was something he could not discuss. "I will tell you when I can."

"Fair enough."

We have an agreement that each of us may omit things the other does not need to know. Neither of us would ever lie, or abuse the privilege, of course, but it does provide some needed room for a couple with rather interesting lives.

At the moment, though, I found I was far more interested in breakfast. My appetite had returned, not surprisingly, and Miss O'Hanlon had outdone herself, with rich brioche rolls, fresh raspberries with cream, and of course eggs and bacon for the gentlemen.

Despite the fact we'd been surrounded by all manner of food offerings over the last few days, this was easily the tastiest and best meal any of us had enjoyed since the first word came about the *Atlantic Star*. We lingered long around the table, slowly sipping a bit of coffee, not making much in the way of conversation, but simply enjoying each other's presence and the warm circle of family.

It was not a family-only celebration for long, however.

Since the *Beacon*, and many others, had put out special editions with the happy news that the last men from the *Atlantic Star* were safe home thanks to the Danes, we had all the good wishes we could manage, and more, pouring in. The first messenger boy had arrived before we even awakened, and the stream of flowers, telegrams, and cards did not abate.

At the apparently decent hour of noon, the first visitors came. Preston and Greta—really family in their own right naturally—merely dropped off a plate of lovely violet fairy cakes, hugged everyone, and headed off to meet Greta's daughter, a nurse in training at Bellevue who had but a half-day off. We would have been happy for them to stay as long as they liked.

A small posy of white roses arrived as I was seeing them to the door. The unsigned card: *Told you he'd be all right.*

Connor.

I pocketed the card and added the roses to the clutch of arrangements we were sending over to the women's hospital. No need for Gil to misconstrue it.

The next visitor, a society matron I knew only slightly arrived as everyone was neatening up for the rest of the day, and was quite put out that she was not welcomed to wait. She dropped a card with a note, the neutral wording of which was entirely undone by the irritation evident in her penmanship.

Once the cast was properly assembled, the Countess and I replacing our simple morning dresses with rather nicer afternoon frocks, quite coincidentally both in happy and frivolous floral prints, hers soft bluish gray, mine a rather sweet mauve—we set up shop in the parlor. After that first brush with Society, we had every expectation we would have to be "at home" the rest of the day. We were not disappointed. Thankfully, though, the first guest was a welcome one: Cousin Andrew.

As it turned out, he came bearing far more than good wishes: a chance to discuss the Lorimer case and give us all something productive to do.

Once the handshakes and congratulations and admiration of the cookies on the coffee tray (entirely for our visitor, considering the late and generous nature of breakfast) had concluded, we settled in to consider the matter.

"So the lady is claiming she brained him because he was attempting an outrage?" Gil summed up Cousin Andrew's careful sketch of the case.

The little detective nodded and took a second lemon cookie. "And when the captain attempted to inquire further, she started sobbing violently and ended the interview."

"Did she have the same reaction with a police matron?" I asked.

"Sometimes women do feel more comfortable discussing such things among themselves," agreed the Countess.

"Flatly refused to speak with one. Now she's hiding behind her lawyer, Alteiss."

Gil smiled. "A very good defender."

"The one I'd want if I were in trouble," Cousin Andrew admitted. "But in this case..."

"She should have no need to hide." The Countess looked to me.

I nodded. "It's absolutely a woman's right to defend herself from attack, and unlike many other women, surely someone like Aline Corbyn would have every reason to expect that she would be believed."

"Well, except for Mr. Lorimer's unfortunate war wound." Cousin Andrew blushed and carefully didn't look at me or the Countess.

"What unfortunate wound?" Gil's puzzled face turned to a furious blush of his own as Cousin Andrew met his gaze and nodded vaguely in the direction of his lap.

"I was under the impression that no one but those closest to Mr. Lorimer knew of it," said the Countess, barreling right past the embarrassment. Very Scots of her, and probably the best way at that. "Certainly no one I met during ladies' at-homes had the faintest thought of it."

"No?" Cousin Andrew asked. "Are you sure?"

A sphinx smile. "Quite certain, my dear boy. I have many more years of experience than you at bringing up things that should not be brought up."

She mistook our mortified silence for interest, and continued quite happily and proudly. "As a Briton used to the property entail and curious about inheritance patterns here in the Colonies, I merely engaged in a little gentle speculation on the provisions for Mr. Lorimer's substantial estate considering he has the two male heirs and apparently no other relatives with a claim. One of the brothers is supposedly not right, having fallen on his head as a child."

"Sad," I said.

"No doubt," she agreed. "But he seems to be properly cared for, which is more than some families do."

We all shook our heads, knowing what can happen to vulnerable people in this harsh world.

"In any case," she continued, "everyone appeared to be under the impression that it had been entirely possible that the poor patriarch could re-marry."

"Really?" I asked.

"Quite." A gleam came into her eyes. "And it was not merely a theoretical issue. There was some youngish female he'd met while doing good works for war veterans, and at least some suggestion that he was considering a re-marriage."

"Which might make life interesting for his sons," Cousin Andrew said as he contemplated another cookie.

"Interesting indeed," agreed the Countess, "since even a late marriage could produce a babe or two. Older gents with younger wives have been known to do so, you know, even at quite advanced ages."

"No doubt, Mother."

"At less advanced ages, too, Gilbert." She grinned wickedly. "I would very much enjoy seeing a grandchild with Ella's lovely eyes and your sister's red hair."

Cousin Andrew cleared his throat and gave Gil and me a sympathetic glance as we shared an utterly volcanic blush. "Katie's mother started a baby quilt two days after the wedding."

The three of us shook our heads in shared exasperation. There is truly nothing more embarrassing than the expectations of the older generation. Aunt Ellen had engaged in far worse in recent weeks—but, of course, only among women.

"At any rate," the detective said firmly, "the Countess is quite right. A woman who defends herself should have nothing to fear from the law or from telling the truth. Especially not a woman in Mrs. Corbyn's high position."

"Which makes one wonder why she does not want to talk," Gil took a sip of his coffee.

"At least not to the police." I could not, of course, break Hetty's confidence about her interview with Mrs. Corbyn.

"To her lawyer," Cousin Andrew said carefully. "Who has been known to play the papers."

"Yes." I nodded and held his gaze. I would say no more.

"It raises considerable suspicion," observed the Countess.

"Well," the detective began, his unhappy aspect lifting a little, "if she does talk to the press, it will be quite useful."

"It will?" I asked.

"Yes. Because once she tells her story, she's stuck with it."

Gil nodded. "A matter of record."

"Precisely, Barrister. I hope she *does* talk to a paper." Cousin Andrew smiled and stopped himself as he reached for another cookie. "I wonder if you folks might do me a favor."

"What's that?" Tommy said it, but we all nodded.

"Keep your eyes open at the Lorimer funeral?"

"Oh," I said, feeling Tommy and Gil watching me carefully. "We weren't really that close...but I have no doubt we'd be welcome."

"I thought perhaps." The detective gave a canny smile. "The service is Saturday, I believe. May I invite myself over for tea in the afternoon?"

"Of course," I nodded to him and the company.

"Excellent." He took another sip of coffee and resolutely turned away from the cookies. "Katie will murder *me* if I don't have an appetite for the lunch she so sweetly made for me."

Tommy, Gil, the Countess, and I shared smiles. Our detective was quite adorable in his newlywed bliss.

"I'd best be going. Thanks for the coffee and the insight, folks."

"You are always welcome." I said it, but the others joined in with warm smiles too.

"Ah, well, time for much less pleasant work at the station house."

Chapter Eleven

In Which We See Several Lightning Bolts

Visitors were quite simply the order of the day that Wednesday. I managed to escape to the studio for a few minutes to feed Montezuma and vocalize with him, but the doorbell just kept ringing. More floral tributes, more notes, and of course, more well-wishers. Some better than others.

"Mr. Coyne, miss." Sophia said with a giggle, walking in at the same time as Tommy's and my cousin Rafe, son of the devout and rather terrifying Aunt MaryKat. He has a particular effect on the ladies and is completely oblivious to it. Rafe believes he is having cheerful and polite conversation with the crowds of females who gather wherever he appears, and is equally charming with all of them, regardless of age or aspect.

In fact, most women cannot spend more than a few moments with Rafe without developing at least a mild crush. He does not realize this, and would never take advantage of it, which is how he has managed to survive into adulthood without being murdered by some jealous swain.

The charm is not necessarily tied to his looks; Rafe has dark hair and the same greenish-blue hazel eyes as most of the family, and he's tall and presentable, today in neatly kept black pants and gray jacket, but not especially remarkable. Until he smiles, and appears to be occupying his own magical spotlight, drawing women in like moths to the flame.

"Well, it looks like Mother's novena worked." Rafe grinned at the sight of

Gil. "We'll never hear the end of it."

"No doubt." I returned the grin, as did Tommy and everyone else. After a round of hugs and handshakes, Rafe settled in with tea and cookies happily provided by the Countess, who is every bit as susceptible to his charms as the younger set.

"Glad to see you're all doing so well," Rafe said. "I'd intended to come over yesterday, but had to study for an exam, so..."

A round of sympathetic nods. Rafe, though currently a handyman, is just a few courses from his accounting degree and his dream of spending the rest of his working life "fixing the books instead of the stairs," as he jokingly puts it.

"An,d of course, you now come into a much happier house." Tommy reached for a violet cake with only a tiny smile at the fact that he had to shift for himself, unlike the well-served Rafe.

"And thank God for that."

Everyone nodded in relieved agreement.

"Now you can start thinking about the wedding." Rafe gave me a teasing smile. "I'm sure you're up to your eyes in dresses and flowers and such."

"Oh, yes."

"Mother's a bit put out, you know."

"Because we're having an Episcopal service?"

Rafe nodded. "She thinks you should at least have a priest there and maybe say a few words over you...just to be sure it counts."

Smiles from Tommy and me...cautious expressions from the Countess and Gil.

"It's all right, Barrister," Rafe said quickly. "That's actually awfully modern for my mother, who's been known to say that those Unitarians are going straight to Hell."

"Why Unitarians?" Gil asked, puzzled.

"She heard once that they believe in everything." He shrugged. "I don't think she's ever actually met one."

"We will have a priest in attendance, you know," Tommy pointed out. "Father Michael is coming."

"And giving us a blessing before the ceremony," Gil added. "I wrote him a month ago and asked him to."

Rafe's eyes widened. Never mind mine. I looked to Gil.

"I am not the first Northerner ever to marry a Catholic," he said with a small, shy smile. "Or to marry a woman who has close friends who are clerics."

I smiled, too. "Very nice."

"And now Mother won't have to think you're living in sin." Rafe gave us all that impish grin and took another cookie.

Gil and I, as was expected of us, shook our heads and blushed a bit. Tommy and the Countess just laughed.

"Anyhow, hopefully you'll have a little quiet until the ceremony," Rafe went on. "You're doing a lot better than those other society brides."

"Really?" I asked.

"Mrs. Lally, the one marrying the Polish prince, is putting up tapestries and paneling all over her house for the wedding breakfast. Wants it to look like 'a medieval keep' for her man."

Gil snorted and tried to hide behind his teacup.

Rafe chuckled. "I figured you'd get a laugh out of that. Do they really have princes in Poland?"

The Countess took that topic. "I think there is still some Polish nobility about, though of course most of them have been absorbed by the Russian Empire and don't rule much of anything."

"I bet they don't live in medieval keeps," Rafe said.

"No," the Countess replied, "and anyone who's actually lived in such an old castle would certainly not want to do so. No decent heat—or hygiene—arrangements."

Tommy grimaced. "The medieval time may have been romantic, but it wasn't very comfortable."

"Romance is in the eye of the beholder," Gil observed. "I, for one, will always vote for starting with clean and warm."

"So will I."

We shared a smile, and I knew the others were enjoying watching the happy couple.

"Perhaps she's hoping the tapestries and dark paneling will set off her jewels," Rafe suggested. "I've never seen anyone wear so much sparkle as that woman."

"Vulgar." The Countess sniffed. "One may have wonderful things, but one wears them appropriately."

"Absolutely," I agreed. Gil had offered to buy me a large and glittery engagement ring and other jewels, but I needed no replacement for the Countess's little circlet of flowers, and I wanted nothing but a simple band of gold as the symbol of our union.

I supposed, at some point, I would have to wear whatever family pieces went with the coronet, but I did not suffer from the frequent diva obsession with jewels, and quite frankly, found them cold and heavy.

"Not in this crowd, Countess." Rafe took another cookie with a laugh. "I don't know how that Mrs. Lally moves her hands with all the bracelets—and the ring."

Gil's gaze sharpened. "The ring?"

"Great big diamond and emerald thing. And you know she's got those pudgy little hands, not like our Ellen here with her pretty long fingers. Just looks silly."

"This one *could* wear something more substantial," Gil pointed out with a significant glance to me, "but she won't, and I don't mind."

Rafe chuckled. "Don't need to mark your territory, Barrister?"

"I know who I belong to." I intended it as a light aside, but Gil's eyes caught mine as I said it, our gaze holding for a moment too long.

"A little more tea, Heller?" Tommy asked, giving me a wickedly amused smile that told me he'd seen it.

I quickly picked up the pot and got back to my work as the serious hostess, not that anyone was fooled.

"Well," Rafe said, once he was properly refreshed and provided with another cookie, "at least tell me you folks are out of that mess from the opera reception."

We all exchanged guilty glances, not sure how much we wanted to share with him.

He sighed. "All right, just as well then. I can tell you and not have to go looking for the copper in charge."

Four teacups went into their saucers as we all looked to Rafe.

"I hung the new doors at the Lorimer house a few weeks ago, and I heard the daughter-in-law complaining about Grandpa."

"The sort of complaint that might raise suspicions?" Gil asked.

"Not really." Rafe put down his own cup. "I wouldn't have remembered it except that all of this happened. Just rude and mean, the way some of these people are."

"Rude and mean..." I encouraged, taking a sip of tea as I noticed my companions taking their cups up again.

"There's a younger brother who's not right in some way, apparently, and I heard her complaining about how much they pay his caretaker."

"Not kind," Tommy said.

"He's well out of that house, for sure. That woman seems to hate her whole family. She said to some other society female, I don't know who—but I didn't recognize her: 'Do you know that old fool is actually thinking of marrying again? Can you imagine we could have to share his estate with some snip of a girl?'"

Everyone once again put down their cups. Good thing none of us was especially thirsty.

"There's more. The last thing I heard was: 'Good God, why am I cursed with the longest-lived father-in-law in New York?'"

Tommy's face tightened, and he said it for us all: "Not anymore."

"Do any of these people teach their children ethics? Or at least how to behave decently?" The Countess seemed to have reached the limit of her forbearance with the society folk.

"Sorry, generally not." I patted her hand. "They call them robber barons for a reason."

She sniffed. "You children learned better morals and manners in a tenement than these people did in their mansions."

It was absolutely intended as a compliment, and we took it as such, Tommy and I swallowing our smiles.

Rafe didn't notice, because his attention was diverted by the latest serving of tea. Or rather, by she who brought it.

"I thought you might like some freshly brewed, miss." Mary O'Hanlon said, walking in with the pot and a cautious smile.

We all got to see it happen. Rafe Coyne, the incorrigible charmer who had never taken any serious interest in a female, looked into the sweet gray-green eyes of Miss O'Hanlon and stopped cold.

The lightning bolt.

"And who—" Rafe began, his voice coming out odd and squeaky like a nervous boy's. He cleared his throat and managed almost his usual easy smile. "Who have we here?"

"Miss Mary O'Hanlon," Tommy began, "our cook and confectionery artist *par excellence*, meet our mostly respectable cousin, Mr. Rafe Coyne."

"*Entirely* respectable, miss," Rafe said quickly, rising to take the small tea tray as he recovered his manners.

"Entirely respectable," I echoed, meeting Miss O'Hanlon's confused gaze. "He's gainfully employed, finishing his accounting course, and the son of our very pious Aunt MaryKat."

"And absolutely unmarried," Rafe added as he bowed, "not, of course, that you'd be wondering about that, Miss O'Hanlon."

She laughed, her face lighting up wonderfully in surprise. As pretty as she is, she'd had a very hard life in the last few years, and she might never have had a decent man court her. I would have bet good cash money that she'd never seen one make such a fool of himself—because we surely hadn't.

"Nice to meet you, Mr. Rafe Coyne." She returned the smile, and I almost heard a little swish of cupid wings in the background. "I hope you like the tea."

"It's absolutely beautiful."

Poor Rafe was, of course, not speaking of the convivial beverage.

Mary O'Hanlon took up the empty pot.

"Thank you very much, Miss O'Hanlon," I said, keeping my voice and face neutral, even as the Countess cut her eyes to me with a twinkle.

"Of course, miss. Let me know if you need anything else."

She started to walk away, then turned a few steps before the door to look back at Rafe, who clearly had not yet lost all of his appeal. "And thank *you*, Mr. Coyne."

Rafe just smiled, completely beyond speech at that moment.

Tommy glanced to me and held out his cup. "I, for one, would like a bit more."

We shared a grin as I poured. I didn't have to look to Gil to know he was smiling, too.

Rafe sat back down, not even trying to return to his usual demeanor. "Who is she? I thought your cook was some nasty dragon from an agency."

"That one only lasted a few days," I said. Back in February, at that! Rafe had clearly not been listening closely during his chats with Rosa and Sophia, neither of whom had been enamored of the unlamented Mrs. McKinney. "We weren't good enough for her."

He didn't catch the intended joke, once again looking toward the door in surprise. "Well, this one is an angel."

"Miss O'Hanlon has had a difficult life, Rafe," Tommy cautioned. "Spent some time in service at the Waverly Place Hotel and had a few unpleasant experiences."

I shot the Countess a quick glance, making sure she didn't jump in and expound on the particularly distressing incident from which she'd helped rescue her. If Miss O'Hanlon wished to share any of the details of her earlier life with Rafe, she would. She had nothing to be ashamed of, naturally, but it was not the first thing he should know about her.

Tommy's vague comment, though, was quite enough to spark Rafe's protective instincts. His eyes narrowed, and he shook his head. "That sweet girl? She's far better off with you."

"And us with her," I assured him.

"She is an excellent cook and a delightful girl," contributed the Countess, who had clearly decided to help speed the course of true love. "Modest and well brought up."

"Not to mention quite devout—she goes to Mass every Saturday evening with Rosa," I said, then realized I sounded just like my matchmaking future mother-in-law. "But she's also quite young and in no hurry to wed…so you can take your time and approach carefully."

"That's good." Rafe nodded. "I'm not yet able to make a proper offer."

Tommy smiled and handed him another cookie. "You will be soon enough."

"And I may just have found my proper woman."

Gil cut his eyes to me as he nodded to Rafe. "If a man's the marrying kind, that's all he needs."

Chapter Twelve

San Francisco and a Honeymoon Baby

We had the chance to discuss the Lorimer matter from another angle later in the da, when Rowan Alteiss dropped by on his way back to his office and rooms a few streets away. Just as his lady love was subtly glowing with happiness in the bloom of their new connection, so too was he.

Tall and rawboned, and normally quite severe-looking in a rather Lincoln-ish way, the defender seemed a good bit younger and more relaxed and definitely better kept than he had before. His suit and shirt were less rumpled, and while his deep green tie did not exactly suggest the dandy, it very definitely spoke to a man taking a bit more trouble with appearance.

"Good to see you safe, Counselor," he said, addressing Gil lawyer-to-lawyer as they shook hands.

"And you. Looking well and happy."

Alteiss laughed. "That I am. I don't think I'm talking out of school if I tell you I'm courting Miss Hetty."

"Not at all. And much joy to you."

"To you as well."

Once the latest pot of tea was poured and a fresh plate of dainties passed and admired (though taken only by Alteiss), conversation inevitably turned from anodyne matters of weather and wedding plans to homicide. Everyone present would have been quite bitterly disappointed if it hadn't.

"Of course, you can't discuss cases in detail, dear," began the Countess, "but why does that awful Corbyn woman think she needs a lawyer?"

"It is always wise to have representation." Alteiss offered neutrally.

"No doubt." Gil met his colleague's gaze. "And wise to get one's case out."

A grin that warmed the defender's stark face. "Always good to have a friend in the papers. You may wish to read the *Beacon* in the morning."

"No doubt we will," I agreed.

Tommy joined the smile for a moment, but then his face clouded. "It truly is sad for the Lorimer clan."

"Indeed it is," Alteiss agreed. "Chester was a very good man. Gave a great deal of money to the veterans and orphans funds. I was on a few Republican party committees with him over the years."

"Did you know him well?" Gil asked, his eyes suddenly sharpening with interest.

"Fairly. Not enough to know much of his private life or habits."

"Did you know he was courting a young woman?" The Countess, of course.

The lawyer burst out laughing. His laugh, a full-out guffaw, is one of his most appealing features, but it was quite a shock to see it then.

"What on earth?" asked the Countess.

"He wasn't courting her, ma'am," Alteiss said, returning to proper demeanor with a little cough. "He was looking out for her."

"How so?" Gil asked.

"Well, as I understand it, Elsie was the daughter of a man who'd saved his life during the war, and he'd run across her working at some charity or other for the widows and orphans. Apparently, he took a fatherly interest. That was all."

"Of course." I nodded.

"Though I suppose, now that you mention it," Alteiss went on, "some of the nastier-minded society types might have seen it differently, especially since he was planning to set her up with a small dowry."

"Dowry? Do they still do that here?" The Countess looked puzzled.

"Not really, outside some very Old-Country communities," Tommy contributed.

"No, but well-off fathers do often settle a bit of money on their girls when they marry so they have something of their own." Rowan smiled a little. "Chester was planning to do that for Elsie."

"Which might annoy his family a bit," observed the Countess.

"I suppose. I don't know them." The lawyer shrugged. "I was surely shocked when I heard what happened."

"And yet you're defending Mrs. Corbyn," I said.

"Everyone deserves a defense," Alteiss gave the Countess and me an apologetic glance. "And one never really knows what might happen between a man and woman in private."

"Well, that is true." Tommy agreed. "Though one might wonder why a man who's never done such a thing before in a long life suddenly..."

"Ah, Thomas, there's more under heaven..." Alteiss trailed off and took a sip of his tea. "We shall see what we see. And it is a matter of principle for me that a woman should be believed in such instances unless there is a grave and serious reason not to."

"For me as well," Tommy nodded.

"And me."

The men shared a glance. The Countess smiled proudly, still glad to see her boy—as she no doubt thought of him—doing right. As for me, the sight, especially Gil's serious and protective face, warmed me right to my toes.

Truly nothing so wonderful as good men working together.

"Quite appropriate, gentlemen," the Countess interposed. "I will never argue with you on that principle. Since we are veering quite close to uncomfortable matters for Mr. Alteiss, perhaps we should move on to the current baseball season?"

Alteiss' eyes widened. "You're a baseball fancier?"

"Not in the least, dear boy. But I *am* curious about everything."

"Well, in that case," I started. "Tommy and I follow the Giants, but Marie, living in Brooklyn, prefers the Superbas."

"The Superbas?" crowed the Countess. "I do think I would prefer a team with such a marvelous name..."

By early evening, everyone was quite exhausted with the company, and we were grateful for a lull before dinner, relaxing in the parlor, the Countess with a book she was not reading, and Gil and I on the settee, not really looking at my postcard album. Tommy, never one to fancy excess visitations, had slipped away for a while.

He walked back into the room, carrying a letter.

"San Francisco wants the *Princes*."

"San Francisco?" asked the Countess. "How lovely. A second honeymoon, perhaps...and just possibly I'll come along as well if I may."

Tommy chuckled. "Why not? We'll just pack up the whole show."

"When do they want us?" I asked.

"December. A three-week stand capped by a New Year's gala. There's enough time after the fall *Xerxes* at the Met to prepare and get out there, so why not?"

"That would be lovely," I said. "And fun for all."

The Countess gave me an odd look. "December? That's more than six months away."

I nodded. "The Met run ends in early November. It's perfect."

"Well, dear, unless you are blessed right away..."

As the understanding dawned, I looked to see Gil watching me closely, and I could not stop the blush.

Tommy, too. He coughed. "Well, perhaps you and the Barrister need to talk about your plans in that direction and we'll decide what to do later?"

"No time like the present. The poor dears haven't been alone all day, after all." The Countess picked up her book and stood. "Thomas, didn't you tell me the roses were blooming in the park? Why don't we go for a little walk before dinner..."

Gil and I, now really alone for quite possibly the first time in our acquaintance, sat there on the settee staring at each other for probably a full stanza.

Finally, he broke the silence. "It is, I suppose, a reasonable question."

"Yes. Marie told me that many women want to avoid a honeymoon baby at all costs."

"You can talk to your doctor about that, I suppose…"

"I am planning a very frank conversation with her next week."

He stared at me. "A very frank conversation…"

"About—about the things married women need to know. I did not need to know them before this."

Gil's turn for a volcanic blush. "And you—"

"Will know what I need to know, don't worry." My reassurance sounded empty, even to me.

He held my gaze. He didn't look any more optimistic than I felt. "I know you've been virtuous, but you've spent your life playing men. Surely you have a fair idea of…"

"Anatomy, of course." I nodded coolly.

He gave me one of those searching barrister glances. "But what one does with it…"

"I've never needed to know much about such matters until now," I said in my best sophisticated tone. "Of course I'll remedy that, and perhaps you'll help me."

I had intended the comment as mildly flirtatious, but he just shook his head.

"You know, it's very good that you're virtuous," he began, carefully composing his face, "and I should be pleased and honored that you're bringing your innocence to our marriage bed…"

"And you're not at all."

"I could wish your aunt or one of your married friends had at least acquainted you with the principal facts in evidence."

"Not my aunt," I said, unable to control a giggle.

Gil waited.

"She told me my man will tell me what I need to know on our wedding night."

"Good God." He put his head in his hands. "It's not just some horror story whispered among men."

"Not a bit of it. Hence the very frank talk."

He looked back up and just stared at me for another long moment in shock or confusion.

"But," I said, taking his hands, "there's something more important here."

His dubious expression suggested otherwise.

"I don't agree with those other women," I continued.

"What do you mean?"

"When you were missing at sea, I realized that if you did not come back, I would not have any consolation at all..."

I had no intention of telling him who had given me that realization.

"No consolation..."

"I don't want to wait to have a baby." I forced the words out, shocked by their bluntness.

Gil gave me a long, assessing glance as his hands tightened around mine. "No? What about San Francisco?"

"We'll cancel if we have to, or I'll just be a very fat Henry Tudor in a tunic." It was a joke, of course. No woman would really perform in the late stages of a delicate condition.

He laughed, easing the awkwardness of the moment.

"I'm willing to risk it," I said.

"You're sure?"

I nodded. He let go of one of my hands and traced the line of my face.

"I love you, *mo chridhe*."

"I love you."

He pulled me into his arms and kissed me. Carefully, gently, lovingly—with none of the nearly ferocious passion of the night before. The reserve was back again.

I wanted to cry.

"What?" he asked as he pulled back.

"Nothing, just—last night was different."

"Last night, I had just come back from peril on the sea," he said rather stiffly, "and I did not remember that I am dealing with a very innocent woman who deserves to be treated with great care-"

"Not that much care. It was rather wonderful."

Gil's eyes widened. "Really?"

"Really."

"Well, have your very frank conversation with your doctor,"

"And a whiskey with Marie."

He gave me a rather relieved smile then. "Whiskey?"

"She promised me a good talk before the wedding."

"Have your talk and whiskey, then, and we'll take up this conversation after the wedding."

"In the meantime," I said, moving closer to him. "You might try kissing me like that again…"

Gil looked down at me very seriously. "No, I'd really best not."

"Why?"

"Because it's entirely possible that the next time I kiss you like that, I won't want to stop."

"That might be a good thing."

"Not if we're not married and you don't know what to expect." His face was stern and grim in a way I hadn't seen since the first day we met. "It's a very serious matter, love, and I'm not going to ruin it for you."

"All right." I did not even bother trying to hide my disappointment.

He kissed me, then, with even more caution and less passion than usual. "We'll sort it out after the wedding."

That was when I was absolutely certain he was at least as scared and confused by it all as I was. And that we'd have done a lot better to just pick up where we'd left off last night and leave it to Mother Nature.

Chapter Thirteen

The Wheels of Justice

The next morning, Hetty and I started the day in one of our favorite ways: a good, relaxing velocipede ride before her shift at the *Beacon*. She'd managed to sneak a quick call from the news office with the idea late in the evening, and I'd quickly agreed, needing the spin and talk as much as she clearly did.

I wasn't ruining any other plans; Gil had made some vague comment about a busy morning when he escaped to his hotel soon after dinner, much as Tommy had slipped out to the Holy Innocents rectory for an evening of checkers and relaxation with Father Michael, which likely went well into the wee hours. As for the Countess, she was flatly exhausted from the social whirl coming on the heels of the terrible days of waiting. So, no one else had been stirring when I, in full sports costume, tiptoed downstairs.

It was only when I picked up the *Beacon* from the step that I understood at least part of the reason Hetty wanted to meet: to engage in a little friendly crowing. Her interview with Aline Corbyn was on the front above the fold. It wasn't the banner—that belonged to disturbing new developments in the Boxer Rebellion—but it was still in quite a plum spot.

And the work was worthy of it. She'd managed to draw Mrs. Corbyn out, allowing her to tell her story in florid terms, just oblique enough not to offend the family readership. Despite Mrs. Corbyn's questionable story and rather unpleasant nature, she'd treated her with respect and professional objectivity—leaving it to the reader to draw her own conclusions about the lady's story.

This reader knew exactly what conclusion she would draw.

Also that my dear friend is a brilliant reporter.

I left the paper on the little occasional table in the foyer for Rosa, and later, Tommy, and slipped out to enjoy my morning.

The sun was up, of course, but the day was still so new that even Mrs. Early, the beggar woman who frequents the park, was not yet there. Hetty was, though, and clearly exercised in mind.

"I could just *shake* Rowan!"

Before I even got a chance to congratulate her on being on the front above the fold, her furious comment warned me this was not going to be our usual relaxing velocipede ride.

"Really?"

"Of course, he was a dear for setting me up with the interview with Mrs. Corbyn."

"Not that it didn't help his case," I pointed out as we mounted our wheels.

"True enough. Even if she lied her face right off." Her furious expression faded for an instant, then came right back. "But what he said last night!"

"Tell."

"Well, we went to that most improving lecture on Renaissance palazzos at the Architecture Appreciation Society..."

"Of course." I nodded. Hetty and Rowan might be a crack investigative reporter and a top defender, but in the eyes of her family, they were any other courting couple, and restricted to the proprieties as such. An improving lecture was one of the very few acceptable ways to get an evening out together, and since the Architecture Appreciation Society meetings were within a short walk, perhaps even a few minutes to talk privately.

Since it was all entirely public, one's reputation, of course, was in no danger at all. If one wished to take one's swain's hand for safety on a dimly-lit street, say, no one would think ill of it.

"So when we were walking home, he praised my handling of the interview and his very difficult client, which was very sweet."

CHAPTER THIRTEEN

"He admires all of you, you know. It's wonderful and rare."

"True. Which makes this all the more upsetting." She sighed as we slowed for a moment to turn down another path. "After we talked about the piece, I said, 'Well, of course, you know she's guilty as sin.'"

"And?"

"He gave me that serious lawyer-y look and said, 'I don't care.' How could he not care!"

"Because he's a professional with a code, just like you."

Hetty scowled. "My code doesn't let me ignore a murder."

"Neither does his. But it does require him to put up the best defense possible for his client. So he may not want to think too hard about whether she's guilty."

"Is this a lawyer thing I am going to have to get used to?"

"Probably."

We pedaled in silence for a few measures.

"You could come up with something like Gil and I have."

"What's that?"

"We have an agreement that we don't have to bring up things the other does not need to know."

"Useful if I were working on a story."

"Or he on a case." I nodded. "And then you don't have to worry about fighting over something that has nothing to do with the two of you."

"True."

As we made another turn, I gave her a sharp look. "You didn't fight."

She blushed. "Not really. And we made up…"

I giggled. "I do enjoy the making-up."

Hetty laughed. "I wonder if men know we enjoy sparking as much as they do."

"Sparking, Miss MacNaughten?" I tried for a stern scowl.

"Oh, stop. I know you're an old-fashioned Irish girl, but there's nothing wrong with two respectable adults sharing a kiss or two before the parents walk into the foyer."

"Nothing at all." I grinned. "Even three."

81

"Well, when they're rather amazing kisses."

"With your proper man," I added. "Who has nothing but the most honorable intentions."

"Don't send out the wedding invites yet, Ells. I'm still trying to figure out how we can manage our two careers and a marriage."

"You'll find a way."

She shook her head. "Problem is, once you start enjoying the kisses and the conversation, you start wondering what you'd be willing to give up, to keep it."

"Really, now?"

Our eyes held.

"Not the same as you, and you know it. You have a lot of control over when, where, and how you work. I'm tied to the *Beacon*."

"Maybe. I still think you can find a way." I pointed to a nice long, empty path spoking out from the fountain. "In the meantime, let's enjoy this glorious day…"

A few turns later, I remembered something she said. "Lied her face right off?"

"Oh, yes. You were absolutely right. She was not telling the truth about the attempted assault. I know how women sound when they talk about it…and she definitely did not sound that way."

There was a great deal of dark subtext here, and it showed in Hetty's sharp expression.

During an earlier misadventure, Hetty had confessed to killing a man and claimed he'd been attempting an outrage. It was in good faith; she had been trying to protect the innocent girl she fully believed had done it in self-defense.

But all of us who are close to Hetty had known she was lying about the attempted assault, and she was still deeply embarrassed about having done so. Even for the best of motives—protecting a young victim—it is a terrible thing for a woman to lie about because it hurts those who have really been harmed.

"You wrote it up very nicely and neutrally," I assured her. "No one would know what you thought of her."

She smiled faintly. "I made sure Rowan did, though. But he's still defending her."

"Because it's his job, just as you have yours."

"And he is grateful for the insight," Hetty allowed, turning onto a path that would bring us closer to the fountain.

"How grateful?"

"Roses. Coral-colored ones that look like a sunset."

I tried for a carefully innocent tone. "And how grateful were you?"

She glared, her face erupting in a blush. "None of your business, Miss Signed-Marriage-Contract."

I sighed, which drew a knowing, and entirely misguided, smile from Hetty. I had not told her—or anyone—of my concerns about Gil's reserve in our private moments. Even if I'd been able to find the words, which Heaven knew I wasn't, I would have felt I was betraying him.

We would just have to work this out on our own. But not now. Hetty was getting away from me, and I couldn't have that. A little velocipede speed was exactly what I needed at that moment.

Chapter Fourteen

In Which the Dollar Princess Calls

The phrase "dollar princess" calls to mind images of some poor innocent heiress sold to a titled bounder for her family's prestige. That does happen occasionally—witness sad young Consuelo Vanderbilt—but dollar princesses come in several varieties, and the sheep to the slaughter is only one.

More than a few are anything but unfortunate innocents, being well-off widows in pursuit of a second (or third) husband who will give them a little glitter…in return for the docility enforced by a wife who holds the bankbook. Pearl Lally was that type, writ large.

That's not intended as an unkind reference to her size, though Mrs. Lally would have fit in well with the fleshy lovelies in Mr. Rubens' paintings. Rather, it's a reference to the fact that she was clearly buying herself a Polish prince just the same as she bought a fine mansion on Fifth Avenue and elegant clothes at a Paris atelier (sadly *not* Mr. Worth's—he is known for preferring sylph-like ladies) each season. Pearl Lally wanted to be a princess, and it was Jerzy Mrzawzy's job to make her one. Also to gaze adoringly at her and keep his mouth shut.

At least, that was the impression we received when the happy couple stopped by on Gil's second afternoon of safety.

By then, everyone had recovered somewhat, and we were all returning to our routines. For me, that meant a good vocalization session with

Montezuma, and a fencing lesson with the *Comte du Bois*, otherwise known as Mr. Mark Woods of the Bronx. For the Countess and Gil, an expedition to the Ladies' Mile, because she was looking for a few last-minute items for the wedding.

I did not ask further questions on that, assuming it was not a matter for my concern. My trousseau was now in the exceedingly capable hands of Anna Abramovitz and Rosa, and aside from offering a few suggestions about my preferences on color and style, (anything light purple, and nothing requiring tight lacing!) I left it to them.

She might also have been looking to the flowers or other decorations for the ceremony; I had made a plea for simplicity in all arrangements, which my sensible Scottish mother-in-law-to-be had happily accepted. But her idea of simplicity and mine could well be far different.

Her insistence on bringing Gil along pointed in a particular direction: my bouquet. We—the Countess and I—had agreed to follow the lovely old tradition of having the groom supply his lady's posy, but knowing Gil, he would likely have needed some help with the order.

All of this was merely the beginning of the wedding whirlwind, which I knew would only intensify as we came closer. For my money, a couple of quiet hours of vocalization and fencing came as a relaxing treat.

Which is likely why the advent of Mrs. Lally and her swain was so depressing. I had just changed into a sweet, fluffy lilac-colored lawn afternoon dress with a satin sash in a slightly darker shade for the rest of the day, on the hope of looking pretty for Gil's return and taken to my chaise with my current book, a study of the flora and fauna of Australia, a most thoughtful gift from his sister, who lived there with her Foreign Office husband. On the flyleaf: Every bride needs exotic and absorbing reading for distraction! Much love and joy, Madeleine.

I hoped we would find ourselves in the same corner of the globe soon. In the meantime, I now had the concentration to read her lovely book...at least until Sophia dragged into the room and announced in a truly tragic tone:

"More visitors, Miss!"

Poor little thing, she'd really been worked to a frazzle over the last couple of days.

"Thank you." I closed my book and rose, leaning over to her and whispering. "Do you need some time off?"

"Oh, miss, I couldn't—"

"We have no social plans for the next few days. Take a half day tomorrow. Tell your father and brothers to leave you alone and sleep in. And make sure to take some of these extra cookies and whatnot so you can bribe them."

Her droop immediately gave way to a grin. "Thank you, miss."

I returned the smile. "Rosa gets a lot of perks as lady's maid...but you know we appreciate you too."

Sophia beamed. It's not easy to be the little one. "Thank you."

"Glad to. Now let's see who we have."

"I put them in the drawing room and called for tea."

"Excellent."

I smoothed my skirt and walked in, to an extraordinary scene. Mr. Gibson could not have drawn a better one.

Pearl Lally, who had a good ten years and twenty pounds on me despite being several inches shorter, was sitting on the settee. She was wearing a dress unfortunately very similar to mine, though candy-pink, with an extravaganza of a hat, piled with a veritable mountain of silk roses and topped with a jeweled pin and plume. The ensemble was finished with diamond jewelry entirely unsuited to the occasion: a series of heavy and intricate bracelets and a pave chain necklace that most ladies would only have worn with an evening gown.

"Oh, my dear! How nice to see you under happy circumstances!"

She stood and took my hands, stunning me with the familiarity. True, women can be rather florid in the expressions of affection—and some of us exchange letters with our dearest friends that are quite warm and intense indeed—but only when we know each other well. I vaguely remembered seeing Mrs. Lally backstage once...years ago.

"Yes," I said quickly, managing to turn the attempted kiss on the cheek into an airy embrace, "we are very relieved."

Up close, I noted that Mrs. Lally was both rouged and powdered and that

86

the carefully styled fringe peeping out from her hat was a slightly different chestnut brown than her knot. The lady did not scruple to take help where she found it. I also noticed that her eyes had a canny gleam I would not have expected.

Perhaps a bit of steel with the fluff.

Behind her, an unremarkable figure who must have been the prince rose from the settee.

"Jerzy, dear, come say hello to Miss Shane. We're going to be connected, of course, being royalty and all."

If Prince Jerzy Mrzawzy was aware I was actually joining the aristocracy, not a royal family, he gave no sign, simply smiling and bowing over my hand and clicking his heels, *Mitteleuropa* style. He mumbled something, not even enough for me to be sure of what he said, never mind how he said it.

For a giant matrimonial prize, the prince was rather unimpressive. Middling height, receding mid-brown hair, and vaguely pleasant features, neither powerful nor slight, with a faint trace of tummy carefully hidden by good tailoring, there was nothing especially memorable about his general appearance. His eyes, though, did rate a second look, being brown and rather sharp.

Another surprise. I suspected the prince was a good bit less of a nonentity than he played.

I would not—however—get much of a chance to explore that theory. Miss O'Hanlon appeared with tea and a couple of plates of very good but utterly plain sugar cookies. She could have been exhausted from the recent onslaught…but she could also have been commenting on the guests, as her predecessor Greta Dare had been known to do.

"Well, aren't you looking well," Pearl Lally began.

I took a breath to offer thanks, but it was unnecessary.

"Of course, it's quite exciting to be preparing for a wedding, isn't it? And to be marrying into a title. You are so lucky that the Duke's mother is here to help with arrangements. Jerzy's parents are long gone, so I am entirely on my own and quite at sea. Oh, *so* sorry to put it that way, darling."

She did not stop for even a full breath as her beloved flicked a modest glance, and I wondered what deathly extremity would be required to make me address Gil so familiarly in company. I remembered that when we had, in fact, seen deathly extremity, neither of us forgot to treat the other with absolute respect.

I had plenty of time for my contemplation, since my guest was barreling on: "I don't even know what to tell people to call me when we're wed…"

Well, I could help with that and even jumped in fast enough to do so. "Likely Your Serene Highness."

The lower style was usual among the Eastern European houses, most of whom had not ruled much more than their own castles in centuries.

"Serene Highness." Pearl Lally took a sip of tea and beamed. "Oh, that's pretty. Sounds less stiff than Royal Highness, too. My Serene Highness."

Her prince smiled and patted her arm; I assume *accidentally* resting his fingers on the complex of bracelets.

"You're marrying on the same day as us, aren't you?"

"Yes." I smiled, happy to be allowed into my own conversation. "An early evening-"

"Well, that's just so sweet…we're having a morning ceremony and a nice breakfast before we leave for our honeymoon. Poland, don't you know, to see Jerzy's family castle. Where are you going, dear?"

"Niagara-"

"Isn't that lovely?" She kept right on going. "I am so fortunate to have met Jerzy. And he me…do you know he told me he saw the elephant when he first set eyes on me?"

My eyes widened. What an extraordinarily unkind and incautious thing to say…and to get away with!

"It's an old Polish expression for finding the love of your life."

Indeed, it was not! I knew I had heard it somewhere, and I was quite sure it was not Polish. And that it definitely did not mean finding one's true love.

Not that I could remember where I'd heard it in the middle of the conversational barrage.

I took a sip of tea and debated whether I should attempt to intrude into the monologue, stealing a glance at the Prince, who was holding a pleasant face with completely vacant eyes. He was somewhere far from here, and who could blame him?

I rather wished I were.

"Dear Ella, I see you've met Mrs. Lally."

I am never unhappy to see the Countess or Gil, of course, but I have rarely been so relieved to see the two of them striding into the parlor. Or so amused: both quickly took the temperature of the room and slipped with imperceptible ease from their usual unpretentious North-of-England demeanor into The Duke and His Lady Mother.

Our guests, as Preston and the sports writers would say, never knew what hit them.

"Oh, Countess!" Pearl Lally spoke the title as if it were a name as she and her prince rose in unison. "Such a treat to see you!"

"Likewise."

"And the Duke! I don't believe we've met." She suppressed a giggle as Gil bowed over her hand and very subtly cut his eyes to me. "And, of course, you know Jerzy. Prince Mrzawzy."

The prince bowed over the Countess's hand, complete with heel-click... and offered a friendly shake to Gil. I saw the flick of my fiancé's eyebrow at that and marked it to ask later.

At the moment, we had all we could manage with polite conversation.

Aside from Mrs. Lally's extraordinary assumption that her prince and my duke must be relations or close friends and her apparent lack of understanding of protocol, there was the simple fact that one cannot converse in a monologue. Mrs. Lally talked us all under the table, and I blush to admit I stopped even trying to follow the thread.

She didn't seem to mind. I kept nodding and smiling and pouring for what seemed an infinite time. The Countess studied Mrs. Lally with the fascination she normally reserved for arcane mummification implements at the Museum, and Gil seemed to be content to observe the prince.

Finally, Mrs. Lally looked at the mantel clock. "Why, look at the time! I have a dress fitting. You know how that is, dear."

"I do." I hoped my relief did not show in my face. "So kind of you to come."

"Are you going to Mr. Bridgewater's dinner party next week?"

"We are."

"Delightful. We shall see you there."

She embraced me again. The prince bowed.

After the door closed, the Countess said it:

"They are a pair, aren't they?"

"At least," I agreed. "She's extraordinary...and he said three words the whole time."

"If they were words." Gil shook his head. "You met them before, Mother?"

"I did. You were still at sea...but he had just come in safely on the Cunarder."

"That's right." Somehow, I had not thought of that in the middle of the whirlwind we had just survived. I looked to Gil. "He was on the *Atlantic Star*, too."

My fiancé gave me one of those careful, opaque looks that means he's working on something he can't tell me about. "He was. In the first group of men who made right for the lifeboats, grabbing any convenient woman or child to give him an excuse."

"Disgraceful." The Countess was watching her son closely and clearly saw the same thing I did. "And I did wonder about the handshake."

"As did I," Gil nodded and looked to me. "You caught it, too."

"There was something off, yes."

"European royalty, even—maybe especially—the vestigial Eastern ones, don't go in for much touching," he explained. "They tend to hold themselves rather aloof, even from people of the same class."

"And a Continental prince, even a paltry Serene Highness, would not see you as the same class, would he?"

"Precisely."

"Pretentious nonsense." The Countess made a small annoyed noise. "Not to mention that our ancestors were ruling Scotland when his were still trying to figure out how to grow cabbage."

Gil shot me a quick glance, and I swallowed my chuckle and amused comment since this was clearly a matter of considerable gravity for his mother.

"That's as may be, Mother, but he definitely does not carry himself like an Eastern royal, even a minor one."

"Well, better Mrs. Lally than us, for certain," she pronounced.

"What about Mrs. Lally?" I asked, moving to more fruitful ground. "Was she like that when you saw her?"

"Oh, more so." My future mother-in-law allowed herself a musical chuckle. "She had quite a lot to say about that nasty Mrs. Corbyn...and all I had to do was mention her name and listen. Gossip has its uses."

"Sometimes," Gil agreed thoughtfully.

The Countess looked from him to me. "You poor children. You haven't seen each other at all today, and it's almost dinnertime."

Gil and I exchanged sheepish glances.

"Why don't you go for a nice walk in the park, and I'll make sure Miss O'Hanlon is proceeding well on dinner."

"Would you care to see the roses, Shane?"

Chapter Fifteen

Among the Roses

With a quick stop in the foyer for a parasol and a broad-brimmed hat (freckles are not becoming on a bride!), we set out for our allotted time alone, such as it was.

I had no illusions.

At our gate, I took Gil's offered arm. His aspect seemed a little tense and concentrated. He needn't worry...I had no expectations of sparking in the park.

On the way to the gate, as usual, I stopped to give some coins to Mrs. Early, and she smiled up at me. "You're looking so happy, dear."

"I am."

"Enjoy it while it lasts—and God willing it will."

"Thank you."

Gil glanced back at her as we went on. "Is there anything more we can do for that woman?"

"I don't know. She's not sick enough for the old-age homes, so she scrapes by and spends most of her time praying at Holy Innocents. Father Michael helps her, too. I wish we could do more..."

He nodded. "Well, perhaps we talk to the Father."

"Yes."

"We need to speak to him before the service, at any rate."

I nodded as we walked into the park. "There's the expectation of a little chat for premarital advice. Even Preston and Greta sat down with him."

"It does no harm."

"None. Though we have already mastered the most important thing."

For a moment he looked almost stricken, and then he remembered what I meant. "I was wrong, and I'm sorry."

"Precisely." We had said it to each other—him first—when we settled our argument over the marriage contract, both of us giving on the final sticking point. Him first, though. I smiled and patted his hand. "As long as we remember that being right is less important than being together…"

"Just so. Will you arrange a cup of tea at the rectory someday soon, then?"

"Of course. He will be delighted to give us a blessing before the ceremony."

"If that's all that we wanted."

"What do you mean?"

"I am not at all certain I want to be married by some doddery Episcopal priest Mother has dragged in on the advice of the Consulate."

"Why not?" I'd accepted the Countess's suggestion of the Protestant minister because it was the closest available to the Church of England. I had simply assumed it was important for Gil as a Peer.

It was not for me. As the daughter of a Catholic father and Jewish mother, who follows both my parents' faiths where I can, I am a good bit less doctrinaire about religious matters than most people. I was quite certain that God would be at our wedding, since He had brought us together, and not especially concerned about *how* we asked for His blessing—as long as we did so.

So, I was rather puzzled by Gil's concerns. I waited for him to continue.

"Well," he said, patting my hand on his arm, "it's actually rather simple. I know and respect Father Michael. He's Tom's best friend. He's essentially a part of your family. I think, after everything that has led us to this place, that I want him to do the honors."

My throat tightened, and I thought I might cry. "You—you don't have to do that for me."

"It's not for you." He shrugged. "I simply don't want to say my vows with some random cleric."

"But with all of the history of the English and Catholics and—"

"Remember, *mo chridhe*, I am a Northerner. Several of the great families in the North are Catholic, and there is a fair degree of intermarriage. So we can be wed in a private ceremony with the priest of our choice, and no one will say a word."

I nodded. I couldn't speak.

"And," he took my hand and laced fingers. "I will make certain that no one dares say a word about our lighting candles, either."

I looked up at him again. I had caught the *our*.

"I am not a religious man, Shane, but I have never felt such love and joy as when we light candles with your family and mine. I think we should do that for ourselves and our children."

My eyes did fill then. "Yes."

"I will buy you a pair of good silver candlesticks if you like."

"No. Just my mother's."

He nodded, understanding immediately. "Of course."

For a measure or more,e we stared at each other, surrounded by the love and warmth between us.

"Isn't this a pretty scene?"

We turned to see Aline Corbyn, decked out in an elegant willow-green walking suit and broad-brimmed hat topped with an entire actual pheasant. If the presence of the dead bird, staring at us with amber-bead eyes, wasn't disturbing enough, there was the unpleasant juxtaposition of the matron's social smile and poisonous gaze.

"So glad to hear you are home safe," she said to Gil in her best carefully sweet tone.

He bowed over her hand, and then she and I exchanged an appropriately loose embrace. So close I could feel the tension radiating from her, and once again, I wondered about what we had learned about Chester Lorimer and his death.

"It is very good indeed to be here with my fiancée." Gil gave me an only slightly exaggerated adoring glance.

"I'm sure." Mrs. Corbyn's expression left little doubt that she was thinking

94

of the daughter she'd tried to throw at him, only to have the young lady decide she far preferred to choose her own man…a livery cabbie.

"We are very lucky," I said simply and accurately. "And, of course, we look forward to seeing you at our open house after the ceremony."

Mrs. Corbyn's face lit up like a child on Christmas Morn. "Oh, how delightful. My social secretary did not tell me he had received the invitation."

"Oh, dear." I sighed rather theatrically. "It must have been lost. I am so sorry. Of course, the Dowager Countess would have sent you an invitation. She is so fond of you."

Fond of watching you make a fool of yourself, I did not add, as the matron preened.

"Well, I shall greatly look forward to it. Many congratulations to you, Ella dear."

"Thank you so much." I did not give her the satisfaction of gritting my teeth.

We bowed. She bowed.

As she walked away, Gil turned to me. "You really want that woman at our open house?"

"I want her where I can see her."

"That's a way to put it."

I slipped my hand through his arm again, and we resumed walking.

"You know, I did not miss the insult, Shane."

"I'm sorry?" I had hoped his command of American etiquette was a little weaker, but this is, after all, the Barrister.

"One does not generally congratulate a bride. The implication is that she has won something, namely the groom, and it is considered at least mildly offensive."

I shrugged. "People have been sending all manner of barbs, veiled and otherwise, toward me all of my life. I only respond to the ones that require it."

"So you will not permit me to empty the punchbowl on her head."

"You would not."

"If she insults you like that again in my presence, I am not responsible. I am, you will remember, half Highlander."

He was only half joking.

"Well," I said, pulling him closer to me, "let's see if we can't soothe the savage beast with a good meal. I assume you are staying to dinner and not eating in your bachelor rooms."

"You assume correctly." For a measure or so, he held my gaze. "I am strictly obeying the proprieties, but I will seize every second with you, sweetheart."

"Good."

"Also, I think it may be better to inform my mother that she has to tell the vicar to go away over dinner."

"You do?"

"Mother is much more likely to be compliant after a good meal."

"You can do no wrong in her eyes, my love," I assured him. "Nor mine."

"Rather a high bar, *mo chridhe*."

I snuggled a little closer to him. "You're equal to it."

Chapter Sixteen

Yet Another Caller

By Friday, we were becoming quite weary of callers. Which, of course, did not relieve us from having to entertain and refresh any number of people we hardly knew. At least I had a rehearsal for our part of the *Atlantic Star* benefit with Marie and Louis, followed by a great big family Sabbath dinner to look forward to. But I had to get there first.

I had my doubts at midday after the Countess sped off to the florist and Tommy uptown to hide at Cabot's and perhaps slip away to the Giants' afternoon game, the wretches leaving me to hold the fort. Gil, naturally, was nowhere in evidence, having no doubt found his own good reason to disappear until dinnertime.

Probably, I should have put on a nice afternoon frock, but with only a couple of hours until rehearsal, I decided to skip an extra costume change and put on my working clothes, worn blue cavalry twill breeches and a puffy white shirt from some previous season's Romeo, soft and well-washed. I planned to don a pretty dress and loosen my hair from its snug dancer's knot before candle-lighting of course, but I wanted to be comfortable now.

Which is why I was at such a disadvantage in my first meeting with Landgravine Charlotte von Stade.

"Miss! There's a landlady here for you!" Sophia said, sliding into the living room beside an impressively elegant woman.

"Landgravine, dear," she said to Sophia, more gently than reprovingly, then turned her gaze to me. She had the most extraordinary eyes, clear and very pale green, fringed by thick, dark lashes. If the eyes hadn't been so lovely, one might have spent a fair amount of notice on her mouth, which was generous and definitely lightly rouged. "Charlotte von Stade."

I took the offered hand for a very light clasp, which told me that whatever her title currently was, she was originally from Britain. "Ella Shane, at least for the next few days."

The polite smile widened a bit. "Duchess of Leith in a week or so."

"Yes."

Charlotte von Stade looked me over for what felt like a very long measure or two. This wasn't the usual society matron game; she wasn't deliberately trying to make me feel inferior, though I was keenly aware of her elegance in a trim light gray suit and lacy pale-mauve shirtwaist that accentuated her figure, which offered exactly the sort of luscious curves men tend to fancy. Nothing ostentatious like Pearl Lally, either in form or style, though, just subtle hints of luxury.

The pin at her neck had a sparkle far too crisp to be paste, her flower-piled hat was recognizably from a top Paris milliner, and her wedding ring and bracelet were thin bands of pave diamonds in platinum. There was a faint trace of a floral perfume I didn't recognize that I suspected would be quite heady, but only if one were very close.

Meanwhile, me, in breeches and not even a swipe of lip salve.

"Well," she said, patting my hand. "That's why I came to offer good wishes, dear. Gilbert is an old friend of my family."

"Oh. How wonderful," I managed, now forced to entertain the embarrassing thought I was appearing at a disadvantage with someone whose circle I would soon share. "Please excuse my appearance. I have a rehearsal in an hour or so. May I offer you tea?"

"That would be delightful." She nodded and gave me a genuine smile that verged on a grin. "I actually *envy* your appearance."

"You do?"

"Quite. You're comfortable, and surely every woman wishes she could wear breeches and have them fit so well."

I turned to call for tea as a way of hiding my blush.

Soon, we were suitably settled with tea and a plate of Miss O'Hanlon's delightful fairy cakes, this time with a strawberry icing in a pale pink that picked up the tint of the Landgravine's shirtwaist.

"How nice to finally meet you," she said. "I've seen both your Romeo and the *Princes* in London, and I've always wondered what you were like off stage."

"Just myself," I shrugged. "You know His Grace?"

"My brother is in the Lords with him, and we moved in the same circles. I'm so glad he's finally found new happiness."

As best I could tell, she was entirely sincere, but there was something in the way she spoke of Gil…I could not put my finger on it, but her face and voice softened in a manner that suggested—more than acquaintanceship.

I reminded myself I probably looked much the same when discussing Connor Coughlan because of our childhood bond.

"And, of course, since I had to sail over for that horrid Lally wedding extravaganza, I decided I might as well make acquaintances with you."

"Are you a friend of Mrs. Lally?"

She sighed. "I would not put it that way. Her sister Ruby is married to my brother. It was well before your first run in London, of course, but the two of them were among the first bunch of American girls to come title shopping. Pearl did not meet with success, being a bit more forward in the wrong ways, but my brother fell head over heels for Ruby, and she deigned to accept a mere Earl."

"I see."

Charlotte von Stade laughed. "Oh, you know family. Everyone has relatives who are less than edifying."

"Oh yes."

"But Pearl seems quite happy with her Polish prince, even though I have my doubts."

"About…"

"All of it, dear. She met him in Baden-Baden, and there seem to be some definite gaps in his family tree. But people do as they do."

"Do you think he is an impostor?"

"I haven't seen enough to know, and I'd never presume to impugn someone without evidence."

I waited. She was offering the disclaimer the same way Gil, or Tommy and I, might.

"That said, I'm rather familiar with obscure fiefdoms, being a Landgravine and all."

"Yes—it's originally from the Holy Roman Empire, isn't it?"

A chuckle followed by a rueful smile. "Von Stade was a very appealing young Prussian soldier attached to the Empress Frederick's suite at the time I met him. I was not setting my cap for a Landgrave."

"Any more than I set my cap for a Duke, perhaps." It was a bit over the line of polite conversation, but she'd crossed first, and I wanted to encourage her. Also, I was really starting to like this woman.

"Quite so." She looked around the drawing room. "Have you actually *read* all of these books?"

"Most of them. My cousin and I are voracious bookworms."

"No wonder Gilbert is so drawn to you. He always tried to get me to read all manner of improving things, and I always told him I was quite satisfied with my novels and the occasional volume of love poetry."

"Tommy and I will read almost anything." I shrugged. "And we love to talk about it."

"And argue about the finer points of the story or the author's approach?"

"Of course."

Charlotte von Stade gave a musical laugh, much like the Countess's. "You really are the only woman for him."

Nothing to say to that, especially not with another odd note in her voice.

"At any rate, I had never heard of the Princes Mrzawzy until I met Pearl's fiancé, but that does not mean they do not exist. Von Stade's holdings were nearer to Austria than Russia."

"Although..."

"Although he does not seem like most of the minor royals I've met."

"Hmmm."

"None of my affair." She took a sip of tea and tried for a small smile. "Pearl seems well pleased in her new husband-to-be, and the rest is none of my concern."

I sipped my own tea and looked at a fairy cake, then decided against it.

Charlotte von Stade favored me with that musical laugh again. "Worried about the wedding gown?"

"Of course."

"Ah, we all do it. I wanted to have a handspan waist for Von Stade…"

I blushed. "That will never happen with me. Opera singers can't lace tight, you know."

"Nor would anyone want you to imperil that glorious voice."

"Thank you." I met her gaze with a smile. She really did seem to be kind and friendly. I wasn't entirely sure what to do with a society woman who was not trying to intimidate or look down on me.

It wasn't the same, after all, coming from Gil's mother, who was not a voluptuous beauty.

"Miss! The Duke!" Sophia dashed in, managing to get a step ahead of Gil.

He was smiling at me when Charlotte von Stade turned to him, and his face froze for a moment. Then the smile returned, though I recognized it immediately as the polite expression he uses to cover less appropriate emotions. Something was definitely going on here.

"Gilbert!" she said, standing and holding out her hands.

"Charlotte von Stade, what an unexpected treat." He took her hands and planted a careful kiss on her cheek. "I see you've met my fiancée."

"Yes, and a perfect match she is. She tells me she actually reads books—and talks about them with you."

"Among other things." Gil seemed a bit awkward…but also genuinely pleased to be showing off his bride to his old friend. "A pleasant surprise to see you."

"I'm in town for Pearl's wedding, of course."

"Of course. And what do you think of the Polish prince?"

"I wish her joy in her new marriage."

101

Gil saw exactly what I'd seen but chose not to pursue it. "Just so."

"Well," she said, standing, "I promised Ruby I would meet her and Pearl for a shopping expedition, though I cannot imagine what else the woman needs."

"No?" I asked.

"Let's just say she's gone very deeply into the trousseau." Charlotte von Stade laughed. "And I understand you have a rehearsal."

"I do."

"Well, then, best wishes to you both. Perhaps we can manage a tea before I must return to England."

"England?" I expected her to be going to Germany for her Landgrave.

"Oh, yes, dear. Poor Von Stade's been gone these twenty years. I have a very nice little dower house and a quite fulfilling life in London meddling in my daughter's affairs when she lets me."

Gil's ears were turning pink.

"Delightful to see you again, Charlotte," he said, moving to escort her to the door.

"The same for me. Your fiancée is a treasure. I'm so glad you found each other."

Only after he'd seen her on her way with a bow did he turn to me.

"Charlotte's family and mine are close. She was very kind to me when I was in London."

"Ah. She seems like a lovely woman."

"She is." Gil nodded and left it at that.

So did I, though not for lack of curiosity.

Chapter Seventeen

Family Sabbath

Sabbath candle-lighting is always special to me, but this week, even more so with Gil home and safe. In an ordinary week, if I am not performing, we have the happy habit of having friends come over for Friday dinner, and under these rather extraordinary circumstances, we were blessed with most of the cast, from Father Michael to Cabot to Preston and Greta, plus Marie, Paul and the three small Winslows. That was quite all right, because Anna and Louis brought their toddler son Morris, known as the Morsel, and Aunt Ellen rounded up her last two at home, Kat and Suze, who were more than happy to supervise a junior dinner in the parlor, in return for the unexpected treat of being the oldest people in the room and therefore in charge.

Of course, we moved all breakables up to the highest shelves.

Not to mention making sure the Parcheesi board, the stereoscope, and the hamper of toys we kept for visiting wee ones were at the ready. Kat and Suze are their mother's daughters, but even they cannot command obedience from four small people without at least a few distractions.

Also a full cookie jar as a final resort. I've found that bribery is an excellent last-ditch strategy with cranky children. Though now, considering the possibility of having to bring one of my own up properly, I'm not entirely certain I would want to rely on it.

In any case, we were quite as ready as anyone could be for an evening with small and medium-sized guests.

Aunt Ellen, as it turned out, was buzzing with more than wedding excitement and the prospect of an evening free of watching over the young ladies. She pulled me aside as the girls dashed inside, and after a thorough hug, informed me of the latest visitation from the second sight.

No, I do not really believe Aunt Ellen actually possesses some supernatural power.

However, in the wake of several eerie experiences, most recently her disturbing vision of flames just days before the theatre fire that nearly killed us all, I have come to the conclusion that she occasionally picks up something. Our modern science, after all, is still explaining the workings of the brain, and it's entirely possible that every once in a while, there is something so disruptive in the atmosphere—say, the fancies of a madman—that a sensitive person might catch it.

So, that night, when she informed me that she was seeing something, I had to at least consider the possibility.

"I don't know what it is, child." Aunt Ellen shook her head. "But after that fire in the winter, I can't not say something."

"Of course."

"It's the wedding. I see you two turning away from the altar—married—and then people rushing in. I don't see them."

"And that's all?"

"Isn't that enough? Someone rushing in on your happy day?"

"Well, if you don't know who it is, or what their intentions are, how do you-"

Aunt Ellen sighed. "You think I'm borrowing trouble."

I smiled at her use of the same expression as the Countess. "I don't know if you are or not. But it's not much to go on. And who knows, maybe it's just the rest of the guests rushing in to congratulate us."

"Perhaps." She thought for a moment. "It is true that all of those other folks are coming after the ceremony."

"Right, so?" I didn't want to launch another discussion of why we were having a small service followed by a larger at-home, lest we get stuck in the whole question of whether even a wedding performed by Father Michael would count outside a sanctuary.

Aunt Ellen was not nearly as picky as Aunt MaryKat about such things, but I had no need to know her thoughts on the validity of a marriage celebrated in a parlor.

She gave me a rueful smile. "Maybe you're right."

"I might just be." I patted her arm. "After what happened in the winter, you'd naturally assume that any vision might be of something bad."

"That's true."

"Haven't you had good visions?"

"Well, of course." A grin. "The first time I set eyes on Fred, I had a vision of myself standing up with him. Didn't know then it would take five years of saving...but he was worth it."

"Well, then." I returned the grin...and then realized what she'd just said. "Wait. You and Uncle Fred waited five years to marry?"

"Yes," she agreed.

"So why were you pushing me to run to the altar with Gil?"

"Because we met when we were in our teens, silly girl." She put her hand on my arm with a wise smile. "You'll want to get to work on filling the nursery right away."

Fortunately, no one else was close enough to hear the comment. Or see my volcanic blush that ended the conversation. And equally fortunately, it was time for candle-lighting.

The entire cast, except for Cabot's giant mastiff Noble, who was happily demolishing a soup bone in the foyer, gathered in the dining room for our little Sabbath ceremony. I lit the tapers in my mother's tiny pewter holders, and Anna offered the blessings as she did whenever I could convince her to do so because her Hebrew is so much better than mine. She agreed this time, even though she prefers to avoid the attention of such large groups, because I convinced her I was too emotional to speak. It was nothing more than the simple truth, and she knew it as she smiled at me, standing there between Tommy and Gil, surrounded by everyone I love the most.

In the wake of all that had happened in the last few days, with the prospect of all that was coming, I found myself unable to fight off the strong emotions. My eyes filled, and I realized I was perilously close to sobbing, not from fear or sadness, but from the sheer unaccustomed joy of the moment.

Gil slipped an arm around my waist and gently rested his chin on the top of my head, a surprisingly intimate gesture for any fiancé, even husband, to make in public, but especially my reserved Northerner. It told me more clearly than any words that he, too, might have questioned whether he would find himself safe in this room on this night.

Tommy caught my eye, just smiling reassuringly, and I nodded.

My men looking after me together.

My other protector made his presence known after the last of the blessings. Preston, who was behind us, cleared his throat, and Gil immediately let go of me.

"You're not quite married yet, Barrister." Preston's tone was teasing, but there was a tiny edge of steel in his gaze.

Gil coughed and put his hands in his pockets, which told me that he'd been fighting tears too…and had no idea what to do with his hands just then.

"Climb down a bit, Pres." Tommy shook his head. "We've all had a rather frightening few days."

"Haven't we, though." Preston patted Gil's arm. "If I'd been stuck at sea wondering if I'd see Greta again, I'd probably hang onto her too. It's fine in the family…but it looks a little much, you know."

Gil nodded. "Quite right."

Preston gave him a wide smile. "Not long now, Barrister. I went through it last winter. Nothing worse than those last few weeks."

Gil blushed. So did I.

"Being lonely, of course," Preston said quickly, clearly worried we'd taken the comment the wrong way. "You don't realize how much you've missed having another person in the house until you're about to have one again."

"Absolutely." Gil cleared his throat again.

"I believe Miss O'Hanlon has tried a new recipe for escalloped potatoes to accompany the roast chicken tonight," I cut in quickly, taking both men's arms and shooting a quick glance to Tommy.

"And she might even be willing to share it with Greta if it is a success," Tommy added.

"Well, we can't miss that."

Even at family dinners, it is not usual for couples to sit together, the idea being that they have plenty of time to talk at home, so they should socialize with others. Engaged couples and newlyweds sometimes get a dispensation partly because everyone knows they just want to be together…and also because nobody wants to hear the lovebirds gush about one another's perfections.

Since it was my table and my fiancé, I decided to take advantage of that prerogative despite the knowing smiles from the others. In the usual few fluttery moments of sitting and settling, Gil leaned over to me.

"I hope I didn't embarrass you, *mo chridhe*," he whispered.

"Not at all. I could enjoy a great deal more of the same, though."

A trace of the blush returned to his cheekbones, and he took my hand, pulling it to his lips for a kiss. "In due time, my love."

My turn to blush.

Chapter Eighteen

For the Faithful Departed

S aturday began with a sad duty, the funeral of Mr. Lorimer. None of our party was especially pleased to be attending the obsequies, which would bring a grim reminder of our own various losses. The Countess, in fact, decided against attending, ostensibly because she had some wedding matter to attend to, but I strongly suspected she did not wish to be brought back to Gil's father's death—or some other that I did not know.

But when we arrived at the Presbyterian Church, it quickly became clear this was like no service any of us had attended. Except for Preston, who was already there when we arrived, alone in a back pew.

"Kid!" he said, standing as he saw me, Tommy, and Gil walking into the church. He was in a black suit with matching tie and none of his usual dandyish touches. The only color was a medal on his lapel, a brass medallion with a red-white-and-blue ribbon, and a plate reading "Gettysburg Veteran."

I'd never seen it. Nor had I ever seen anything like the church, which was filled with flags and bunting. It felt more like we were about to witness a celebration or a call to war than a funeral.

I took Preston's hands, marking but not acknowledging his worn expression. "We wanted to pay respects."

"With a little encouragement from your detective friend?" he asked.

"Cousin Andrew tries to avoid society events," Tommy began, shaking hands with Preston, "but this does not look remotely like one."

"Not a bit." Gil agreed, taking his turn to greet Preston. "My great-uncle was a Crimean War veteran, and this seems quite reminiscent of his service."

Preston nodded. "Very sharp, Barrister. Lorimer's getting military honors, as he should."

The church was full, many of those present, old enough to have served with Lorimer. I saw, to my surprise, that Grover Duquesne, Captain of Industry, was there, in a back pew on the other side of the church, clearly so absorbed in his memories that he saw no one else. Perhaps there really had been a decent man lurking somewhere in there all along.

The service itself was unexpectedly simple, Lorimer's flag-draped casket borne into the church to a rather anodyne organ processional, followed by a few psalms and prayers, all in English, with a minimum of emotion. I was unsure if the Presbyterian service was actually so cold, or if it was some misguided effort to ease the family's pain by allowing no expression of feeling at all.

Whatever the truth of the matter, the service seemed surprisingly brief and plain for someone of Chester Lorimer's standing, as if all of the effort for his farewell had gone into decking the church in flags and bunting, and there was no need for further tribute. I found it all puzzling, and quite honestly rather disturbing.

I was not the only one. A slight dark-haired woman I strongly suspected was Lorimer's protegee clearly did as well, sobbing quietly into her handkerchief from her seat a few pews very deliberately back from the family. Her placement was the clue; a relative, however distant, would not have been seated carefully outside the view of the chief mourners.

Not that they seemed overly concerned. Gertrude Corbyn Lorimer, the wife of the older son, seemed rather bored by it all. She might have started as a lovely blonde girl, but now, likely well into her thirties, she had that overfed, ruddy, blowsy look that some society women develop in a life of late nights and large meals.

Her mother, somewhat surprisingly, was not in attendance. I suspected the early hour, since I doubted Mrs. Corbyn would otherwise forego the chance to brazen it out. Unless she were taking her lawyer's wise advice to avoid the scene.

Though there was little enough to confront. The service felt almost like a demonstration at a seminary. *And now, class, we read this blessing...*

It was only during the final Psalm that I reached the unsettling conclusion that perhaps Chester Lorimer had not made clear his final wishes...leaving it to his family to arrange the farewell. They could not in any propriety deny him the military honors he had so dearly earned. But they *could* make his service as brief and perfunctory as possible.

I remembered what Rafe had overheard from Gertrude. If her mother had hoped to help matters along...

My reverie was broken by Gil's hand on my elbow, as the gentlemen stood for a final blessing. We would have much to share with Cousin Andrew later today.

The pallbearers, baby-faced cadets from some military academy, took up the flag-draped casket, looking nervous, well aware that they were toy soldiers in a room full of real veterans. Preston and many of the other men had already been mustered out to face life after the war when they were younger than those boys.

I glanced over to Lorimer's family, wondering if his sons felt guilty at missing what many might see as a last duty to a father: bearing him to his rest. The older son kept sending nervous glances at his wife, Gertrude, as if he were afraid of her. The younger was sobbing uncontrollably, and when he looked up for a moment, I understood. He was an adult, but his face was as open and simple as a child's.

I remembered what the Countess had said of a whisper about him falling on his head as a boy.

Many families hide people away if they are imperfect in any way, and I suspected this might be the only time we would ever see the younger Lorimer son. It spoke well of somebody that they made sure he was able to pay final respects to his father.

Not Gertrude, for certain. She leaned over and hissed something sharp to her brother-in-law, and he stifled another sob and was quiet. Even for a daughter of Aline Corbyn, it was cruel.

I could not help hoping that wherever the poor man normally kept his home, it was far from Gertrude…and that people were kind to him.

We all bowed our heads as the minister intoned a simple final prayer with the same professional calm as the rest, and then, for a measure or so, there was nothing but the sound of the boys' booted feet. Beside me, Preston was ramrod-straight, standing at attention as he had so many years ago on that blood-soaked field in Pennsylvania.

Gil and Tommy were holding carefully respectful stances, but I knew both of them were remembering other caskets they'd seen borne away. It was the one small luxury of losing my father so young that I did not remember him or his death. A Christian burial service holds fewer painful echoes for me.

What few flashes of memory I have from watching the rabbi say the words over my mother are far different. A cold, mostly empty, room at the Jewish charity that had buried her, Hebrew blessings, surprisingly beautiful and musical…and as Aunt Ellen guided me away, someone handing me a tiny *yahrzeit* candle, and telling me to light it for her at home.

Nothing like this crowded, banner-draped sanctuary or these very deliberately non-musical English words apparently meant to impose some kind of cool rationality on the mystery of life and death. The least rational thing known to humanity.

I could feel the men beside me tensing, all carefully hanging on to demeanor in the near, and nearly unbearable, silence.

And then, suddenly, ripping through the quiet like the first shot must have done on a humid July morning at Gettysburg, a raspy, impossibly ancient voice intoning:

Mine eyes have seen the glory of the coming of the Lord….

"The Battle Hymn of the Republic." Because there could be nothing else. On the second line, Preston joined in, and so did several others, all apparently older gentlemen and veterans, too:

He is trampling out the vintage where the Grapes of Wrath are stored…

As he reached the last word, Preston patted my arm and nodded to me, and I joined him:

He hath loosed the fateful lightning of his terrible swift sword...

Then, encouraged by Preston and the others, Tommy, Gil, and the rest of the congregation began to sing along as well, Lorimer's younger son joining loudly despite Gertrude's efforts to shush him:

His truth is marching on...

Glory, Glory, Hallelujah!

Now everyone was singing, except Gertrude Corbyn Lorimer and a few other society women, who looked genuinely confused and offended. Lorimer's protegee put her hand on her heart as the casket passed, proudly singing through her tears. So did the younger Lorimer son, standing at attention with his brother, both clearly doing as their father had taught them.

The veterans, singing one more lost comrade out, were no longer aged and decrepit but alight with pride. All standing straight, carrying the spirit and the memory of those who never came home.

It was only as we started the second verse that I looked to Gil, realizing then he actually knew the words. Another surprise from my beloved.

As we reached the final chorus, the congregation marched after the family onto the church steps, now more proclaiming than singing as we went:

Glory, Glory, Hallelujah!

Glory, Glory, Hallelujah!

Glory, Glory, Hallelujah!

His Truth is Marching On!

As the last notes faded in the heavy June air, the boys gently placed Lorimer's casket in the hearse, standing together for one last silent salute.

God give him rest.

Chapter Nineteen

In Which We Walk Away Unsettled

We all watched as the horses began to step away with their burden, everyone once again quiet, but having somehow burned off the worst of the sadness and pain by joining together in the Union song. At least for the moment.

Lorimer's older son quickly guided the younger to a carriage, as if he were trying to protect him from Gertrude's wrath—which he might well have been. Rafe was right, Gertrude did seem to hate everyone.

Grover Duquesne nodded to the casket and walked away, never even looking at the rest of the congregation.

Most of the crowd was still standing on the stairs or just below, watching the hearse go, little other sound than the clop of the hooves and faint squeak of wheels.

Preston turned to us.

"That's well done. A proper send-off."

"As it should be," Gil agreed.

"And how do you know the words, Barrister?" Tommy asked.

A modest shrug. "Ah, well, I've made a study of Lincoln. Why would I not?"

We all managed small smiles, unwilling to break the extraordinary moment, the feeling that we had just witnessed—and taken part in—something amazing.

"What a disgraceful display!" Gertrude Corbyn Lorimer was upbraiding the elderly veteran who had started singing and Lorimer's young friend, who was standing with him. "We were hoping to give Father Chester a dignified farewell, and you—"

Preston turned, his face tight and flushed with fury. Tommy, Gil, and I started to move toward him...only to realize we'd been trying to stop the wrong confrontation.

"You're not fit to say his name!" The slight dark-haired woman, God love her, actually raised her hand to slap Gertrude.

"Now, ladies. Come along, Miss Elsie." Rowan Alteiss, who'd been on the other side of the steps, quickly put a gentle hand on Lorimer's friend's arm. "We're all quite overwrought today..."

"We're mourning one of our own, young woman, and we'll do it our own way," the elderly man chimed in, with a determined glare at Gertrude.

Alteiss watched but didn't try to stop him.

A tiny, stooped gent who had to be eighty or more, he wore the same Gettysburg medal as Preston, along with a few others on his outmoded but immaculate coat. He continued with a fury in his eyes and whiplash tone of voice that would have wilted most people. "And you'll shut up and like it."

Gertrude had clearly inherited her mother's sense of self-importance. She huffed for a moment, her plump little face turning an unflattering shade of puce. "Well, I never!"

"Go back to your castle and wait for Chester's money," the old man said, his voice breaking on a rusty laugh. "If you think you're going to get any of it, that is."

"Colonel Vandergrift." Rowan's voice held a tiny trace of lawyerly steel. "That's not a conversation for today."

The Colonel nodded. "Quite right, son."

Gertrude huffed once more and swept down the stairs toward her carriage.

The younger woman wilted a bit, and the old man patted her back.

"It's all right, dear. You did right by Chester."

"As did you, sir." Preston came up to shake hands with Colonel Vandergrift.

"All we can do for a fallen comrade, right?" The old man patted Preston's arm and gazed up at him. "Drummer boy?"

"Started out that way."

They nodded grimly together, long-ago horrors binding them together in ways we could not understand.

"Well, that Gertrude's always been a nasty little piece of work, just like her mother." Vandergrift shook his head. "You always knew her eye was on the bankbook. And when Chester took a kindly interest in Elsie…"

"He was like a second father." Elsie's voice broke on the last word, and tears spilled over.

Vandergrift, though stooped and a few inches shorter, patted her back and tried to offer manly reassurance. "There, there, dear. We know."

"Thank you so much." She nodded to all of us. "On another day, I should like to meet you, but I truly wish to mourn privately if I may."

We all nodded and watched her walk away, her carriage straight, her steps sure, though anyone who had seen her face would not doubt her pain.

"Poor girl," said Vandergrift with a shake of his head. "It's like burying her father again. Chester had done his best to watch over her."

"Young Mrs. Lorimer thought something else was in play?" Gil asked.

The old colonel's eyes widened a little at his accent, but he nodded. "Nasty-minded people can only see nasty things."

"So true," Tommy agreed.

The Colonel nodded to Tommy and then turned to Alteiss. "Are you going to stop defending that horrid woman now?"

"I can't, sir." He shook his head. "I've promised to provide her an effective defense, and so I shall."

Gil's brow quirked, and I knew he was parsing some aspect of this. I marked it to ask later.

As for the old man, he shook his head. "Just like *your* father, Alteiss, honorable and too da- er, blasted — stubborn. Sorry, Miss."

I swallowed a smile.

"Thank you, Colonel," Alteiss said. "A high compliment indeed. May I present my friends?"

"Well," he said, turning his still sharp hazel eyes on me, "this pretty thing is

Miss Ella Shane, the singer. I'd know that voice anywhere. Which probably makes the big boy her cousin, the Champ, and the one with the fancy accent her fiancé."

Of course, on the steps of the church after a funeral, we could not give in to a laugh, so we contented ourselves with friendly smiles and handshakes all around before resorting to a bit of polite conversation before moving on.

As it happened, the Colonel had bought a ticket to the *Atlantic Star* benefit, and we invited him backstage. He declined quite decidedly, saying he would be happy to have us to tea some afternoon, but his mother raised him far better than to visit a young lady in her dressing room.

After that electrifying comment, we walked down the steps to find another surprise: Cousin Andrew, a few yards away, watching the scene.

He gave us a sheepish little smile. "Just because I could not attend did not mean I could not watch the stairs afterward."

"Why don't you walk us home, and we'll tell you what we've learned?" offered Tommy.

"Would there ever be a cup of coffee at the end of the walk?"

I laughed. "Of course, there would. Even a married man can't be expected to have proper provisions at all times."

Chapter Twenty

Intermezzo and Interrogation

By the time we reached the townhouse, we had acquainted Cousin Andrew with what we had learned at the service, and he had acquainted *us* with the fact that Lorimer's son, married to Mrs. Corbyn's daughter, was likely the only heir to a sizable fortune and a large house besides.

Cousin Andrew seemed as curious as we were about what concerns Lorimer's fatherly interest in Elsie might have sparked with the Corbyn connections and asked us to keep our ears open. We happily agreed and then got down to the real business of the visit: coffee, cookies, and family talk.

I didn't go very heavily into the coffee and cookies since I had a fencing lesson in an hour or so, but I was more than happy to catch up on the doings of the detective and his new wife. The former Katie McTeer was a college-educated primary school teacher, and she was initially unwilling to leave her work in a city public school and marry him. Then, though, Cousin Andrew found a private progressive school on the West Side that was thrilled to have a Mrs. Riley as a part-time instructor, clearing the path for their happy ending.

Now, in the heart of the summer, Katie was setting up their new home, a sweet little apartment a few blocks from the precinct house and working on her lesson plans for fall. Gil, Tommy and I exchanged subtle glances, as the detective waxed eloquent about his wife's cooking and his pride in her ambitions for her new students.

We were near the bottom of the pot of coffee when Miss O'Hanlon and Rosa appeared in the foyer, giggling.

Cousin Andrew and Gil gave Tommy and me puzzled looks.

"The young ladies are going walking out," I explained.

"Walking-out?" Cousin Andrew looked dubious.

"A couple of printers, apparently." Tommy didn't know much more than I—and probably Rosa, over the last few days—had told him. "They're going for a turn around the park."

"And the fellows are coming here to meet Toms first." I nodded to Gil.

"Just as it should be." Gil nodded.

"Rosa! Mary!" I called, "Come in and say hello."

The young ladies in question walked into the parlor, and we all stared for a moment. In their black uniforms, even with Rosa's embellishments, they look rather ordinary and perhaps even a bit plain. But in pretty afternoon outfits, they turned into the attractive young girls they are.

Rosa had a light-brown jacket with red trimming over a soft red and tawny floral dress, topped with a sweet hat in the same red as the jacket trim. Her brown eyes sparkled, and there was no doubt that she'd taken my example and bought a tin of rose-petal lip salve at Chalfont's Pharmacy.

Our Irish maiden was a vision in green, a green sprig-print dress and light wrap, finished with a broad-brimmed straw hat trimmed with plenty of green leaves and ribbons. She'd done her bit with subtle cosmetics too; I suspected she'd added a dab of the rose petal salve to her cheeks for color, since her skin is almost translucently pale, and it's easy to look a bit washed out. Heaven knows I've resorted to it on occasion!

"Looking quite lovely, ladies," Gil said as they walked in. "Do I hear you are meeting friends?"

"Going walking-out." Rosa grinned. "I'm not sure they're that interesting, but it's awfully nice to be asked."

Tommy laughed. "Hopefully, the walk itself will be the treat and not the asking."

"Well, the dressing-up was a treat, too," Mary said. "Rosa helped me make over my hat…they'll have to do pretty well to live up to this."

"Indeed they will," Cousin Andrew joined in with a smile. "Now, we're sure these are nice fellows?"

"Printers," Rosa said. "We met them just outside Holy Innocents when we were doing the marketing."

"They go to Mass every day, they say," Mary added.

"Well, that's as good a recommendation as any for a walk in the park," Tommy said just as the bell rang.

Cousin Andrew rose. "I'd best be going, and I'll give the fellows a nice hard look on my way out."

Gil reached for the newspaper. "I think I will do well to stay out of the way. All of you will be quite terrifying enough."

Tommy and I were laughing as we headed into the foyer, trailing the girls by a few important feet. Rosa opened the door, and the two young men carefully stepped inside.

They were, as advertised, one blond and one dark. The blond one was rather tall, and the dark one was a bit shorter, but there was nothing otherwise memorable about them.

They did seem to gawk a bit at the house, studying the scene with a curiosity that might have concerned me if I hadn't seen it on any number of deliverymen over the years. Tommy and I are rather a thing, and people are always curious about our home.

For the first few years, I'd been concerned such visitors might have nefarious intentions, but eventually, I realized the gawking type just wanted to stare, not burglarize us. A little disconcerting, but harmless.

The fellows caught us watching them and quickly stopped staring, looking embarrassed at being caught, as any reasonable person would.

The blond one stepped past Rosa to stand a hair's breadth too close to Mary, as the dark one followed more slowly, greeting Rosa with a friendly smile.

"Nice to see you two," Cousin Andrew said before introductions could be made. "I need to get back to the police station."

Both paled a bit, as was intended and were silent until Rosa closed the door behind the detective.

"Now, then, who have we here?" Tommy asked, turning to Mary, giving her the prerogative of introductions.

"Jim and Tim, Mr. Tommy," she said.

"James Collier, sir," the blond one began, offering his hand to Tommy. "You're the Champ, I know."

"I am, at that." As he held the handshake, he allowed just a tiny thread of menace to creep into his voice. "And we're very protective of Miss Mary and Miss Rosa."

"Don't blame you, sir. It's a scary world sometimes, and we have to protect our young ladies."

"Exactly." Only a tiny flick of Tommy's eyelid suggested that he found the answer just a touch too perfect, but he said nothing, only turning to the next contender. "And you are?"

"Tim Gardner." The dark-haired one reached out to Tommy. "Honor to meet you, Champ. My Da and older brother saw you fight."

"Thank you." Tommy shook and nodded. "So, where are you going?"

"Just a walk around the park," Tim said.

"We may stop for an ice at that nice little ice cream parlor nearby, too," Jim added.

"That's a lovely idea," I contributed, merely to remind them of my presence. Whatever my feelings on male prerogatives, this event was very much a thing among men. Tommy and Cousin Andrew were reminding the fellows Rosa and Mary are well-protected and they had best treat them with respect. Or else.

"Their lemon ice is very tasty," Tim agreed.

I prefer violet ice cream, but I had no intention of getting drawn into the perennial discussion of which flavors are best…because that could take longer than anyone had for that walk.

"Well, then, have a wonderful time," Tommy said, giving the fellows a graceful bow and the official signal that they'd passed muster for the moment.

"Thank you very much, Mr. Tommy," Rosa said, with Mary echoing her.

"Of course." Tommy opened the door.

We watched as they walked down the steps and paired off, the fellows reaching the bottom first and offering their arms, as is appropriate. At least in my circles. But it seemed just a tiny bit too polished by half for a pair of printers.

Still, the sun was shining, our girls were perfectly done up, and their swains were reasonably acceptable. Tommy and I watched them for a moment, waving when they turned back to look before stepping off in the direction of the park.

After he closed the door, we returned to the parlor, where Gil was absorbed in an article on the latest turns in the Boxer Rebellion.

"What do you think, Heller?"

"A little slick...but probably harmless."

Gil looked up from his paper.

"My thoughts as well," Tommy agreed. He turned to Gil. "They seem nice enough, but there's something that bothers me—just a little."

"What?"

"If I knew, I would do something about it," Tommy said. "As it is, I don't see any danger in a simple walk in the park on a busy Saturday."

"Just so." Gil looked at us both. "And it is possible that you are a bit overly protective of the girls."

"Well," I said. "They're very young to be courting..."

Gil laughed. "Not that young, Shane. Plenty of girls marry at eighteen."

"Not Irish girls," I reminded him. "We marry later because we want to save up money for a decent start on a life."

"Or," Tommy said with an arch smile at me and my fiancé, "because they haven't met their proper man."

"Well, true," I admitted.

"I'm not entirely sure of those fellows either, Heller," Tommy said. "But we'll do better to let the girls find out for themselves that they're not worth much."

"And at least they'll get an ice cream out of it."

Tommy and I turned to Gil, who was blushing.

"I have a sister, you'll recall." He shrugged, quite adorably. "Until she met her husband, Madeleine enjoyed the dressing-up and the treats offered at least as much as the actual company kept."

We all laughed.

"But I agree," Gil continued. "At least as it stands now, those two are merely a diversion for our young ladies. And good thing."

"Absolutely." I smiled.

"I suspect there isn't the man-made, who interests Rosa more than writing," Tommy observed. "At least not right now."

"There wasn't the man-made, who interested me more than singing…" I began as my beloved's eyes lingered on my face. "Until recently."

Tommy laughed and smacked my arm. "Until you met your proper man, you mean."

"Well, yes." I looked away to avoid Gil seeing the worst of the blush and saw the clock. "Oh, drat!"

The men looked at me.

"I have a fencing lesson in ten minutes. I'm going to go throw my clothes on…"

I dashed for the door, hands on the buttons at my collar, as I'd done hundreds of times before…only this time, I saw Gil was watching me.

Both of us froze for an instant, as I realized what he was thinking…and he understood that I knew.

Probably the worst shared blush yet.

"Um, I'll be back in a few minutes," I said quickly, dashing for the stairs.

Behind me, I heard Tommy chuckle and the very determined rustle of the paper as Gil sought refuge in the Boxer Rebellion. At that exact moment, it was probably a safer topic.

Chapter Twenty-One

Fencing and Other Matches

By the time I changed into my fencing kit and splashed a little water on my face (to cool it from the run upstairs, not anything else!), I was back to my normal calm and appropriate demeanor. I was coming down the stairs, making sure my hair was securely pinned into the tight dancer's bun I wear for fencing lessons when the bell rang again.

"Oh, the Comte is here." Tommy spoke as he walked out of the parlor with Gil behind him.

Gil offered me a hand I obviously did not need at the base of the stairs, but I was glad for the excuse to touch it, even if it did send me right back to another blush. Glad, too, for the appreciative gaze he always had for my fencing outfit. He would never be so vulgar as to admit he liked looking at my legs, but I was reasonably certain that was the case and not in the least offended.

"I don't suppose you'd be interested in joining the fencing lesson..." I offered.

He shook his head. "I'm sorry, sweetheart, but I have an errand this afternoon."

"Oh."

"Shane," Gil said, taking my hands, "very little would give me more pleasure than crossing swords with you, but I've promised a friend at the Embassy that I will meet him for tea."

"All right."

I hated the petulant sound of my voice. Especially since I recognized his tone: it meant he was involved in something he could not tell me about, and it was my duty not to ask. Just as it was his duty not to ask when I was involved in something I could not discuss.

And they're very good ground rules, in general.

But it's damnably hard to follow ground rules when you're a bride who wants to spend time with her man.

With an apologetic smile, Gil leaned in and kissed me on the cheek. "I will owe you a good duel."

"I will hold you to that."

For a measure or so, his lips rested on my skin. What had begun as an innocent gesture suddenly felt like much more as his fingers tightened around mine and he pulled me closer.

"*Mo chridhe...*" Gil's voice was low and husky, nothing like his normal cool tone.

Never mind fencing. *This* was the match I wanted.

"Monsieur le Duc!"

Gil and I broke apart as the Comte's voice rang through the foyer, guiltily clasping our hands behind our backs.

My diminutive gargoyle of a fencing master strode toward us with a floridly outraged scowl. "What is this?"

Clearly, at the edge of his forbearance, Gil tensed and glared right back. "Listen, you little frog—"

The Comte burst into laughter and held his hand out. "I believe congratulations are in order."

Gil blushed, laughed, and took the offered hand. "They are indeed. You cannot be unaware that Miss Shane is doing me the honor."

The Comte grinned. "You are a lucky man."

"I am indeed, Monsieur le Comte." Gil nodded to me and Tommy. "A very lucky man who unfortunately must go."

"All good wishes, Your Grace."

"Thank you kindly."

124

At the door, Gil turned back to look at me.

The Comte chuckled. "Ah, love. Don't worry, Monsieur le Duc, your beloved will be well occupied. How many days until the wedding?"

"A week."

A wicked grin from the Comte. "We'll do well to keep you two away from the swords after today."

Tommy laughed. Gil, Lord love him, just shook his head and gave into a laugh too. What else could he do?

Upstairs, Montezuma greeted the Comte with a cheery chorus of *La Marseillaise*. The match was surprisingly normal. The Comte is probably the best fencing partner I've ever had, and I've only defeated him once. Exactly as it should be; fencing on the stage is work, and my matches with Gil are fun, but sessions with my instructor should be all about improvement.

Though, of course, when you have two highly-skilled duelists, it's also plenty of fun!

We were both in our best form today, and it was a good, hard fight…to a draw.

I didn't give it to him, nor he to me. But it was a perfect end to my last match as an unmarried woman.

When we bowed, the Comte shook my hand and took a long look at me.

"Do you intend to continue fencing after your marriage?"

"Oh, of course." I shrugged. "His Grace has demanded no limitations on my stage work."

"Not that you would give them."

"Precisely. He likes to fence on occasion, too."

A grin from the Comte, which strongly suggested he understood that Gil and I took a bit more joy in the fencing than was strictly proper. "No doubt he does, Mademoiselle. You are very skilled."

"It's part of my work," I reminded him, walking over to put my foil in the cabinet.

"Yes, and a pleasure to teach someone who takes it so seriously." The Comte sighed. "Unlike many other ladies who fence."

"Many?" There had been a brief vogue for fencing among women years ago in France, but I hadn't realized it came here.

"Oh, every so often, it becomes the thing." The Comte carefully put his sword into its case, "That does not mean they make any effort to become good at it."

"No?"

He chuckled. "That Mrs. Corbyn—she tried last winter."

"She did?"

"Not for long. Nearly took my eye out."

I had to stifle a laugh. Not at the thought of my dear instructor being injured, but his beleaguered expression. "I'm sorry to hear that."

The Comte grinned. "Oh, don't be. I was glad to not have to teach her anymore, if only because she was not especially prompt with payment."

"What?" It was the second time I'd heard about Mrs. Corbyn's questionable financial habits. Perhaps she made a habit of paying late or not at all with more than young artists.

"Oh, yes. I had to have a very pointed conversation with her, and we decided to part ways. Of course, this is for your ears only, Mademoiselle."

"Of course."

"Most ladies are just fine, of course. Not especially proficient, but willing to learn...and to pay on time."

"Which is quite all you need."

"Indeed." We had reached the studio door, and he turned, grinning up at me. "Enjoy your wedding celebrations, Mademoiselle."

"I will do my best."

The Comte's gaze sharpened on me. "And don't worry about your man. Weddings terrify even the finest gentlemen."

"What?"

He laughed. "All of this public adoration and declaration is rather difficult for a man, especially one like yours. Remember, Mademoiselle, you are used to being the star of a show. He is not."

"Oh."

"Yes, all he has to do is offer his arm and recite a few words...but it probably seems like a much bigger task than it does to you."

CHAPTER TWENTY-ONE

"Perhaps."

"And marriage makes men *just* a little nervous."

"Why?"

"It's the way we're made, Mademoiselle. A man may want nothing more than to stay by his hearth with his beloved…but he may not want to say so to the world. It seems a bit less manly."

"Ah." I managed a sophisticated nod. I would have to talk to Marie about this later.

"In any case, he adores you, and all will be well."

His reassuring smile was absolutely sincere.

"Thank you."

"And I'll see you after the honeymoon. Niagara Falls, really?"

"Really."

"Well, enjoy the scenery, then."

We walked down the stairs and shook hands at the door.

"All good wishes, Mademoiselle."

"Thank you, Monsieur le Comte."

We bowed, as we always did at the end of a lesson or match. Whatever momentous things might happen between now and our next lesson, we would maintain our forms.

After I closed the door, I went downstairs to check on dinner plans…and our young ladies' afternoon out. I heard a giggle as I stepped in.

Miss O'Hanlon was shelling peas, and Rosa had a lap full of work.

"Back in place, I see," I said, returning the impish smiles.

"And glad to be," Miss O'Hanlon replied, her grin giving way to a wry scowl.

"Not the pleasing companions you hoped for?" I asked.

Miss O'Hanlon let a handful of the peas trickle into her work bowl. "Oh, not even a little."

"They can't all be the Barrister, miss," Rosa said with a sigh as she picked up a skirt whose hem needed mending.

"But they should be interesting to you."

Mary O'Hanlon laughed. "Then these two aren't the ones."

"No?"

"Not a bit of it." Rosa shook her head. "We were bored silly. All the way to the park they talked about how wonderful they are—their good jobs, and good prospects and such. And then they got all nosy."

"Nosy?"

"Oh, you know. You probably get it with the society ladies sometimes. What famous people we've seen, who we know, all of that."

Miss O'Hanlon giggled as she pulled another handful of peapods from the brown paper sack. "Can you believe Jim thought you knew Miss Sarah Bernhardt?"

I joined the giggle. "I think I saw her once on the street in London."

"And Tim asked if Mr. Tom brings the Giants over in baseball season."

"Our carpets would never recover." I shook my head. "What a strange pair."

"It's quite all right," Mary O'Hanlon said, "I'm sure there are plenty of other men out there."

"And better ones," Rosa added.

"On that, ladies, I think we can all agree."

I was smiling as I headed back upstairs.

Chapter Twenty-Two

Sunday Dramas

Sunday morning began as it always did when we were home, and not sleeping off a performance night: with Mass at Holy Innocents. After the eventful day, we had all decided in favor of a very simple dinner and an early night, so Tommy and I were quite well rested when we walked over for the service.

While Aunt Ellen always insisted on the early Mass when we were children, Tommy and I much prefer the late-morning service. It's not laziness, truly—we are often working into the night. Or, as we were on this day, we spent the early part of the day clearing other obligations so we could enjoy the afternoon and evening in family time.

Tommy locked himself in his office and worked on arrangements for the fall production of *Xerxes* at the Met and groundwork for the San Francisco stand if we decided to go through with it. He planned to talk to Henry Gosling later, to see if there was any good guidance on what singers with family expectations did with their calendars.

I doubted there was, quite honestly. Marie had stopped singing except for the occasional benefit for about two years, from a few months before Jimmy's birth to the end of her confinement with Polly. She'd returned to work for a few years before Joseph arrived...and was back on stage within months of his birth.

For my part, I had no intention of filling a nursery and less of leaving the stage for any extended time. But there was no doubt that we needed some kind of plan for the next year or so, while we were, as the Countess had rather bluntly put it, "working on that baby."

In any case, Tommy had a very busy morning of paperwork and letter-writing in his office, considering contracts and all the other matters related to the Met production. It would surprise no one to know the Met has its own expectations and way of doing things, and that it required considerable adjustment from the Ella Shane Opera Company way.

My early morning was far more enjoyable: a good vocalization session and then a few fencing and physical culture exercises just so I would not forget what I'd learned the day before with the Comte. That, and the walk to and from Holy Innocents, would be quite enough activity for the day, all things considered.

And a very pleasant walk it was, at least on the way to the service. Tommy and I assembled at the door in summer Sunday church clothes: a light gray suit, light-green foulard tie, and gray trilby for him. For me, a simple but not dull pale-lavender lawn lingerie dress with a big straw hat trimmed up with lavender roses. By no means my most elegant or expensive outfit, and very much as it should be. Church is not the time for showy diva costumes or airs, and I always "dress down" a bit.

Tommy offered his arm, and we walked the few blocks happily together, enjoying the sunshine and the pretty day.

"The Barrister doesn't go to church, does he?"

"Not often. Apparently, aristocratic males only attend church on Christmas, Easter—or when their women make them."

Tommy shook his head. "Probably doesn't even know the comfort he's missing."

"Probably not." I shrugged. "But he does want the Father to marry us."

"Really."

"Yes. And to light candles together on Friday nights."

Tommy smiled. "You are going to bring him into the same patchwork as us, whether he wants it or not."

"Probably so." I smiled back. "It will likely be good for him too."

"It's certainly good for us. Has he told the Countess?"

"Of course. She was actually quite relieved not to have to drag in some unknown priest from a Consulate list and try to explain everything."

Tommy's eyes gleamed. "I can imagine that conversation. 'My son is marrying a woman who's Catholic and Jewish…but she's agreed to an Episcopal service. If you behave yourself.'"

"The behaving himself is not negotiable."

"Not even a little. I'm glad it's going to be Father Michael."

"So am I."

"Candles every Friday, eh?" Tommy smiled warmly. "So much for the hidebound aristocracy."

"He's not just any aristocrat," I reminded him with a small scowl. "He actually loves the ritual."

"And why not." We were at the door of Holy Innocents, and a few of our acquaintances were walking up the stairs. Time to be quiet and behave *our*selves.

The service was wonderful, as always. Father Michael favored us with a homily on the importance of love, all kinds of love, reminding us that the greatest thing we can do is love others as we love ourselves.

You'll never find anyone at our house arguing with that. (Or at least not anyone who's welcome for long!)

Outside the church, we spent a few minutes talking with the priest after he greeted the congregation. We knew it could not be too long, though, because clouds were gathering, clearly pointing to an afternoon storm.

"Good thing the weather was fine yesterday," Tommy observed with a chuckle. "Or else the girls would not have gotten their walk with their new swains."

"New swains?" asked Father Michael.

"Apparently, a couple of your parishioners," I said. "Printers named Tim and Jim? They come to the morning Mass after work."

"Tim and Jim? Printers?" the priest looked confused.

"They took Rosa and Mary O'Hanlon walking-out yesterday." Tommy explained. "A tallish fellow with light hair and a shorter one with dark.

Cousins, they said."

Father Michael's eyes narrowed. "I've seen a couple of fellows like that a few times in the neighborhood, but only once at Mass. They are *not* regular churchgoers."

"Perhaps they were just trying to impress the girls," I suggested.

His face relaxed a little. "Probably so. And how better to seem safe and appropriate than to claim to go to daily Mass?"

"Every mother's dream." Tommy nodded.

"Except that the young ladies weren't especially impressed with them." I hadn't had the chance to share the whole story with Toms, and I was quite glad for the time now.

"No?" Tommy asked, a wicked sparkle coming into his eyes.

"Sadly, no. Apparently, they bored the girls silly with talk of how wonderful they are…and sillier questions about all of the interesting people we must know."

The priest nodded. "Well, the girls are well out of it if they're braggarts who stretch the truth."

"Indeed."

"Should I be keeping my ears open for a match for the ladies?" asked Father Michael. "They're awfully young for that, aren't they?"

"Much too young," I agreed. "And you've got another match to worry about right now."

"Ah, yes. The Barrister came by to ask if I might be willing to do the honors."

"And?" I asked.

"Of course I will."

"But," Tommy put in, evilly amused, "you'll have to have a pre-wedding talk, just like Preston and Greta did."

"Oh, I don't mind that at all," I said, reminding myself that brides of years and discretion do not stick their tongue out at their annoying cousins on the church steps. "We already took your advice on 'I'm wrong and I'm sorry.'"

The priest beamed. "It is still the best advice I have ever heard or given for friends or married couples."

"No argument here." Tommy nodded.

"So when would you like to come in for a cup of tea? We'll pretend it's a serious premarital talk, even though it's not really necessary for you two. I have an hour Tuesday morning."

"That will be just fine." I nodded and did not even cut my eyes to Tommy. "We'll look forward to it."

"So will I." He smiled at me. "It's a real honor to be asked, Ella. After everything that's led us here, I'm just delighted to have the pleasure of bringing you two together."

"We would not have it any other way," I said.

"He will hear about it at home, though, won't he?" Father Michael asked.

"You don't really think he cares about such things, do you?" Tommy asked. "We would not be here if he did."

"True. Still rather brave of him. And you."

"It's not me," I said. "I told him all along I would respect his conscience, because all that matters to me is having God's blessing on our marriage. But it's especially wonderful that you'll be giving us that blessing."

We three shared a happy smile.

"It's certainly not what I expected all those months ago when I met him." the priest said. "A British Duke, in an Irish house—"

"Not your usual Duke," I said.

"Not even a little. And good for him." Father Michael nodded. "He's a good man, and he adores you."

"And Heller adores him...at least a little." Tommy chuckled. "She'll never admit it, but he's the only man for her, even if she fights him at every turn."

"A good Irish woman never makes it easy for her man." Father Michael patted my arm. "Nor should she."

"Exactly. We don't want them getting spoiled."

A rumble from the sky.

"We'd best get home, Father," I said.

"Yes, and I've got to make sure the altar boys have put everything away properly and gotten home safely. See you and the Barrister Tuesday."

The rumbling continued as Tommy and I walked home...and we ended

133

up running the last half-block, as the raindrops started. Of course I hadn't bothered with an umbrella, and I wasn't about to ruin my new hat!

No sooner had Tommy and I hung up our respective toppers and settled in with some after-church tea, though, than we found ourselves moving from the impending happy ending to the current romantic plot. That, apparently, was not running smoothly at all.

"Mr. Coyne, miss," Sophia announced, clearly suppressing a giggle as Rafe stomped into the parlor, shaking off rain and looking like a thundercloud in his own right.

"What sort of ruffians are you letting her walk out with?"

"Good to see you, too, Rafe," Tommy said calmly, pointing to the tea-tray. "Like a cup?"

"Did you allow the girls to go walking with those two questionable men yesterday? I was on my way to hang a door on MacDougal Street, and there they were—"

I shook my head. "Tommy—and Cousin Andrew, for that matter—met them and looked them over. I do not think you need to worry."

"Why? Did you *see* them? The way that weaselly blond one was looking at Miss O'Hanlon?"

"All they wanted to talk about was the neighborhood and our house and the interesting and famous people we might know," Tommy said. "The girls were bored silly. Jim and Tim will have to find someone else to squire next week."

"Oh." Rafe folded onto the settee, his anger deflating.

"Now, have a nice cup of tea and calm down." I poured.

"I guess I'm just worried about missing out because I won't be in a position to marry for at least a year."

"Miss O'Hanlon is nineteen, Rafe." Tommy picked up his cup again. "And she's just found a very congenial and happy situation with good friends."

"You mean she's in no hurry to wed."

"Precisely." I sighed. "I told you much the same when you met."

"I wasn't hearing anything much that day." He blushed. "I've made a fool of myself. Fortunately, with you, and not her."

"Very true." Tommy sipped his tea with a carefully serious expression.

"You're in no position to marry yet, but why couldn't you just ask her to go walking out?" I asked.

Rafe, clearly, had been so caught up in the impossibilities that he had not taken time to consider what could actually happen. "Can I?"

"As long as you're honest with her about your position—and your feelings—why not?"

Tommy smiled at me. "Heller's a bit of a matchmaker, but she's got the right idea. Mostly."

"Mostly?" I asked, with a pointed glare over my cup.

"You'll scare her silly if you march down to the kitchen and say you want to go walking out, but you won't be able to propose for a year."

Of course, Toms was right.

"So?" Rafe asked.

"So," I began, acting as if Tommy and I had been in agreement all along, "just ask her to walk in the park next week. Maybe find a friend for Rosa if you can. Leave all the other things. You'll get to it soon enough."

"But I don't want her thinking I'm-"

"At the moment, Rafe," Tommy said gently, "all she thinks is that you are our respectable cousin."

"All right."

"We can't stop you from slipping down to the kitchen to say hello on your way out," I reminded him.

His confused expression gave way to a smile.

"Especially since the rail on the stairs is loose..." Tommy added, giving him his excuse.

Rafe beamed and stood. "Do you mind if I—"

We were laughing as we returned to our tea.

Chapter Twenty-Three

In Which We Rehearse...but not for the Wedding

T he benefit for the *Atlantic Star* families had quickly mushroomed from a few opera friends putting together a small event into a full-scale project. Whether because of the public interest in the tragedy, or the people putting together the event, we soon had a full slate of performers, not to mention a good Broadway venue, and plenty of society— and other—folks clamoring to fill it.

The Countess stepped in to organize the society matrons, and Aunt Ellen took over tending the crewmen's families, both excellent ladies pitching in according to their talents. Which was essentially what happened with the bill as well.

Most of our opera friends, plus some instrumentalists, a ballet ensemble, and even a few popular Broadway stars, wanted to show off their talents for the good cause—and the attention it would bring. With his usual diplomacy, Tommy set it up so everyone could have their own short turn. Since Marie and I were the lead organizers of the event, no one could argue with us taking the last spot on the bill, singing our death arias from the *Princes*, and then bringing out the rest of the performers for a rousing final number.

(Letting the divas finish also neatly ended a very nasty little argument amongst the Broadway performers over who was the most important. Marie and I, after all, are simply divas by profession. Some of the legitimate stage folks, male *and* female, are divas by temperament!)

It would be the only time the *Princes* ever survived the Tower, not to mention sharing a stage with Richard III (Ruben), Ben Hur, the Camellia Sisters, Siegfried, Cleopatra, and a couple of stray Valkyries.

Not surprisingly, we had to rehearse the whole thing at least once. So everyone gathered at the theatre Monday afternoon to run it through.

Most of us appeared in appropriate practice clothes and gave a proper rehearsal. The ballet dancers and the Camellias were especially impressive; I dance well enough, of course, but I'm always awed by the quicksilver movements of real ballerinas.

A few of those Broadway stars, though, felt the need to impress us with their style and importance and showed up dressed to the teeth and posed through their pieces. The star of the current sensation, *Ben-Hur*, was particularly annoying.

Marie and I, both in comfortable and appropriate rehearsal breeches, were backstage talking with the Swan Queen and her friends when he stepped off and favored all of us with a leer, all the more offensive for being indiscriminate.

"And that, boys, is why you get into the theatre. Where else can you see so many wonderful legs in one place?"

Behind him, Tommy cleared his throat.

Mr. Ben-Hur turned so quickly, his camel-hair coat almost fell off his shoulders to meet the Champ's gaze. The look Tommy saves for moments like this.

"Ah, well, good to see you, ladies," the star mumbled, managing a bow in our direction before walking off with more energy than anything he'd shown on the stage.

"Thank you, Mr. Hurley." The Swan Queen gave Tommy a grateful smile. "What would we have to do to get someone like you at the ballet?"

"Sorry to disappoint you." He laughed. "There's no one else like me."

Marie and I joined in the laugh, and so, after a moment, did the Swan Queen and her friends. We'd promised to ask Tommy if he knew any likely boxers who might be willing to tolerate the ballet in return for the ballerinas' gratitude when our music started.

Of course, Marie and I turned in a very good run-through. Almost perfect, though, of course, one is never entirely flawless.

After the rehearsal, she and I were in the hall outside the dressing rooms, back in our pretty spring day dresses, when Ruben came up to us, straightening his tie.

He's quite the dapper fellow, with dark hair and eyes, and an immaculately-trimmed Van Dyke beard, today in a much simpler and better-fitted suit than anything Mr. Ben-Hur might consider. "I'm so glad I ran into you two."

"Are you coming out for tea?" Marie asked. Most of us were heading out together for some post-show refreshment. Even Marie, who usually prefers to go home to her children, could not resist sharing a table with *this* mix of characters.

Ruben shook his head. "I can't—I have so much work to do."

"You do?" I asked.

"Well," a sheepish grin. "I've been offered a Wotan in Prussia. The Russian Imperial Opera stole their basso, and the director had seen me in Paris, so…"

"Prussia?" Marie asked, glancing at me.

My eyes widened, and we both looked to Ruben.

"You both look like my mother now."

With good cause. Ruben is Cuban by way of Birmingham, Alabama. Inside our small, tight circle, we know he's really the son of freed slaves. Outside, all anyone will ever hear is that he was born in Havana, and any records were destroyed in one of the many hurricanes there—so no one can say otherwise. Certainly, neither Tommy nor I nor any other friend ever would.

"I thought you were going back to Paris this fall," I said cautiously.

"Oh, I am. But the production is good, the money is ridiculous, and it's only a few weeks."

"Of you singing Wagner in Prussia—Imperial Germany?" Marie's brows quirked. "The Prussians are very caught up in that whole Fatherland idea…"

"I'm aware of that." Ruben sighed. "It's a very liberal little enclave—the Dowager Empress is a patron."

"Hmm." I'm sure I didn't sound convinced, since I'd heard that the Dowager Empress, formidable daughter of Victoria and Albert, was in failing health and likely would not have the time or energy to protect a singer at some small company she once endorsed.

"And the money…" He shrugged. "It's worth it. I'm trying to put back a bit."

Marie's eyes sparkled. "Are you, now?"

"Yes." He blushed. "There's a girl."

"Oh?" We weren't trying for unison, but Marie and I said it together.

"She's a dancer at the Paris Opera. Really sweet, reads the same books I do…"

We smiled at him, let him talk.

"She knows—enough. And she hasn't run." His face was just glowing with love and joy. "Says she cares who I am and who we'll become together, not who my grandparents were."

Marie patted his arm. "Enough of a reason to risk a couple weeks in Prussia."

"Exactly." Ruben shrugged. "And the company director is looking after me a bit."

"Not impossible, then," I said. "Is your mother coming along?"

"No, she'll stay in Paris. Celeste will keep her company."

"They've met?" Marie asked.

"They're thick as thieves. And both tried to talk me out of taking this engagement. I think it looks worse if I don't."

"Maybe," I admitted.

"In any case, I'm sorry I'll be missing the wedding, Miss Ella."

"It's all right…I know weddings aren't exactly a big attraction for most men."

"Unless you're one of the participants," Marie added with a wink.

"True." Ruben's blush intensified to two bright sienna patches just above his beard.

I decided not to join in the teasing, and simply patted his arm. "We'll just have to welcome you back with some kind of extravagant celebration on your next American visit."

"I shall look forward to it."

Hugs all round, and then Ruben took off to pack and prepare.

"Do you know anyone in Prussia?" Marie asked as he walked away. "I'm not at all sure of the Dowager Empress and some company director."

"Neither am I." I thought for a moment. "I'll ask around. There must be someone who can keep a friendly eye..."

"Let's hope he doesn't need it," Marie said.

"Better to be ready if he does."

Chapter Twenty-Four

Tea and Intrigue

Theatre-district coffeehouses are not my usual haunt, of course, but there's nothing even slightly inappropriate about a company of respectable artists going out for a bit of refreshment after a rehearsal. At least not in the middle of the day, in a nicely-run establishment.

One could wish the establishment had better offerings, but of course, that wasn't the point.

Just as well the tea was too weak, the coffee too strong and the baked goods barely adequate. I didn't need any temptation with that wasp-waisted white dress just days away…and none of us needed distraction from the conversation, which was quite worth the effort.

Much of the pleasure came from catching up with my colleagues on their various tours, performances, and other doings. One of the Broadway stars had toured with Tommy and me in a featured opera role a few years back, and it was good to see her doing so well. The tenor who was giving Siegfried had performed with Marie and me in a few benefits, and he sat down between us to enjoy a good gossip.

Marc Koziewicz, known as Kane on the stage, looked and sounded like the living rule for the *heldentenor*, tall and strong, with a thick shock of blond hair and piercing light blue eyes. He could have been a great favorite with the ladies, if he were so inclined. He's not.

Marc is the life of every backstage gathering, with an impish smile that belies his heroic roles and a wicked glee in sharing colorful stories balanced by a surprisingly sweet nature.

"So, how's our lovely bride?" he asked with a laugh. "I don't see much in the way of maidenly sighs and blushes."

"I'm saving it for the honeymoon."

We all laughed.

"Good thing." He grinned. "A real treat to see you three out in daylight, after everything."

Tommy shook his head. "It was a rather interesting winter."

"Too interesting," Marc said.

"Isn't that the truth," I agreed. "You haven't been exactly sitting at home waiting for your next engagement."

"Of course not. A fella's got to make money where he can. Haven't seen either of you on the society musicale circuit in a while. Too bad, Ella, you could have put away a nice penny for the trousseau with what some of these robber baron types pay these days."

Marie and I blinked.

"Really?" she asked. "I stopped doing musicales forever ago because the pay was so awful for the effort."

"And you're right," Marc said, "it usually is. But folks like that woman who's marrying the Polish prince—Pearl Lally? They've got more money than sense and want to throw it around."

"Too bad I'm almost off the circuit for good." I laughed. "Was it a terrible bore?"

"It wasn't wonderful. She clearly knows next to nothing about opera, just told me to sing 'some of that heroic *Wag*-ner stuff.'"

"Wag, as in dog tail?" asked Marie.

"Yes." He shook his head. "Look, I'm as self-educated as everyone else—I talked about discovering Oscar Wild-ee until a friend corrected me—but if you're going to get into a world..."

"You should make at least a little bit of an effort." I nodded. "Nothing like money for confidence."

"Isn't that the truth. She's a weird one. Thinks she's the loveliest beauty in the room and flirts like a sixteen-year-old. Even batted her lashes at me."

"Bet that went well," Tommy said with a chuckle.

"Let's just say I have a new understanding of what the ladies go through at these things." Marc shuddered. "The insane part was that she followed me around right in front of the prince. Most of the Polish men I know would have taken me out behind the barn."

"You should know," I said. Marc was from a struggling Polish Catholic neighborhood in the Bronx.

"Must build 'em different in castles." He shrugged and picked up his cup, then took a sip and winced. "We come here for the companionship and the prices, not the quality."

Marie grinned. "That we do."

"Marco!"

The basso roar from the next table made Marc turn. Giorgio Dragone, who made a very nice living singing villains in Italian opera and playing them in melodramas, was surrounded by ballerinas and clearly needed a little masculine support.

"I'd better go rescue George from the swans." Marc kissed Marie and then me on the cheek and shook Tommy's hand. "See you when you get back, Duchess. Don't let the tiara go to your head."

We all laughed.

"Give me that!"

The snap from the other end of the table made us all look.

One of the Camellia Sisters was doctoring her coffee with a flask, and one of the other three did not look happy about it.

"Don't worry, Iris, I'll save some for you," said Rose, who was apparently the leading Camellia. She was definitely the eldest, with a few lines at her brow and smudges under her big blue eyes that owed nothing to leftover eyeliner.

"Promises, promises, Mother." Iris snatched the flask right out of Rose's hand. Her *mother's* hand.

That was actually more of a surprise than the drinking. If I were in the habit of carrying a flask, I would certainly have used it on that coffee.

143

Rose shook her head at us and shrugged. "Girls today."

"Some of them are definitely a bit much," I agreed. "But their hearts are usually in the right place."

"I care more about her feet being in the right place on stage, honestly." Rose took a slug of her coffee. "We do all right. But don't let your friend fool you."

"About what?"

"All of those new rich types aren't big spenders." She drank a bit more. It was clearly better with the addition of a medicinal drop. "That Corbyn woman is a skinflint and a cheat."

Marie's eyes widened, but Tommy and I just nodded.

"You may not know since you're on the road a lot, but we also perform as a chamber ensemble." Rose smiled modestly. "Sixteenth-century motets, Primrose even plays the virginals."

"Oh, the irony!" drawled Iris, sipping her own special coffee.

One of the others, I assumed the offended Primrose, slapped her arm. "Take that back!"

"Calm down, Primmie," said the last sister, Lily, who was a little taller and more serious-looking than the other two. I'd seen her reading a thick book backstage and wondered if she might have chosen something other than the family business if she were free.

"Chamber ensemble?" I asked, trying to bring them back to the story.

"Oh, yes." Rose shot her daughters an impressive glare. "We're quite the fancy act."

"I don't doubt it." Tommy gave her an encouraging nod.

"Naturally, not as the Camellia Sisters, but as the York Family Chorale." Rose ignored a snort from Iris and rolled eyes from the other two. "She booked us for one of those nasty musical evenings the matrons give."

"Nasty indeed." Marie's nose wrinkled.

"Nothing like a roomful of stuck-up women looking down on you while their men leer." Rose picked up her coffee cup, shook her head, and motioned to Iris, who handed back the flask. Once she'd added another splash, she nodded. "But we expect to be paid for our trouble."

"As you should be." Tommy's scowl showed his opinion of anyone who takes advantage of artists. "So she booked you and just didn't pay at the end?"

"Mumbled something about having her secretary send me a check, which of course never came. Only after I asked around backstage did I find out that she'd done it to a bunch of others."

"I'd heard that," Tommy said. "I don't understand why people keep performing for her."

Rose shrugged. "Because we were booked for six other dates after that night at her place...including the Lally woman. She really does pay stupidly well."

"So Aline Corbyn gets away with it," I said.

"At least for now. I can't think she'll be able to do it forever." Rose drank a bit more, took a deep breath and sighed. "Must collect my little angels and get moving soon. We are sold out right through July."

"Won't need to take many outside jobs with that kind of run," Marie pointed out.

"Ah, there's where you're wrong, sweetie. This one—" she pointed to Lily, "wants to go to college and become a teacher. We need to make our money while we can."

"Mother, you know-" Lily began, blushing to the roots of her hair.

"I know that the stage has done very well for us, my dear. But I don't want you three to spend the rest of your lives in this world unless you choose it."

Tommy, Marie, and I blinked at her. We'd all seen plenty of stage mammas, and not one who ever gave such consideration to their child's wants.

Rose squirmed a little, possibly embarrassed at being caught out as a good mother. "I'm softhearted—or maybe soft in the head—but I want them to be happier and safer than I was."

"Isn't that what we all want for our children?" Marie asked.

"I certainly do." The stage mother drained her cup. "Come along, duckies. We're still stars for the moment."

The girls dutifully picked up their bags.

"See you at the benefit," Rose said. "And if you hear of anyone who can sing alto harmony and play the mandolin, let me know."

Lily blushed again, and the other sisters just shook their heads.

"Well," Marie said, picking up her own cup and quickly putting it down again. "The refreshments were awful, but the conversation was extraordinary."

Chapter Twenty-Five

The Prince of What?

When Tommy and I returned, he took one look at the clock and gave me a shove toward the stairs. We had only an hour before it was time to get ready for Cabot's dinner party.

"Oh, I'm sorry, dear!" The Countess almost walked into me as I stepped onto my landing. "How was the rehearsal?"

"Quite wonderful…and fascinating as well." I would have happily shared what I'd learned, but she seemed only slightly interested.

"Delightful. You can tell me about it—and the dinner party—tomorrow."

"Tomorrow?"

"I'm sorry, dear." An awkward smile. "In all of the wedding kerfuffle, I managed to forget that I was dining with old friends from the Consulate tonight. I phoned Mr. Bridgewater, and we'll meet him and his darling auntie for tea after your honeymoon."

"Oh."

"Old—and rather boring—friends of long standing. No escape, I'm afraid."

"Of course."

"I'm quite sure you'll have a better time, but one must." She hugged me quickly and started for the stairs before turning back. "Wear that pretty lilac gown from the recital. Gilbert will love it."

There was no time to sort out the puzzlement, of course.

Rosa had laid out the lilac gown, no doubt on the Countess's advice, and it took far less time than the males of the species imagine for her to help me into it. A large but simple heart-shaped amethyst pendant Tommy had given me for my birthday a few years ago was the perfect finish. I don't like to wear much jewelry when I perform, but of course, I was a guest tonight.

Hair took a bit more time, but Rosa's quite skilled—and speedy. By the time I swiped on a bit of rose petal lip salve, stepped into a pair of lovely satin slippers, and grabbed a slightly shiny crochet lace shawl, I was not exactly running late...but I wasn't early, either.

Not early enough, though.

"Heller, get down here!" Tommy called. "The cab—and your man—are waiting."

As I stepped out onto the landing, Gil stopped mid-chuckle and just stared at me. I guess the dress was indeed pleasing.

Never mind the cab; I'd have been happy to spend all night just basking in his appreciative gaze. The respect and admiration in his aspect always makes me feel like a work of art, but tonight, there was something more, something warmer.

And this from a man looking as fine as it was possible for a male to look in black tie.

Oh, dear.

For a long few seconds, we just stared at each other.

"The cab?" Tommy asked with a laugh, breaking the moment with an almost audible snap.

Gil managed a laugh, as I stepped briskly down the stairs. "I believe this is the first time I've had to wait for you."

"Rehearsal—and the tea after—took longer than expected." I smoothed my skirt. "But proved rather instructive."

Both looked at me.

"If the cast were Aline Corbyn's jury, she'd hang." I smiled. "She is not known for paying artists on time...if ever."

"But..." Gil began.

"But that does not necessarily imply she'd kill."

"Only that she's cheap and nasty, which we already knew." Tommy shook his head and walked to the door. "Why don't we leave Mrs. Corbyn for the moment and enjoy our evening?"

"A capital idea," I said.

And a fascinating evening it was.

Cabot, as one might expect of a Knickerbocker, was an excellent host, welcoming us in luxurious but not pretentious style. Seating was protocol-perfect but arranged to allow for enjoyable conversation. Gil and Toms were on either side of Cabot's Great-Aunt Cecily, which seemed like a good bargain for all.

I didn't have much cause for complaint, either. While I was saddled with Prince Mrzawzy on one side, I had the pleasure of Cabot's cousin Nicholas Ten Broeck on the other.

The Ten Broecks, as it turns out, share many of Cabot's political sympathies and are quite modern of mind, despite having been in the former New Amsterdam at least as long as the Bridgewaters. So Nicholas and I had a lovely discussion of woman suffrage, only enhanced by the appreciative gleam in his deep blue eyes.

Respectfully appreciative, I should add.

And I quite appreciated him, too.

I should also mention here that Mr. Ten Broeck spent a fair amount of time explaining that much of his support for woman suffrage stemmed from his admiration for his wife, who had left early to summer with their children, leaving him free to squire Great-Aunt Cecily. His obvious love for his fortunate spouse only increased his charm.

Unfortunately, there was not much in the way of charm on my other side.

This time, Prince Mrzawzy was decidedly more talkative, though that did nothing to allay my questions about him. I tried to draw him out in conversation, listening closely to his peculiar accent, which sounded like a strange hybrid of Russian and French, not remotely Polish.

He did, however, have the act down, as we performers like to say. The only memorable things he said were in praise of his fiancée, mostly for her sweetness and loving nature. At one point, he did dwell on her loveliness... and in rather peculiar terms that I marked.

From Gil's expression, shooting me the occasional sharp glance from his spot between the vivacious Great-Aunt Cecily and an unnervingly flirtatious (and décolleté!) Pearl Lally, I suspected I was going to be asked for all of the details of the conversation. So I did my best to give the prince a good, careful look. I also made sure to glare a dagger or two at my fellow bride-to-be…and share a smile with Great-Aunt Cecily.

Dinner, as happily catered by Greta Dare, was a delicious but not pretentious crown roast with escalloped potatoes and simple accompaniments. Cabot doesn't follow the old ways of men lingering with port and cigars while women go off and discuss embroidery, so the entire company adjourned to the library for more wonderful conversation.

At least ours, Great-Aunt Cecily's and Nicholas Ten Broeck's was.

Finally, Tommy decided to stay for a whiskey—and probably an assessment of the event—with Cabot. I didn't blame him in the least and, in fact, hoped for further good stories in the morning.

Great-Aunt Cecily, waiting for Nicholas Ten Broeck's carriage to be brought around, watched Gil hand me up into the hansom with a wicked little smile. Wrapped in her midnight-blue velvet evening cape, she seemed impossibly tiny, though still beautiful in at least her eighth decade, with large, lively blue eyes.

"Quite nice," she said. "Back when Alexander and I were engaged, we weren't even allowed to be alone in a room for an instant, lest we misbehave."

Gil and I both blushed.

"Of course," she continued, the smile widening into a grin, "with a week until the wedding, no one should say anything other than to wish you a happy evening."

"Indeed, ma'am." Gil bowed to her and wished her the same.

He looked at least as embarrassed as I by Aunt Cecily's assumptions when he sat down, and quickly moved into a much less uncomfortable topic.

"What did you think of his Serene Highness?"

"He may be a prince, but Jerzy Mrzawzy is no Pole."

"Really?"

"He doesn't even say his own name like one."

150

"Are you sure?"

"As sure as I can be." I took a breath. I never enjoyed talking about my childhood, but this was necessary. "When I lived in the tenement with my mother, several of our neighbors were Polish. Some had been in the City for a few years, but others were right off the boat...so I know how real Poles talk."

"Do you speak any Polish?"

"My mother spoke it well—she helped the neighbors sometimes because her English was better." I shook my head. "I never learned anything beyond a word or two."

"If he's not Polish, what is he?"

I thought some more about Mrzawzy's odd speech pattern and much-too-good English. "This is going to sound crazy."

"But?"

"I'd almost think he was American. At least, I think he may have learned his English in the West. There are a couple of expressions that people in San Francisco use that come from the Gold Rush."

"Tell me."

"Pearl Lally told me that he said it was like seeing the elephant when he met her."

"What an unkind thing to say. Mrs. Lally does have a bit of avoirdupois, but—"

"No, no." I put a hand on Gil's arm. "It's not a reference to her size. Seeing the elephant means finding gold. A theatre manager in San Francisco told Tommy and me that he saw the elephant when we brought *Capuleti* to town."

"Ah."

"The Prince passed it off to her as a Polish expression meaning finding one's true love, but I knew I'd heard it before. And tonight, he said Mrs. Lally looks quite beautiful when she titivates."

My fiancé's expression was rather priceless. He clearly thought, as I had the first time I heard the expression in San Francisco, that it meant something scandalous.

I chuckled. "I know how it sounds, but no. It simply means when she fusses over herself, pretties up."

He laughed. "Good heavens, but it sounds quite—"

"Yes. Tommy once very nearly broke a mineral magnate's jaw for telling me that he knew I would be lovely if I would trouble to titivate."

"I might have done the same."

I giggled at the memory. "It was backstage. He was attempting to tell me that he wanted to see me in female attire, but of course, we didn't know the slang."

"And, of course, you remembered it."

"Hard to forget that. Even in Prince Jerzy's weird pretend Polish accent."

"You seem very sure about the false accent."

"I am." My laugh died as I thought about the real Poles I had known. "I heard a lot of Polish as a little girl."

Gil nodded and took my hand, his eyes sharp on my face. "Well done."

"Thank you." Despite my determination not to let the memories of my early life intrude, my voice wobbled a bit. I wasn't shivering yet, at least, but I felt distinctly off balance, as if an upset might be coming.

"When was the last time you heard Polish spoken?" he asked gently.

He knew.

"The morning..." I could not finish the sentence.

For him, I had no need to. He knew exactly where I was.

The morning in the middle of winter more than a quarter-century ago, when my teacher, worried because she hadn't seen me in a week, found me curled up beside my mother's body in our frigid tenement room. She'd died of consumption in the night, but I had somehow hoped, probably pretended to myself, that she would wake when it was light. The neighbor women heard Miss Wolff knocking hard enough to attract attention and followed her in. She was calm, and so was I, but they filled the room behind us, wailing and exclaiming over the scene in Polish.

I was eight. Cold, hungry, and sure I was going to the orphanage.

I would have, and probably died unloved and unwanted there like so many others, if Aunt Ellen hadn't swept me up.

Occasionally, usually only when I get very cold, or if I am foolish enough to take up a needle, reminding me of the piecework we did to scrape by, I find myself back in that room, shivering like the terrified child I was.

I do my best to avoid such embarrassing upsets.

Gil had seen it a few times before and always treated me with great care and gentle reassurance.

Without another word, he pulled me into his arms. Immediately, I felt warm and protected, as I always did in his embrace. I snuggled into him, rested my head on his chest, listening to his breathing and the faint sound of his heartbeat.

"You're safe, *mo chridhe*." His voice was low and soothing, the Northern accent more noticeable as it often was in our private moments. "Safe and warm."

I nodded, burrowed a little closer.

"Dear God, I love you," he whispered, resting his chin on the top of my head.

"I love you."

There was nothing else we needed to say or do. We stayed twined together, enveloped in the closeness, and affection until the hansom reached the townhouse.

When the cab stopped, we pulled apart slowly, reluctantly, and our eyes held for a measure. Love, understanding, the knowledge that—as Marie said of her husband—you had found the other half of your soul. All pretty, lyrical ways that got close, but didn't fully describe how the deep and true connection between us actually felt at times like this.

He handed me down and walked me into the house, leaving with a quick kiss and goodnight, both of us still wrapped in the warmth of our ride home.

As I walked up the stairs, despite the lack of a passionate farewell that a fiancée might have reason to expect, I felt much more optimistic.

Whatever problems we might have with marital matters, I had no doubt, at least that night, we would find a way to work them out. Anyone, after all, can share a bed, and many do. Very few people are blessed with the connection Gil and I share. Surely, that will pull us through.

Chapter Twenty-Six

Premarital Confessions

It was a good thing the conversation was the point and not the coffee the next morning at Holy Innocents Rectory.

The beverage was weak and wretched as we all discovered once seated in Father Michael's study, and an obviously bored girl about Mary O'Hanlon's age set out the tray.

"Virginia is a very nice young lady," the priest said with an apologetic wince at his first sip, "but she is far happier working at the shirtwaist factory than pitching in for her mother."

"I don't really blame her," I said. Father Michael's regular housekeeper these days is a very competent and kind widow, but she had a younger child who was still in school and sometimes sent her eldest in her stead if she was running late.

"Neither do I." The priest chuckled. "Service—in general—is miserable work, and she doesn't want anyone to get the idea that she'd be good at it."

"I do not think she need worry." Gil sniffed his coffee and put it down. "Factory work is not especially safe or easy, but some people find it more dignified."

"Well, it is," Father Michael agreed. "You're simply coming in, doing a job for a period of hours, and going home."

"The same with service these days," Gil said. "Isn't it?"

"Not really," I started carefully. I had cleaned houses with Aunt Ellen before Madame Lentini took me on. "Even if you're not living in, people expect a certain kind of behavior from their staff."

"Some don't expect it," added the priest. "They demand it."

"Oh." Gil nodded. "The Servant Problem, so called."

"Which usually means servants who are insufficiently servile," I agreed. "In any case, we don't have servant problems at our house."

"Are Miss O'Hanlon and Miss Benedict doing well?" asked Father Michael. "Not pining for their two printers?"

"Not hardly." I laughed.

Gil chuckled, too. "I do not think we need to worry about broken hearts from that direction."

"That's very good. Because I asked around about those two."

We waited.

"I don't like the idea of strange men sniffing around young ladies." The priest shrugged. "It's a dangerous world, and anything we can do to protect them is good."

The men exchanged one of those grim little male nods.

I swallowed a smile despite the seriousness of the topic.

"I could not find a printer who knew those men. And you know, though it is a very big city-"

"We live in very small worlds." I nodded.

"Any further thoughts, Father?" Gil asked.

"Rather odd, is all. If they were looking for comely young ladies, surely they might find them any number of other places."

"You think..." I began

"I don't *think* anything, Ella." He sighed. "And I certainly don't wish to alarm you so close to your happy day. I just think we would do well to keep our eyes open."

"On that, Father, we all agree." Gil nodded. "Caution is not a bad thing."

"Now," began Father Michael, picking up his coffee, then putting it back down. "About your happy day."

"We have already taken your most important advice to heart," I said.

"I was wrong, and I'm sorry." As Gil spoke, he held my gaze, both of us clearly remembering the night he'd been the first to say it, followed by me, opening up the compromise that led to an agreement on the marriage contract.

"That is indeed the most important thing." The priest smiled. "You two always seem to find a way to fight to a draw."

"We do."

Unison wasn't our intention, of course, but it almost happened. Father Michael's smile widened into a grin.

"You two seem to be doing just fine. Do either of you have concerns about marriage?"

"Concerns?" Gil asked, his voice rising a bit.

"Well, anything worrying you about married life or—anything?" Father Michael looked from Gil to me. "You know, even though I'm a priest, I do know about—marital matters."

I carefully did not look at Gil. He carefully did not look at me. Both of us *very* carefully kept our gaze on the large cabbage roses of the rectory rug.

"Ah, well." Father Michael let out a relieved chuckle. "I always feel I should ask, just in case."

We looked back up to see him smiling, easily as glad as we were to move past that part of the discussion. Gil and I both smiled in relief, too.

"In any case, it's been a long time since I've seen two people more in love and more determined to make a happy life together." He watched us both for a measure or more, clearly picking up a bit of the tension between us.

"A wee bit of advice from my Gran?" he asked finally.

We both nodded.

"Be good to each other, and everything else will sort itself out."

It was probably what he said to every engaged couple, and I strongly doubted it really came from Father Michael's Gran, but it was excellent advice, nonetheless.

"Just so, Father." Gil smiled. "Then you judge us ready for the altar?"

"Rarely have I seen anyone more ready." The priest nodded toward the door. "Now, why don't I walk you out since I clearly need to step down to the coffee shop for a cup?"

We were all laughing as we walked out of the rectory, ending the session with handshakes and hugs.

As we turned out of the rectory, I took Gil's arm.

"To the park, perhaps the long way home?" he asked.

"An excellent idea."

For a few steps, we were silent, enjoying the beautiful day and simply being together.

Then, Gil took a deep breath and spoke in a very measured tone. "Our conversation with the Father suggested to me that perhaps I need to make a confession."

"Confession?"

He cleared his throat. "I'm told that men are expected to clear their consciences of indiscretions before the wedding, especially when marrying an innocent and virtuous woman."

What horror is this?

"I've never believed in it," I said quickly. Preston had briefly considered some such nonsense before marrying Greta, but Tommy talked him out of it, and good thing. When Toms, rather concerned that he'd encouraged Preston to hold back something important to his marriage, told me what he'd done, I backed him without the least hesitation. Then, as now, I saw no way that such a foolish expedition into the past could help the new marriage and many ways it might harm it.

Nothing good comes of making a woman think about whatever her man might have done—and with appealing other females—before he came to her. There be dragons.

And now I had to stop Gil. I had no need, and most especially no desire, to know how he had filled the ten years of his widowhood. It was none of my business, and I wanted it to stay that way. Perhaps another tack. "You can't have confessed all to your first wife before the wedding."

He managed a small bitter laugh. "Sadly, there were no indiscretions requiring confession."

"None?"

"Truly. I was in love with the law until I married her." Gil blushed. "The lack of a confession ended by being a confession in itself, now that you mention it."

"Well, you have no need to tell me anything. I assume that you were not lonely during the ten years after her death, and I equally assume that it has no bearing on us."

"Generous as always, *mo chridhe*." His face tightened. "But you should know, because we would not be here if it had not happened."

"All right," I said slowly. I did not understand what he was trying to say, but I could see it mattered a great deal to him. "Please, no names or—specifics."

"Of course not." His blush deepened. "There was only one woman, and it was only important because she showed me that I was not dead after all."

I waited.

"An adventurous widowed friend, who made me her amusement for a season or so. I had been absolutely certain that I would not love again, nor marry, and she convinced me that I might not wish to be alone."

"Ah." I tried for a sophisticated face.

"She reminded me of the—advantages—of having a female companion, though it was very clear that she had no intentions of being that woman for any significant time."

"No?"

"None. We had no connection of mind or spirit as you and I do. I doubt she and I had read two of the same books in our lives. Though, of course, it was not about reading matter."

We both attempted a sophisticated laugh and barely managed it.

"More, I am, as she pointed out to me, the sort of person who wants a spouse, and she most definitely is not."

"I'm sorry," I said, then realized I wasn't in the least sorry. If she'd wanted a husband, *she'd* have married him.

"It's all right, Shane. I was just an—amusement—to her. But she was a gift to me. Because soon after she went on to her next adventure, I had to investigate a family matter in New York…"

"You did?"

"I did." He rested his hand on mine on his arm. "And met a woman like no other I've ever known."

"Who discovered that *she* might well want a spouse."

"With a bit of encouragement."

We smiled together.

"True. And your—friend—she is happy in her new adventures?"

"Very. She was married once and decided that was quite enough for her."

"Though you asked." I didn't mind, really, but he needed to know that I understood he would have done so.

"I did. It was the right thing to do." He shook his head. "She handed me my hat—and that was the end of the adventure."

"Then I owe her my thanks." I snuggled a little closer to him.

"You probably do, but it will be far easier if you don't offer them."

Which, I suddenly understood, meant that I knew her. And if I knew her, there was only one person it could be.

Charlotte von Stade. No wonder she was so concerned about him, and so kind to me. The comments about what a perfect match we are…

"Yes. It's what you think." His eyes held mine. "Kindly don't say anything, though."

"Of course not."

He stopped walking and studied me for a full stanza. "You don't seem shocked or upset."

"I'm not. I still think I owe her my thanks, not that I would ever be indelicate enough to offer them."

"Good." Gil smiled. "Not jealous?"

"Not really, though I may have to kiss you quite thoroughly when we get inside, just to stake my claim."

"Will you, now?"

We were almost to the house.

I took his hand and pulled him up the stairs. The foyer was deserted for once, and I just launched myself into his arms. Whether it was my forwardness or the fact that he knew what I was doing and why, he responded with more enthusiasm than caution for once. It wasn't desperate and passionate like the night he arrived, but rather playful—and curious.

Do you like this—perhaps we could try that—maybe *this?*

Yes, yes, oh, yes!

For the first time, I understood why people describe these activities as love play. A game I very much hoped would be part of my marital obligations.

"Children!"

Getting caught was bad enough. Getting caught by the Countess was worse…and worst of all was the fact that she was standing on the bottom stair laughing. Clearly, we were amusing to her.

"Mother," Gil said as I pulled back from his embrace.

I could not have formed words if my life depended on it.

She giggled like the impish schoolgirl she once was. "You two are utterly adorable."

And what could be worse or more embarrassing than that?

Chapter Twenty-Seven

War Stories

Fortunately, this was the day we were going to Colonel Vandergrift's for tea, so we had a respite from our beaming family cupid. The Countess scooped Gil up for a walk to the florist (this time, I was quite certain they were going to pick out my posy), and I went upstairs to put on something a bit more elegant than the simple morning dress I'd chosen for our visit to the priest.

The Colonel would no doubt expect me to show up at my diva best, and I was happy to oblige. Especially since I had invested in a few new summer afternoon frocks on the assumption that I would have teas or garden parties or some such things to attend in the days before the wedding.

For the Colonel's tea, I chose a very demure, but quite fancy, soft lavender silk, with a wide white lace collar and matching cuffs. My favorite summer hat, a large straw affair topped with flowers shading from deep purple to pale lavender, harmonized perfectly.

"Very nice, Miss." Rosa grinned as she fastened the last button in the back.

"You were right about the color," I said. "I'm glad I chose this instead of the blue one."

She laughed. "Blue is not really your color. You see Madame Marie wearing it, and you think…"

"I do." I shook my head, smiling. "Thank goodness for a smart lady's maid."

"I do the same thing myself." She shrugged. "I'm always drawn to green, because Miss O'Hanlon looks so lovely in all those shades."

I looked closely at her for a second. Surely not feeling less pretty than her friend? Rosa was still very young, but it was already clear that she was one of those women who would be beautiful once she grew into her features. Not sweetly pretty like Miss O'Hanlon. Beautiful, in that regal, dark-eyed way Italian women sometimes are.

She had no reason at all for concern.

And she had none. She let out an impish giggle. "It's all right. Mary always pushes me toward the red and tawny shades…and we both look good."

"You certainly did on Saturday afternoon," I agreed. Rosa's red hat had been an exact match for the red trim that sparked up her simple light-brown dress, and Miss O'Hanlon's green hat had brought out the leaf print in her cotton dress and the tint in her eyes, too.

Rosa shook her head. "I just hope we don't see those two around the neighborhood again."

"They're not troubling you?"

"No, but we spotted them in the park on the way to market yesterday and slipped up the other street. I'm not overly worried. Tim had next to nothing to say for himself."

"No?"

"Hardly a word. I asked him what the last book he read was, and he clammed right up."

That would absolutely be the end with our bookworm and wordsmith.

I nodded. "I don't trust people who don't read."

"Me either. I do wonder about Jim, though."

"Why?" My voice had a more cautious edge than I would have liked. I did not want to remind Rosa of the dangers that sometimes lurk near our happy home.

"He seemed very taken with Mary. Kept just looking at her in that way men do. Not like the Duke, but like Mr. Duquesne used to."

"Not nice."

"Not at all. And the last thing she wanted to see, for sure."

"For sure." Miss O'Hanlon had suffered a narrow escape from a predatory employer, and a leering man would find no favor.

"She told me that she much preferred the way Mr. Coyne looks at her ."

"Did she now?"

Rosa gave me another of her very wise looks. "Mr. Coyne likes to play with everybody, but there's something special in his eyes when she's around."

"I agree."

Our gaze held for a moment, unspoken agreement to leave *that* discussion right where it lay.

"I just hope we don't see Jim and Tim again until they've found other women."

I chuckled. "If they're gainfully employed men who claim to go to Mass on a regular basis, someone's mother will snap them up in no time."

The little furrow at her eyebrows eased. "Why do you think I didn't tell my mama, I was walking-out with Tim?"

I shook my head. "You're so young…"

"Mama has been known to remind me that she was a mother at seventeen."

I stared. I knew such things happened every day, but I still had a hard time understanding what sort of mother a child could be.

Rosa grinned. "And I've been known to remind her that we live in a much different world these days."

"That, thankfully, we do."

We shared a nod, and she added another pin to the hat since it was a rather breezy afternoon.

Downstairs, Gil was in the foyer, chatting with Tommy and Preston. The men were dapper in their light summer suits, and all seemed as if we were attending any other social event. Except that Preston was once again wearing the "Gettysburg Veteran" medal.

No doubt for the Colonel's benefit.

The Colonel lived in the old Vandergrift manse, a short cab ride from our house. Even before we arrived, we determined that we would walk back, since it was late afternoon, and it would be the coolest and prettiest part of the early evening by then.

The mansion was one of the older Knickerbocker installations, really just a large and better-appointed townhouse, perhaps twice the size of ours, in unpretentious brick. But it had large parlor windows looking out into the street, telling us it was built at a time when window glass was still a significant luxury. And it was clear the rest of the street had grown up around it, so the Vandergrifts were likely the original owners of much of the land in the neighborhood.

Cabot still owns, and his great aunt Cecily lives in, the original de Brede Wege house a bit further downtown from us. The spacing around it is the same; if you know what to look for, you can often recognize these true treasures.

Tommy was marking the house too, and we exchanged a smile as Preston knocked.

A housekeeper who was almost as old as the Colonel greeted us at the door, her fading blue eyes sweeping over us with momentary suspicion, and then when she landed on Tommy, lighting up with surprise and delight.

"Champ! If it isn't Tommy Hurley, as I live and breathe."

Even though her sentence structure was entirely Irish, her accent was faint and odd, suggesting someone who'd emigrated long ago. I realized she was likely one of the many older folks who'd seen Tommy's victories as a literal punch back to the prejudice they'd suffered when they arrived here decades before.

"Yes, Ma'am," Toms said, taking the hands she held out. "A pleasure to meet you."

"A pleasure indeed. Everyone in my parish was so happy to see you knock out that dirty Polish boy..."

Tommy coughed. "Markus Radzisch was a very good fighter, and quite a champion."

Not to mention a friend Tommy was still happy to see when we went through Chicago on our western swings. Preston knew that. Gil didn't, but it didn't matter. He understood, as well as the rest of us, that Tommy had no tolerance for prejudice of any kind.

"Well, ma'am," Preston said firmly, but not unkindly, re-asserting himself as the senior male. "I'm Preston Dare, and these are my friends. Colonel

Vandergrift invited us for tea?"

"Oh, yes." She nodded at Preston's medal. "A fellow veteran. How wonderful. He commanded a unit at Gettysburg, you know. Such a terrible day."

Preston nodded.

The woman's face clouded. "My brother. Said one way to show we love our new country was to fight for it…"

Preston patted her arm. "Lot of Irish in Union blue. Proud men."

"And us proud of them." She drew herself up and managed a smile. "Come along, then. The Colonel's waiting in the garden."

She led us through a hallway lined with Colonial and Early Republic portraits of earlier Vandergrifts, of quality varying from serviceable to legendary, to French doors that gave onto a lovely courtyard. When the house was built, the courtyard was likely just a nice feature. Now, in our crowded City, where every inch was a luxury, it was quite literally priceless.

The rich, especially the newly rich, were in the habit of tearing down the older mansions and building grander ones. I truly hoped that whoever inherited this jewel of a home would not be so foolish.

"Mr. Dare and his friends, sir."

Colonel Horatio Vandergrift had been sitting in a large wrought-iron garden chair, softened with several generous cushions in a plain, burgundy-colored cotton drill, and he turned at the sound of her voice, immediately moving to rise.

There was no question of us telling him it was unnecessary. From the determination with which he moved and the set to his jaw, he would have risen to welcome his guests if he'd been far more enfeebled. In fact, he moved quite well for a man as old as he must be, pulling himself to his feet and walking the few steps to us very steadily.

Away from the funeral service, Colonel Vandergrift was far different, reminding me of nothing so much as an amiable imp in size, sparkly eyes, and especially, the devilish pleasure in his smile.

"Well, how delightful to see all of you! Mr. Dare—or should I call you Corporal?—Miss Shane and the gentlemen."

"The Champ, Mr. Vandergrift," cut in the housekeeper with a tone something like a growl.

"Of course, Mrs. Muldoon. The Champ and the Duke, I believe."

Mrs. Muldoon shot her employer a mutinous scowl. "I'll get the tea."

"Thank you most kindly." The Colonel motioned to the assortment of cushioned wrought-iron chairs and settees ranged around the table. "Do sit down. The tea will be very good, even if Mrs. Muldoon's attitude leaves a bit to be desired."

"It's quite all right," I said quickly, realizing even as I did that it was unnecessary. The Colonel and Mrs. Muldoon had likely been (mostly) play-fighting for the last forty years and would do so until one of them went to their eternal rest.

The Colonel misinterpreted my awkward stop as I walked toward the seating and patted my arm with a grin. "It's perfectly fine, dear. No one's going to mind if you sit with your fiancé this close to the wedding."

Now I was really embarrassed.

The Colonel chuckled and offered a hand to Gil. "She's a lovely young lady, and you are a very lucky man."

"I am well aware, sir."

The Colonel held Gil's hand a fraction longer than he should, still smiling just like a father or uncle would do. "Just as it should be."

He motioned us to the settee, then turned to Tommy. "Mrs. Muldoon is quite taken with you."

"She is a very nice lady." Tommy shook the offered hand as firmly as he would anyone else's, knowing that however frail the Colonel's form, his spirit was strong as ever.

"No, she's not. But she is an excellent housekeeper and very good at keeping me in line." He turned to Preston. "So, Corporal—"

"Preston is fine, sir."

A nod. "You don't want to be reminded any more than I do."

"True, sir."

"Fine by me. I'd much rather hear why you think that adventuress Aline Corbyn, sorry Miss Shane, brained Chester."

It was a good thing we were all seated by the time the Colonel threw that little grenade. We all stared at him for a moment, eyes wide.

"I'm well aware that you're all rather more familiar than most with violent death, as is anyone who's ever read a newspaper. I would be surprised indeed if you didn't have thoughts on the matter."

I cleared my throat to cover a squeak of surprise.

"Yes, I'm sure even you, Miss Shane. When someone attacks a man practically in front of you, it's hard to keep your mind on arpeggios."

I shrugged. As I knew from Cabot, Knickerbockers were surprisingly practical and unpretentious...except when they weren't. Much like border lords.

My particular border lord had the sharply contemplative expression that suggested he was parsing the case. "I'm sure you're aware that I have a bit of experience in matters of law."

"Do you think this is a matter of law?"

"As a matter of *principle*," Gil began, "the benefit of the doubt should go to the woman in such situations."

The Colonel nodded. "Ladies don't generally lie about such things. Unless there's a very good reason...often worse than the lie."

Preston nodded. "It's quite a tough world for women."

"But it is not a very tough world for Aline Corbyn," said the Colonel. "And she had considerable reason to want Chester out of the way."

"For her daughter?" I asked.

The Colonel nodded. "She probably expects all of the money, prestige, and, of course, that silly overwrought house to go to the older boy."

We all caught the odd way he put it, and Gil gave him the very serious nod that barristers do: please continue.

"I know—because he told me about it—that he planned to put a bit of money into a trust for Elsie, so she'd have something of her own."

"Alteiss said as much," Tommy agreed.

"But what Alteiss didn't know was that he was ready to do a good bit more than that."

"What?" Preston asked.

"He was going to give his house and most of his money to set up a home for Union veterans."

"Really?" Gil said it, but we all thought it.

"He hadn't yet changed his will?" I asked.

"No." The Colonel shook his head. "He wanted to have the house looked at to make sure it was in good shape and see how much money he needed to put aside for the maintenance. But he was going to do it, any day."

"Any day." Gil said it, but we all thought it.

"And instead," said Colonel Vandergrift, in a grim tone, "he didn't survive the opera night. Sorry, Miss Shane."

"The timing is terribly convenient," Preston observed.

"I agree," Gil began, with an apologetic tone, "but only if we can prove that she knew."

"Difficult." The Colonel scowled.

"Who was doing the inspection of the house?" Tommy asked.

"I don't know. He had a regular handyman...but you would need a specialist for this."

That, at least, was a help. Toms cut his eyes to me, and Gil caught the glance. We knew who the regular handyman was and knew there would be no trouble getting his opinions.

Just then, Mrs. Muldoon appeared with a quite decent tea tray. Serious conversation was tabled for the appreciation of dainties, and when the repast was over, the Colonel—who was, after all, well into his eighties—looked quite faded.

As we moved to leave, he took my hand and pulled me down to look into his eyes. "That boy adores you. I can only wish you the happiness I had with my wife."

"Thank you, sir." I hoped he took my flush and wobbly tone for maidenly shyness instead of the suppression of a truly inappropriate giggle at his description of Gil.

"Good to see you all," he said as he saw us to the door. "I expect, now that we've made acquaintances, that you'll be coming round again soon."

We assured him we would not miss it for the world.

We spent most of the walk back to Washington Square discussing the extraordinary Colonel Vandergrift and his home. Not to mention his running feud with Mrs. Muldoon—which had probably kept them both alive.

As we passed the park, we saw a couple of familiar faces near the fountain. Jim and Tim, of walking-out infamy, were sitting in the sun, just watching the passers-by.

"What, Shane?" Gil asked as he noticed me tensing a bit.

"Over there." I nodded to the men.

"Ah." Tommy shook his head. "The famous Jim and Tim."

"Out in the middle of the day, when printers should be sleeping." Gil shared a raised eyebrow with the other men.

"We are not allowing them to walk out with the girls again," Preston said.

"Indeed not," I agreed.

"And we shall be keeping a very close eye out for Misters Jim and Tim." Tommy's tone suggested that our alleged printers had better stay far away from us.

Chapter Twenty-Eight

For Those Lost on the Sea

While the benefit for the widows and orphans of the *Atlantic Star* crewmen had begun with Marie, Louis, and me, it ended as the cause of the moment, with that huge Broadway theatre, the full bill of performers from all arts, and much complimentary attention in the papers. So when the night finally arrived, it was a grand and glorious event, in the way a good cause of the moment sometimes becomes.

That was quite all right in this case. We would raise enough money to take proper care of those two sailors' families, allowing them to grieve without worrying about where their next meal or rent payment was coming from. Not to mention putting aside a good little fund for the children's education.

Benefits like these are perfect for such causes. They aren't so good for continuing problems in society, unless one plans to do a performance for the street urchins every few weeks and bring in huge sums of money every time. Not that we don't try...but this is likely a problem for social workers and governments, not artists.

Artists, however, did very well that night, all of us at our best, offering some of our finest pieces. And at the end, the entire cast joined together for a moving version of "Eternal Father Strong to Save."

I was not the only one whose eyes filled as we reached the line "for those in peril on the sea."

There was not a dry eye in the house when it ended; Marie and I at center stage, flanked by a couple of Broadway stars, our motley ensemble stretching across the front. After the final curtain call, we all exchanged handshakes and embraces, and promises to do this again soon. Who knew if it would happen, but it added a lovely warmth to the evening.

The only unpleasant note came from Ben-Hur. One of the Broadway luminaries who'd taken the star's bow with Marie and me, he pulled me in for a kiss on the cheek in the farewells and, as my fingers itched to slap him, gave me what he no doubt thought was a raffish grin.

"Why's a woman like you throwing herself away on some milquetoast aristocrat when you could have a real man?"

It had been more than a decade since I'd been the recipient of such a direct and repulsive advance. It was not the words, though they were quite offensive enough, but rather the leer with which they were delivered and the insult to Gil. My half-Highlander fiancé is not the only one who occasionally feels moved to violence to defend his beloved.

Ben-Hur seemed to assume I would take him up on his vile offer, quite possibly right then and there. It did make me wonder what went on at the popular theatres; while I'd heard of any number of misdeeds by tenors and perhaps the occasional stolen kiss among the supernumeraries, I had never heard of any opera singer making a quite clearly indecent proposal on the stage floor.

"Thank you, but no. I am well supplied with masculine companionship." I put my hand on my sword hilt and narrowed my eyes a little. "Very well supplied indeed."

Ben-Hur wilted a bit. "Er, sorry, Miss Shane. No—no insult intended."

"I should think not." He bowed and backed off. He was not even out of earshot before I saw him creeping up to Cleopatra. I doubted he'd meet with more success there, but good luck to him.

"What on earth was that?" Tommy, of course.

I sighed. "I believe Mr. Ben-Hur was making a rather ham-handed attempt to send the bride along with a happy memory."

Tommy snickered. "Not that happy if the chorus girls are to be believed."

"Oh?"

"He's got quite the reputation. They call him 'Old Shoot First and Ask Questions Later.'"

We laughed.

"I handed him his hat, Toms. Please don't tell Gil."

Tommy nodded, his jaw a grim line. "I'll have a word with our dear luminary before he goes on his way."

Which meant Mr. Ben-Hur would likely be scared into leaving not just me, but those chorus girls, alone for quite a while. There was absolutely no need for Gil to know any of this, especially since he might well decide to teach Mr. Ben-Hur a lesson in manners far more emphatic than the one Tommy would deliver.

In any case, I was quite glad to retire to my dressing room after that little donnybrook. Since our brush with disaster in February, Tommy and Gil had banned all but family and closest friends from the dressing room, but we knew we could not strictly enforce the new rules that night. It being a benefit, most of the people involved qualified as friends, or at least acquaintances, and they were doing good by helping the families, so we had to at least act as if their intentions were appropriate.

In almost all cases, they actually were.

Almost.

If Aline Corbyn had no scruples about essentially inviting herself to our wedding while still under investigation in the untimely demise of her daughter's father-in-law, why would one have expected her to have any about appearing at a benefit? And yet, I was set back for a second at the sight of her sweeping into the dressing room in watery-green charmeuse with a sparkling aigrette of egret plumes dripping with aquamarines and diamonds.

"Such a magnificent event, Ella dear."

She had adopted the Countess's way of addressing me without ever asking if it was all right. Which of course it was not.

Gil's eyes narrowed, and his jaw tightened. I knew this meant the Highlander wanted to defend his woman. His mother had the same flash in her eyes but was more successful at cultivating a neutral face.

I shot a quick glance to Tommy, who took one look at our Scots and understood that we had mere seconds before things got far warmer on this lovely June night.

I returned Mrs. Corbyn's loose embrace with a careful smile. "So kind of you to come out tonight."

"Well, one must help the deserving."

"One always enjoys helping people get what they deserve," agreed the Countess.

"Just so, Mother. I am a great believer in helping matters along."

There was not a single impolite note or glance from the Duke or the Countess, but something in their aspect and tone wilted Mrs. Corbyn like cheap flowers. She quickly stiffened her spine and forced a smile. "Well, it's quite the lovely night. Of course, we'll look forward to seeing you on your special day..."

"Of course."

If she felt a cold wind at her back as she walked out, it was nothing more than the chill from two pairs of ice-blue eyes.

And the shock of that incident paled in comparison to what followed, though in an entirely different way. The next knock had a distinctive grubby scrape that I immediately recognized. Tommy, too, and his eyes widened a bit, even as his jaw tightened.

"I'll make him go away, Heller."

I drew myself. "You will not. We will be polite. He apologized at the Met reception, if you recall."

"Who?" Gil hissed as Tommy opened the door.

Grover Duquesne, Captain of Industry, for once did not begin by leering at me. Gil caught it, which is likely the only thing saved us from a disastrous scene. Not that it began as a happy moment by any means.

"Mr. Duquesne." Gil's tone would probably have sent polar bears scrambling to their warm dens.

"Why, it's the Duke." The Captain of Industry gave Gil a warm and friendly smile but wisely did not try for a handshake. "What a relief that you came back safely. I hear you helped get some women and children into the lifeboats…"

"Neither here nor there, Mr. Duquesne. One is always glad to help those in need."

"Of course. Why we're here tonight, right?"

"Right."

Gil watched him. He watched Gil. Tommy watched them both, probably calculating exactly how much time it would take him to stop my fiancé from landing the punch he so dearly wanted to throw. If Toms troubled to stop him, which he just might decide not to do.

"Well, I just came back to thank you folks for talking to your friends on the cops about the Lorimer matter…and to wish the bride well."

"Very kind of you." The Countess was cool, but not as unfriendly as she'd been with Mrs. Corbyn. Perhaps offering, our industrialist a chance to behave nicely.

Which, incredibly, he took, keeping the same tone of careful concern. "I've been hearing a few things about Chester's plans."

"Really?"

"Apparently, he was very close to making an announcement that he would be leaving his house and most of his estate for a veterans' home."

We all nodded.

"Well, it makes sense, you know. Of course he did well in dry goods, but the fortune started with his late wife. She was a Knickerbocker, with money so old you don't want to know where it came from. Probably made him promise to do good with it."

Tommy, Cabot, and I nodded.

Gil and the Countess looked confused.

Even in New York, several of the oldest family fortunes stem from slave and sugar trading, and in some cases, the current descendants try to use the tainted money to improve the world. It would likely have appealed to a Civil War veteran to set up a home for his fellow soldiers with money that stemmed from the very evil they fought.

I gave Gil and the Countess a quick "explanation later" glance and kept my focus on the Caption of Industry. We were learning very important things here.

"Wasn't he worried about impoverishing his children, though?" the Countess asked, clearly genuinely puzzled.

Duquesne let out a little bark of a laugh. "Chester had already taken care of them. The older one had the business and was probably set up a bit when he married. Of course, the younger one's not right, and he lives in a nice little place in the country."

"He does?" She hadn't seen the funeral, so, of course, she could ask with perfect propriety.

"Oh, yes." The Captain of Industry was clearly enjoying sharing the local gossip with our matriarch. "Poor boy fell on his head as a baby, they say. Probably fifteen years ago, Chester found the house, and a kindly older couple, to watch over him. Of course, he settled them properly as well."

The Countess nodded. "That's far better than many people do."

"We're not all barbarians, ma'am." Grover Duquesne shrugged uncomfortably. "The boy apparently has his mother's eyes, and Chester said he couldn't stand the thought of those eyes ever being sad. So he made sure they wouldn't be."

"What a lovely memorial to his wife."

"Erm, yes. A very kind thing to do."

"You know," the Countess said, with a tiny, impish smile, "you robber barons like us to think you are quite cold and tough...but many of you have very soft hearts under there."

It was quite possibly the first time I had ever contemplated the possibility that the Captain of Industry even *had* a heart.

"Well, that's as may be, ma'am. But I did want to tell the happy couple here something important."

We all looked at him, probably more sharply than we intended.

"I asked Mr. Bridgewater what might be an appropriate wedding gift for you two, since he knows you all much better, and he had a capital idea."

You will know that it is not often our company is stunned into silence, but there we were. Not one of us could have formed words at that exact second. I managed a numb nod and an interested face.

"Well, I'm sure you have no need or desire for any of the silly decorative items people generally send at such times, so instead, I'm starting a music collection at the main Bridgewater Library in your name, Miss Ella."

"Really?" I gasped. A kind—and entirely appropriate—gesture from *this* man?

"If it's all right with your husband-to-be here."

"Quite all right." Gil offered a hand for a shake, then. "A very good way indeed to honor her—and celebrate our marriage."

"Mr. Bridgewater suggested it. I just went along. Congratulations to you all."

"Thank you, Mr. Duquesne." I gave him probably the first genuine smile of our acquaintance and was shocked to get an almost paternal gaze back.

"Miss Ella, you've proven yourself more of a lady than most of those glittery show horses in the Four Hundred. All happiness to you both."

"What a lovely gesture, Mr. Duquesne." The Countess gave him another of those sparkly smiles. "We shall look forward to celebrating the opening of the new music collection with you."

"It will be my honor."

He bowed over my hand and left. We stood there staring after him for a full stanza at least, until a little voice piped up from behind the dressing screen.

"Well, doesn't that beat all?"

"Rosa, slang!" I said, even as our eyes met and we dissolved in laughter, quickly joined by the others.

"When the words fit, miss, they fit."

"And how!" I agreed.

Chapter Twenty-Nine

A Very Frank Talk...and After

Dr. Silver was not in the least surprised or concerned by my undeniable ignorance about marital matters. She allowed as how she found it encouraging that I had some minimal understanding of the workings of my own body (most of which had been supplied by her over the years!), and the basics of male anatomy, and explained the rest in clinical detail with a minimum of embarrassment.

At least on her part. I was blushing like a volcano.

"Of course, it's not just about making a baby. It's supposed to be enjoyable for both of you, and a considerate partner will do his best to make sure it is." She smiled. "You'll figure it out as you go along."

"Marie has promised to pour me a whiskey and explain a few things."

The smile widened. "Perfect. A good woman-to-woman talk will go a long way to easing your concerns."

"I hope so."

"He's the one I'm worried about, really."

"What?"

She shook her head. "Men are such delicate creatures. They get nervous about the silliest things."

"Really?"

"Really." A rueful nod. "Much of marital happiness is simply managing your man's fragile feelings, one way or the other."

"That's not especially encouraging."

"Probably not, considering all you two have been through." She took off her reading glasses and sighed. "While men place such a store on chastity, some are quite terrified by the reality of an innocent woman in their bed."

"Oh, dear." I understood at least part of what was happening here now. "His first wife was a widow."

"I did not know that." The doctor shook her head. "You'll want to tread carefully then. He's probably more nervous than you are."

"Lovely." If I had correctly understood Gil's oblique comment, he had gone innocent to his wife, and of course, Charlotte von Stade was probably far more accomplished in such matters than he, considering her adventurous past. The thought occurred that I would be happy to become accomplished myself, if only my soon-to-be spouse would give me the opportunity. Surely, one could find a good book on this, too—even if Mr. Comstock would not permit it to go through the mail.

"And if you can avoid it, try not to save his life again right before the wedding night."

I gave Dr. Silver a puzzled glance.

"Ella, dear, having his woman rescue him is rather defeating for even the most modern man."

"I suppose."

"It is, though he'll never admit it. You might wish to find some non-dangerous way to make him feel like your hero. Note that I said non-dangerous."

I shrugged. "I'm not sure how to manage that."

"It's a silly idea. Better for you two to just get on with it. You've come through far worse and come through it together." She smiled. "You'll settle into married life just fine."

As I walked back to the house, I thought about the very frank conversation and the doctor's wise advice about men's fragile feelings. Getting nervous about the silliest things, she said.

Gil had been treating me like I was made of glass since the stabbing. Even after his confession about Charlotte, he was careful and playful, not

178

especially passionate. Except for the night he came back from the sea, when he was too overwrought to think it to death. And good thing.

Would I get that man on our wedding night—or the one who seemed almost afraid to kiss me?

As I turned onto Waverly Place, I realized I did not want to wait to find out. Yes, I was a very good Irish girl. I was also a very good Irish girl with a signed marriage contract. Gil himself had admitted months ago that the service was only the formal blessing of what we'd agreed to in the contract.

The contract. Which for some reason made me think of the Tudor courts and all the disputes over who was married to whom and how married they were. And how one defined whether people were really married or merely promised to be.

I'd read enough about Henry VIII's tangled marital history to be well aware that Gil and I had what was known as a valid pre-contract. A true marriage in the eyes of God and man, if consummated, and back then, most couples did so once the contract was signed, no matter if the public celebration came later.

Even good Irish girls and their men.

In our modern age, we do not talk of valid pre-contracts, of course, but the point was clear: we were as married as we needed to be, and why give him several more days to wait, wonder, and worry?

Perhaps it was time to take the rest of the good doctor's advice and just get on with it.

Instead of returning to the townhouse, I walked to the Waverly Place Hotel and marched up the stairs to Gil's rooms, knocking briskly on the door.

"Shane?" He stood in the doorway, jacket off, tie loose, book in hand, looking absolutely astonishing. And astonished.

"We have a valid pre-contract," I said. I probably should not have opened with canon law, but it seemed safer, considering I was still in the hallway.

"What on earth?" He took my hand and pulled me inside.

It was a small sitting room; I assumed there was a bedroom somewhere. I certainly hoped so.

"Valid pre-contract?" he asked.

"Like Catherine Howard—how she ended up no longer queen and no longer alive-"

"Catherine Howard?" He was genuinely confused. "You came to my rooms to discuss Catherine Howard?"

"No." I shook my head. I had no intention of getting caught on Great Harry's fifth wife—she was just a convenient example. This was not going to plan at all. "About us. We are as married as we need to be—"

A faint smile. "I wondered when you'd figure that out. That's true. If you want me to leave, you'll have to divorce me."

"I'm not here to tell you to leave."

"Good." He studied me for a measure or two, waiting. "Why *are* you here?"

"There is no earthly reason for you to spend three more days treating me like a glass figurine-"

"I'm not treating you like a glass figurine."

"You are."

"I am showing respect to my future duchess, Shane."

Damn him. *Damn* him. The one thing that I, the Lower East Side girl made good, could never, would never, resist. After a lifetime of fighting, sometimes literally, to be taken as a good woman, I could not argue that. Even though I was absolutely certain it was nothing but an excuse for his fears.

I was silent, furious, for probably a full stanza.

"And also, *mo chridhe*, when I have envisioned consummating our marriage, and I have, I did not envision it taking place in my bachelor rooms at this hotel, in the afternoon between engagements."

"I'm not between engagements." Only later would it occur to me that I should have asked if he were. Or at least marked it.

"On your way back from Dr. Silver, no doubt?"

"Yes."

"And wanting to perhaps just finish the whole new bride business?"

I sighed. Damn him again. I knew he had any number of problems here, but he was turning my few, entirely normal, concerns against me. "Perhaps."

"Perhaps also trying to re-claim your territory from the Landgravine von

CHAPTER TWENTY-NINE

Stade?"

I bit my lip. I truly wasn't jealous of her. Not even a little. I was grateful that she'd shown him, that he did want passion in his life. Because if she hadn't, he would never have wanted me.

"I'm actually grateful to her, Gil. But I think I can be forgiven for wanting to enjoy the privileges she did."

"Don't worry, you'll get your privileges." He pulled me into his arms, then, but not in the kind of embrace I'd hoped for; not the beginning of a passionate interlude, just a loving and reassuring hug. "*Mo chridhe*, we may be as good as married, but you deserve better than this."

I knew he meant it. I also knew it was an excuse. And I knew him well enough to know I would not change his mind. So I just snuggled into his arms, enjoying the embrace, since it was all that was on offer.

"Now, why don't I walk you back to the townhouse? I'll tell Mother I ran into you on the street."

I managed a chuckle. "All right."

He picked up his jacket, and after he buttoned it, took my hand, pulling it to his lips. "I love you, Shane."

"I love you."

We walked in silence. His arm was tense under my fingers, his face sharp in thought.

For the first block or so, we were each alone with our reflections, despite being arm in arm. But as we made the turn onto our street, within sight of the townhouse, we almost walked into a young man who was just standing there. I was so distracted by the incident with Gil that I could not say with certainty what he was doing.

But there was definitely a possibility he'd been watching the house.

One that became much more real when I recognized him. "Well, Jim, how nice to see you."

I seriously doubted he was socially adept enough to recognize my politeness as cover for my discomfiture, and I offered a silent prayer to whatever God watches over distracted brides that he didn't notice—or attributed it to some other cause.

"Oh, Miss Ella! Nice to see you. I was just in the neighborhood—ah—going to Holy Innocents to light a candle for my aunt, you know…"

I nodded. "I sometimes light one for my father there."

Jim pulled a serious face. "It's good to remember our lost ones."

"Very true."

Gil cleared his throat. I recognized the sharp assessment in his eyes and knew he was observing something he did not like about young Jim. Good thing Miss O'Hanlon had reached the same conclusion.

"I'm sorry, Gilbert Saint Aubyn. May I present James Collier?"

Gil exchanged a friendly shake and hello, cutting his eyes to me approvingly. I'd guessed right in leaving out the title. That wasn't the main play, though. His cool eyes held Jim's for a very long measure.

"Um, well, I need to be going," Jim said finally. "Please give my regards to Miss O'Hanlon."

"Of course." I did not add that Gil would likely also be giving his unflattering assessment as well.

"Thank you then…um…have a very good afternoon."

Nods and bows all around, and Jim scurried off.

"One of the famous swains, then?" Gil asked as soon as he was out of earshot. "Surely Miss O'Hanlon does not prefer that fellow to your cousin?"

"Not a bit of it. It's fair to say there were no lightning bolts."

Gil chuckled. "No?"

"As I understand it, the two of them bored the poor girls silly. All they could do was talk about their own wonderfulness and ask intrusive questions about the house."

His eyes narrowed. "What questions?"

"Oh, stupid things. What famous people do we know? One apparently thought I knew Miss Bernhardt."

A real, honest laugh from Gil. The first that day. "That is rather a bit much."

"I thought so, too."

"And these two are supposed to be printers?"

"That's what they told the girls."

"Indeed." He held my gaze. "Well, one can't help wondering what a printer is doing running to church to light a candle for his aunt on a weekday afternoon?"

"When he should be sleeping or preparing for his next shift."

"Exactly."

"A day off?"

We shared a very suspicious glance.

"Well," I continued, "in any case, the girls weren't interested in the least, and Mr. Jim won't be returning to the house anytime soon."

"We hope. Do you suppose he's mooning about waiting for Miss O'Hanlon to come out?"

"If we see him again, Tommy will have a word."

Gil nodded grimly. "Perhaps Detective Riley, too."

"You think it so serious?"

"I think we take no chances, considering what has happened in recent months." His face clouded for a full stanza, and I knew he was thinking about February and the brush with death we—and a theatre full of people—had survived.

"That's fair."

The conversation had brought us to the townhouse.

And suddenly, a true surprise. He turned to me with an impish grin. "Perhaps a fencing match?"

"What?" A stunning way to change the subject.

"It will give us something to do and perhaps allow us to burn off some of the bad feeling from our earlier conversation."

I could not argue that.

"I will not give you a draw this time," I warned.

"Then I'll have to earn it."

Chapter Thirty

...and the Fight Afterward

T his fencing match was different.

Cautious to start, even more cautious than the first time we'd squared off more than a year ago. We began slowly, clashing swords in a casual, almost desultory way as if we were merely marking time.

"Perhaps this wasn't the right way to resolve matters," I said after a few light parries.

"Perhaps." He launched a decent enough attack, and I fended it off easily. "Perhaps you don't care."

"Is that what you think?" Gil's gaze sharpened on me.

"I can only go by what I see." This time, I backed him up with a harder attack, and he met it.

"Things are not always simple, Shane." He came back at me sharply enough to force me back a bit.

"Some things should be." I blocked his attack with a quick and hard return. Make him work for it.

"There's a great deal in play," he said, his breathing becoming faster as he fended me off.

"Too much?" I backed him across the studio. "Am I too much for you?"

He let out a little laugh. "Perhaps I'm too much for you."

With that, he launched his own ferocious attack. It took me by surprise—he had nowhere near my level of skill—but suddenly, I was the one who had to work. Though I could usually anticipate his next move, this was wild and unpredictable. The battle was really on: everything moving very fast, the sound of steel on steel ringing through the studio as we clashed, parry and thrust and reverse—and back again.

We'd never sparred like this.

Of course, the stakes had never been so high either.

And then we were at the middle. Swords crossed, each pushing too hard against the other to finish a stroke or parry. Eyes holding as well.

Both of us breathing hard, something entirely different going on now.

We stood there, transfixed, foils locked together, steel on steel, the current between us suddenly crackling in ways I'd never imagined.

"*Am* I too much for you?" I asked.

It was intended as nothing but a fencing taunt. But the valence changed somewhere between my thinking it and his hearing it.

"Never," he breathed. "I'll take all of you."

No question, no nerves, no reserve now.

Damn the consequences, bring it on.

For a fatal instant, we stood there frozen, the way bathers do after a rogue wave has rushed up and drenched them, stunned and staring, shocked by the sheer magnitude of the feeling between us—and the realization of what we might…and could and even *should*—do about it.

Then he reached for me with his free hand. "Shane-"

"*Yes.*" I leaned toward him.

His arm wrapped around my waist, pulling me close, his body warm from the match, his heartbeat fast and hard enough to hear.

I hadn't envisioned the studio as the setting—but why on earth not? I ran my free hand up his shoulder to his neck, reveling in the closeness, his breath on my lips-

"Miss! Miss!"

Gil and I broke apart, as guilty and embarrassed as we'd ever been.

Sophia ran into the room. She looked from him to me, her little face puzzled for an instant. Then, brightly: "Who won?"

I sighed. "No one. No one at all."

Without a word, Gil took the foil from my hand and shook his head. His face was once again cool and inscrutable, the only sign of what had happened—or *not* happened — a faint flush across his cheekbones.

I did not want to think about what color my face must be now. I tried to manage a calm tone with Sophia. "What's wrong?"

"A visitor, miss." She beamed. "A very nice one."

"All right." I turned back to Gil as I followed her to the door.

"Draw?" he asked.

"For now."

He smiled. And in that smile, which held a new trace of the ferocious attraction that had nearly exploded between us, I found some reassurance. There *was* something wrong here, but there were also many other things right. Perhaps, I thought, Dr. Silver had diagnosed it—and all I had to do was find a way to manage my man's fragile feelings.

I had no time to consider it now, because we had a larger matter to occupy us at the moment. A matter well over six feet tall standing in my foyer.

The tall young man had bright-ginger hair and sparkly gray eyes and an elegant air, despite being a bit disheveled in good but not flashy travel clothes.

"More Belle Starr than *belle-mere*," said our new visitor, taking in my fencing outfit, which was a bit more elegant than the lady gunfighter in question would wear—but probably not much. His French accent was very good, suggesting a fine gent who'd just finished his Grand Tour, the final clue to the identity of our new visitor.

And my newest relation.

"Jamie, we would happily have collected you at the pier." Gil had a slightly stern, but affectionate tone as he took the last few steps down, walking to the young man and exchanging a handshake that turned into an embrace, his hand lingering on the fellow's arm as he turned to me. "Miss Shane, as you still are for the next few days, it's my dubious pleasure to present my son, Lord James Saint Aubyn."

As my soon-to-be stepson bowed over my hand with an impish smile just like his parent's, I did not find the pleasure dubious at all. The Saint Aubyn

186

"spare" had sent me a charming and welcoming letter from his Tour on word of the engagement, and we'd exchanged a friendly missive or two since.

Unlike his brother, the heir, who was resolutely ignoring my existence, whether because of class or religious prejudice, or simply an unwillingness to see any other woman in what he considered his late mother's place, James Saint Aubyn seemed quite happy to have me in the family. Though his letters, and his actual demeanor, suggested a cheerful scamp, as his gray eyes held mine, I had a sudden sense of the very sad little boy who'd been sent off to school soon after his mother's death from the Russian flu.

I wondered if Gil had told him that I, too, had buried a mother very young.

This was certainly not the moment for that discussion, though, as Jamie nodded to my attire and grinned. "Fencing match instead of wedding rehearsal?'

"I am not going to be sitting on a chaise eating bonbons after the marriage, after all." I returned the grin.

"Perhaps, if you are a very good boy, Miss Shane will be kind enough to defeat you later." Gil shook his head, but he had a joyful aspect I'd never seen. "It's wonderful to see you, *a bhobain*."

I would ask later for a translation. I guessed something along the lines of little rascal. Not that the rascal was little anymore—the nineteen-year-old was just slightly taller than Gil.

"And you, Pater." Jamie pronounced the preciously aristocratic title with a bit of irony, clearly a joke between them. Whatever had happened in his childhood, the adult Jamie and his father clearly had a strong and loving bond now. "I took care of that-"

Gil narrowed his eyes slightly at his son, who immediately broke off.

"It's a delight to meet you, Miss Shane. And to see Pater so happy."

"A delight to meet you." I bowed to the gents, who clearly had business to discuss. "I am going to go counsel with Miss O'Hanlon about dinner arrangements. She will send up tea, and I'll join you once I change."

Gil held my gaze and nodded. Jamie smiled.

They were quite a pair.

Dinner gave me no reason to revise that opinion.

Jamie apparently had not had a decent meal since he left Britain. That was certainly the unavoidable conclusion at dinner when he tucked into our very simple family meal of chicken and dumplings with a relish I hadn't seen since Tommy's fellow boxers frequented our home. (We were a bit better off than most because I was starting to take singing engagements by then, and we could be counted upon for a generous and well-cooked dinner, thanks to Aunt Ellen.)

The Countess and I exchanged amused glances as we sent the tureen down to Jamie's end of the table for a third time, but Gil was starting to look ever so slightly annoyed.

"James, one would think you had never seen food."

"Oh, Pater, it was a long trip…and this is a very good dinner."

"Miss O'Hanlon will be delighted to hear it." Tommy chuckled. "And some people have a hard time eating well at sea."

"Exactly." Jamie put down his fork and took a sip of wine. "It's good to finally be here."

"And we are glad to have you, Jamie." The Countess patted his arm. And put the lid back on the tureen.

"So, do I hear I've landed in the midst of a murder case in addition to wedding season?" he asked, putting his glass down.

"We're not sure it was a murder," I said cautiously. "Mrs. Corbyn claims she was defending herself."

"And any other woman I'd believe right away." Jamie shook his head. "Not her. That Corbyn lady's capable of almost anything, you know. Even if she is something of a joke."

Eyes widened across the table.

"Do you know something about her, Jamie?" asked his father.

"Charles sure does." Jamie picked up his fork again and took another bite of chicken, as everyone else at the table absorbed the mention of Gil's older son and heir, who was resolutely ignoring the wedding, not to mention my very existence.

"Really?"

"Well, a couple of years ago, she and her daughter were following him all

188

over London. We laughed about it. Everywhere he was, they were."

"They were?" The Countess asked. "What daughter? I thought she had the one who was married to Mr. Lorimer's son—and the one she threw at Gilbert."

Jamie coughed and almost choked on his food. "She threw the same daughter at Charles and Pater? That's —"

"Indeed it is." Gil winced. Charles, his son, would have been almost as good a match.

"Not quite as bad as you think, gentlemen," I said quickly. "There's no way Miss Pamela would have been old enough two years ago. I believe there is a middle daughter, and all I know about her is that she's married."

"Not to Charles." Jamie laughed. "And probably not to anyone in London circles."

"Why?" asked the Countess, having been out of the conversation quite long enough.

"Well, Mrs. Corbyn's husband was up to no good, and she didn't rise above." Jamie squirmed a little.

"What sort of no good?" The Countess's eyes gleamed with inappropriate curiosity.

Jamie looked at me. "With apologies to Miss Shane and Grandmama, he was known to collect chorus girls. Not respectable singers, Miss Shane. We all know—"

The Countess patted his hand a bit too briskly. "We do, James. Continue."

"Well, everyone heard the story. She actually showed up at the stage door to confront him at this—er—place, I can't really call it a theatre, can I? Screaming like a fishwife."

"Really. How extraordinary." The Countess shook her head. "An insult to fishwives, I suspect."

"Definitely." I shook my head. "Whatever stories you've heard about the lower orders and marital misbehavior, women of every class prefer to ignore and rise above whenever possible."

"It's usually only if the man violates some unspoken agreement that the woman takes action," Tommy agreed. "Was Mr. Corbyn very publicly chasing one particular girl, or something like that?"

"Not one—a lot of them." Jamie shook his head. "People snickered about him, and then of course after that incident, they laughed."

"Of course." Gil sighed. "So a great deal of tension in that clan."

"A great deal," Jamie agreed. "And probably more so now."

"Why?"

"Wasn't it his mining company that went bust a few weeks ago? Archer-Corbyn Mineral?"

I was quite embarrassed to realize I had no idea what they were talking about. I read the papers each morning of course, but I admit I occasionally skipped the business pages when Tommy and I were not actively making new investments.

Tommy, though, had not missed it. "I just assumed it was one of his many enterprises."

"So would I," Gil said. "Those robber barons generally own many things."

"Well, that's true." Jamie shrugged. "Probably doesn't mean anything."

"But I must admit I'm curious about her effort to throw the daughter at Charles," Gil said. "Did he have any interest in making the catch?"

Gil's sparkly little glance in my direction completely escaped Jamie, and good thing.

"Pater, you know Charles. He would not even notice her unless she was on a hunter."

"Was she?"

"Thankfully, the one place we never saw her was horseback. Otherwise, who knows what might have happened." Jamie laughed and turned to Tommy and me. "Charles fancies himself the perfect country gentleman. Someday, he'll just marry some girl for her bloodlines and her string of hounds."

We nodded. It did help explain Charles' determined effort to ignore me. An opera-singing stepmother definitely did not fit into that picture.

"He's not a bad fellow, Charles," Jamie continued. "He's just—stuck. In the mud, in his ideas of how life should be. You'll see when you meet him."

I managed a nod and hoped my face wasn't as dubious as my thoughts.

Gil gave his son a sharp glance. "Perhaps we should move the discussion to more pleasant matters."

"An excellent idea, Gil." The Countess picked up her wine glass. "So, Jamie, which city did you enjoy most during your Grand Tour..."

Chapter Thirty-One

With This Ring

On the morning before the wedding, Tommy took off for some kind of meeting with Cabot about one of their library projects, but I had nothing to do after vocalizing. I was on my chaise trying to read when Gil walked in.

"Not out seeing the sights with Jamie?"

"He's gone to the Natural History Museum. I wanted to come back and steal a moment to talk with you before we get caught up in all the preparations."

I waited. His aspect was serious, even worried, and for a moment, I was rather unnerved at what he might want to discuss. I would have been quite concerned indeed if he had not so recently assured me we were as good as married.

Whatever it was, it could not be *too* bad, could it?

Actually, considering the way he'd been acting in recent days, it probably could.

I had to remind myself to breathe.

Then Gil reached in his pocket and pulled out a tiny box, handing it to me with a shy smile. "It's probably some sort of bad luck for me to buy this for myself, so you may write the check for the jeweler's bill."

Puzzled, I took the box and opened it. Inside, a gold band, just large enough that I could tell it was not intended for my hand. Stunned and moved, I truly did not know what to say.

Most men, and certainly most aristocratic British men, don't wear wedding rings, after all. I had not expected that Gil would; it's just a matter of tradition and no slight intended. Though I was aware that Prince Albert had worn a ring, I knew no man who did; in the tenements, of course, it was a major effort to afford even a thin pawnshop band for the bride, and in more exalted circles, it's the gentleman's job to deck out his lady.

A woman generally doesn't have—or expect—the same right to stake her claim.

Preston had recently started sporting a small gold signet on his pinky that Greta had bought him, partly with the first proceeds of her catering, but that was as much about Greta's appreciation of his understanding for her work as a claim on her man. Perhaps that had given Gil the idea, though.

"Well, Shane, it occurred to me that if I'm asking you to go out in the world with a sign and symbol that you belong to me, I should give you the same consideration."

"Really?"

"And," his aspect darkened a little, "it also occurred to me during the mishap on the *Atlantic Star* that while you had my ring on your hand, I had nothing from you."

My eyes filled. "Nothing but my love."

"Trust you, *mo chridhe*." He took my hand. "So, will you give me the ring tomorrow?"

"Of course." I couldn't stop a tear from overflowing.

He carefully wiped it away with his thumb and leaned in for a kiss. Still terribly cautious, but sweet and almost reverent.

Then, finally, as he gently pressed his lips to mine, slowly and so very carefully, I understood.

I had been misreading his reserve.

Every time he pulled away, I'd taken it as a lack of desire or even neglect, but that wasn't it at all. He was afraid of everything that was going to happen between us because he cared too much.

Nursing many of the same fears I was, though from an entirely different angle.

"I love you," I said, resting my forehead on his for a moment.

"And I you."

For a few measures, we just stayed there, close and comfortable, enjoying the love and understanding between us. Surely, that would be enough to pull us through the next two days—and nights.

Then he took a breath and reluctantly pulled away, still holding my hand.

I looked down at the little box, then back up at him. "I will be honored to give this to you."

"Only fair." He shrugged. "One shouldn't ask his wife to do something that he won't."

"And I like the idea of my ring on your hand." It was what he'd said to me the night I accepted his proposal.

He remembered and smiled.

I took a closer look at the box. It was a society jeweler not far from here, on the Ladies' Mile. "I'll go over to the shop and pay the bill today, so it truly is me giving you the ring."

"I admit I'm a superstitious Highlander at times, but I'll be glad if you do." Gil's face sharpened a bit. "Do you know what made me think of having you pay the bill, though?"

"What

"Mrs. Lally was buying hers at the jeweler when I was there yesterday, along with a bunch of gaudy little trinkets for her bridesmaids."

"Really. A band for the prince?"

"No." A wry head shake. "Her own wedding ring."

"So he really does bring nothing but his title and his sensitive soul."

"Rather a high premium to be a princess."

"I think we can safely assume she's buying the title the way she bought that paneling Rafe was hanging."

"Just so."

"Well, I wish her joy of it," I shook my head. "She's going to have to see that blank face across the breakfast table for the next 30 years."

Gil laughed. "I think I have rather a better bargain."

"So do I."

"Though," he said, a blush creeping across his cheeks as he held my gaze and twined his fingers with mine, "it's possible we may be late for the Eggs Benedict on occasion."

I blushed, too. Perhaps he did have 'demands' after all. "Eggs Benedict are a bit much early in the day."

"I tend to agree."

For a moment, we just smiled together, enjoying the play.

"Gil! What an odd hour for a visit!"

"Mother."

The Countess was in a simple but elegant gray walking dress, hat in hand, clearly ready for a morning of errands. She looked at us and beamed. "Just over a day to go, children. Everyone will happily look the other way if you wish to steal a kiss or two."

Another shared blush.

Gil cleared his throat and rose. "No, I was just here to give Shane the ring for the ceremony. I need to go speak with the good Father now."

"There is a place in the Catholic ceremony for the man's ring?" the Countess asked.

"I don't know," I admitted. "But I imagine Father Michael will just bless them both at once."

"It will do." Gil nodded. "I'll see you this evening."

"Of course." I squeezed his hand, and he kissed my cheek.

"Where is James?" the Countess asked her son as she walked him to the door.

"The Museum. I assume you'll see him by dinner."

She gave a musical laugh. "He's still a growing boy. We'll see him at a meal before that, unless I miss my guess."

Gil smiled an indulgent fatherly expression. I hoped I would someday see over the head of our own wee one. "No doubt."

As he swept off, he crossed paths with Sophia, who favored him with her usual adoring gaze as she carried a small parcel to me.

Sophia has a bit of a crush on Gil...and Connor...and Rafe. She's just enough younger than Rosa and Mary O'Hanlon that all she wants or needs from a man is for him to stand around and look nice and perhaps smile at her on occasion. Of course, no man welcome in our house would ever respond to Sophia's adoration with anything else.

"Miss," she said, holding out the box, "another gift. It's from that landlady."

The Countess gave me a puzzled look.

"Landgravine, Sophia," I replied patiently, taking the box and turning to Gil's mother. "Charlotte von Stade?"

"Oh, yes. A friend of the family." She nodded and gave me a smile almost as careful as the one I was giving her.

Which of us would acknowledge it?

Both.

She chuckled, and so did I.

"You know, don't you, dear?" she asked.

"I know enough." I looked down at the box, which was from a very good London store, meaning Charlotte von Stade had brought it with her. "I have no intention of thanking her for anything but this gift."

"Ah. He's told you the story."

"The outlines, at least."

The Countess patted my hand. "If not for her, he would likely have spent the rest of his life mourning poor May."

"That's what I gathered."

"But Charlotte was just—an adventure, for lack of a better description."

I managed what I hoped was a canny smile. "I gathered that, too."

"In her way, Charlotte is a very good woman. She knows exactly who she is and where she belongs."

"I'm sure." I nodded. "I'm not threatened at all. If he wanted to be with her, he would be."

A bright smile. "Just so. Exactly so."

"Well, let's see what she's sent us."

I carefully untied the blue satin bo, and lifted the lid to reveal two engraved silver bookmarkers. Both had what I presumed to be the Leith crest on one side and on the other, one was engraved with a lyre, of course, the symbol

196

of a musician, the other with the scales of justice. "How perfect," I said as I opened the card, signed in a flowing script:

For all of those books you will read and discuss. Much joy to you both. Charlotte.

"A lovely gift indeed." The Countess beamed. "And just perfect for you two."

I remembered Gil's comment that he and "the woman" had probably never read two of the same books and smiled. "Very much so. I will be delighted to write this thank-you note."

I put the card in my lap desk and the small box in the pile of gifts in the parlor. By the time I walked back into the foyer, the Countess had donned her hat, a lovely gray broad-brim topped with a swirl of shimmery tulle and a large soft-pink flower.

"So what else does the day hold for you, my dear?"

I nodded to the small ring box on the table by the chaise. "Well, before I start writing notes, I have to put that safely away, and go pay a bill at the jeweler's, to prevent bringing bad luck down on us all."

"He asked me if he should wear the ring."

"He did?"

"Yes. He'd heard that Prince Albert wore one, and rather liked the idea. He didn't wear one before."

"This marriage is different for any number of reasons." I said it as neutrally as I could. I absolutely did not resent poor dead May, who never got to see her boys grow up. But an ignoble little part of my soul suspected that Gil had treated her with more passion and less fear because she was a widow...and I did envy that one thing.

"As it should be." The Countess's face took on a wistful expression. "The main reason I never remarried was that all of the men I know are too much like Gil's father...with a few crucial qualities missing. You are right for him because you are so different."

"Much different," I agreed. I hadn't intended it to come out so glum.

She studied me for a measure or two. "Have things been—awkward — between you two lately?"

I looked to her, stunned. "At times."

The Countess sat down in the chair her son had just recently occupied. "He's quite nervous, for some odd reason. Worried that you don't know how much he really cares for you."

"He's been rather—distant at some moments," I said, hoping she would get the drift without my needing to pursue it further.

She smiled. "Overly careful with you, perhaps?"

"Yes."

A sigh and a smile. "Ah, men. So predictable."

"What do you mean?"

"Let me explain it in terms you'll understand." She gave me a wise nod. "You spent quite a while fighting your feelings for him, didn't you?"

"Yes. I was afraid of what I might do."

"It's much like that for him, though in one rather specific way." She held my gaze, making sure I knew what she meant. "He's afraid of what he might do because of his feelings for you. And, since I'm sure he knows how innocent you really are, probably terrified of hurting or shocking you in some way."

"So…"

"He's going to be quite timid until you give him a reason not to be."

"What do you mean?"

"Well, I suspect you'd do better to ask your friend Madame Marie for the exact details, but you'll need to be brave and bold enough for both of you at first."

"Brave and bold."

"My dear, it's playing a role. Very little different than what you do on any given night…but this time, it's an audience of one. Sweep him off his feet and let nature take its course."

I took a breath. "All right."

"Talk more with Madame Marie tonight after dinner. She'll have better insight than I…or at least it will be a good deal better coming from her."

I nodded. Probably the absolute last thing I wanted to do in this life, was have a discussion about the details of our private moments with Gil's mother.

"In the meantime, dear, you have a jeweler's bill to pay, and I have a florist

198

to see."

"True."

Tommy appeared as I donned my own pansy-bedecked hat, looking happy and relaxed as he always does after a library visit with Cabot, and invited himself along on the jewelry mission, probably for the sake of spending time with me. Though it could just as easily have been to avoid the Countess's final floral fancies.

"Ready for the wedding, Heller?"

"Mostly." I shrugged. He knew me too well.

"Nervous?"

"Not about the ceremony—that really is a performance like any other. And not about our life together—we agree on all of the important things."

"It's the getting from here to there."

"Exactly."

He patted my hand on his arm. "You two are so well matched. You'll do fine. Stop thinking things to death."

"Probably true."

"Have I ever been wrong?"

"Well, once you thought you were…" I began with a wicked smile.

"But I was wrong."

"Exactly."

We laughed. We were at the jeweler's.

Inside, a number of society women were studying all manner of ornaments. While I've never been drawn to the heavy, ostentatious pieces that the matrons favor, I do enjoy simple but good things like my engagement ring, or a single colorful stone in an unobtrusive setting—that lovely deep-purple amethyst heart pendant on a plain gold chain from Tommy is precisely my style. If Gil is ever overcome by the masculine need to decorate his woman, I will urge him in that direction.

Nothing that appealed to me was on offer at this establishment, which catered to the highest end of the carriage trade. Gil had likely come here because it was the closest trustworthy place.

As Toms and I moved back to the counter, I recognized Mrs. Demeter

Fisch and a few of the other ladies who were browsing, and we exchanged pleasantries, including praise for the benefit, and their best wishes (*not* congratulations!) for the next day. And then, I saw her.

Aline Corbyn, her face tense, with a nasty red flush at her cheekbones, was talking quite intensely with the jeweler, the spectacular aquamarine parure she'd been wearing on the benefit night on the counter.

"Don't acknowledge her, dear," whispered Mrs. Fisch. "No need to embarrass her."

"So true," I nodded to her as I carefully caught the eye of the young lady at the other case, probably the jeweler's daughter.

It was only after I'd paid and accepted the girl's good wishes, and a wistful smile suggesting she hoped someday she would have a man who would want to wear her ring that Aline Corbyn acknowledged me.

By then, the aquamarines were off the counter, and the jeweler was nowhere in evidence, and she was talking quite neutrally with Mrs. Fisch.

"Why, dear Ella and Thomas! How delightful. Buying a last-minute gift for your bridesmaids?"

"Her man's wedding ring," Tommy said, clearly taking a little familial pride in the Barrister's devotion.

Aline Corbyn pursed her lips, reminding me of Jamie's vivid description of her less-than-elevated handling of Mr. Corbyn's indiscretions. "Well, it's all quite lovely at the start, isn't it? Best of luck to you."

"We'll see you at our open house tomorrow."

"Of course. I would not miss it for anything."

There was more than a little poison in her eyes as she turned, and I could not help hoping the police would find a way to shake her story soon. Probably not before the wedding, though.

And after that, I reminded myself, I would be in Niagara Falls for a while, with plenty of other things to consider. Not one of them to do with Mrs. Corbyn.

Chapter Thirty-Two

In the Eye of the Wedding Whirlwind

N o one was especially interested in luncheon, with the various celebrations coming up in the evening, and I had little appetite, so I slipped out for another walk in the park. I've never suffered from nerves, beyond the little tug in my stomach that tells me I care about the performance I'm about to give...but all this wedding nonsense was starting to bother me just a bit. I grabbed my favorite broad-brimmed straw hat, trimmed up with some rather adorable pink daisies, took a parasol, and headed out for another turn around the park.

The lilacs were no longer in bloom, but the rhododendron flowers were out in all their shimmery bright-pink glory. So was Landgravine Charlotte Von Stade, looking surprisingly practical in a simple light-brown walking suit and pale pink blouse. Her hat was almost exactly the same as mine.

"Why, how lovely to see you, Miss Shane!" she exclaimed at the sight of me.

"And you." I held out my hands, and we exchanged a surprisingly comfortable greeting.

"I love your hat," she said.

"And I yours."

We shared a grin.

"Just bought it on the Ladies' Mile," she admitted. "I didn't bring anything suitable for keeping off the sun, and I had no intention of freckling for Pearl's sake."

"Indeed not." I nodded. "And one must have a good walk."

"Well, some of us must. Pearl would not be caught dead outdoors unless she had to be, but I find walking to be most soothing at trying times." Her tone suggested the future princess was trying indeed. Not that she would ever say so. She gazed at me with a warm, if slightly assessing, smile. "Bridal nerves?"

"Perhaps a bit," I admitted with a little sigh and tried to push the conversation away from me. "Likely not a problem for the princess-to-be."

"Well, of course, since it's her second marriage, Pearl isn't facing quite the adjustment you are. But she's also nowhere near as blessed as you."

"He is a very good man," I agreed as I remembered my manners. "And we will make good use of those bookmarks. Thank you."

"I thought you might." She nodded and hesitated for a moment as if she wasn't quite sure whether she should say the next thing. "Not just a very good man, my dear. A very good man who is desperately in love with you and perhaps overly determined to get things right."

"Perhaps." I suspect I knew the things to which she was referring.

"Well, let's just say you need have no concerns in private matters once the initial shyness is over."

I blushed. Was she really—vouching—for him?

She patted my arm and slipped hers through mine. "You'll come out all right. No one could love you more or be more determined to make you happy."

"I truly believe that." I kept a friendly tone as I moved on to something less awkward. "I hope your sister-in-law will have every happiness."

Charlotte von Stade laughed, a glorious, honest guffaw. "I doubt she'll have much happiness beyond being able to call herself a princess, but that will probably be enough."

"I hope I'm not speaking out of turn by saying he seems to bring little but his title and companionship."

"You're not. And honestly, the companionship isn't much." She shook her

CHAPTER THIRTY-TWO

head. "Rather mad what women will do for a title, isn't it?"

"Barking mad."

"I know I'm not the best authority, having been born a Lady and married a Landgrave, but some of your countrywomen will accept absolutely anything to put a word or two in front of their name."

"They truly will." For a moment, I was afraid I might be missing something very important, and asked quickly: "You don't suspect anything—dangerous — here?"

She laughed again, a wonderful uproarious sound. I suspected men found it as fascinating as women found it charming. "Not a bit of it. Pearl would kick his lazy posterior back to Poland if he tried any of that nonsense."

"That's a mercy, at least."

"It is." A wry twist to her generous mouth. "They rather deserve each other. Both utterly shallow and essentially uninterested in anything other than appearances."

I shook my head. "To each his own, I guess."

"Yes. I completely understand why one marries a man for love—I did it once. And I understand why one might marry for companionship or children. *I* wouldn't, but I can see how it might happen."

I nodded, encouraging her to continue.

"But marrying, actually living—even in a big house with separate rooms—with some nonentity simply for the sake of his title? No. I do not understand that."

"I don't either," I agreed.

A warm smile. "You'd marry him if he were the handyman, wouldn't you?"

"I would." I shrugged. "I don't need money and I don't care about his title. All I want is…"

"Him."

Her smile widened into a grin. "Now, you see, that's what a bride should be saying on the day before her marriage. Do you know what Pearl is doing today?"

"I'm afraid to ask."

"Laying out her jewels, changing the wedding breakfast menu, eating bonbons—and shrieking at her staff."

I allowed myself a laugh. "Not funny for the staff, of course, but otherwise, so silly."

"Quite." She shook her head. "Pearl is neither especially bright nor especially kind. It is a poor combination."

"Kindness makes up for a great deal." I sighed. "And my sense is that the Prince is not especially troubled with others' feelings, either."

"He doesn't seem to be troubled with anything at all, dear. The only time I've seen him show interest in anything was in Pearl's diamondrivière."

"Glad he's getting a rich wife for his trouble, maybe."

"Probably." She took a breath and let it out slowly. "Not the joining of two true hearts, for certain. I'd far rather be at your wedding, dear. I hope you'll forgive me."

"Of course. She's a relative. You can't just run away from her service to ours. But the next time we're in London…"

"Dinner—and perhaps a ladies' tea?"

"I would love that. We'll be there in September or so."

"So shall I. My son and I go to Prussia to visit von Stade's connections in the summer, but I like to return by autumn."

"Prussia?" I asked, remembering Ruben's Wotan. "Do you know of a small, modern-minded opera company there?"

"Ah! Did I hear that your Richard III had been booked for a Wotan?"

"You did." I nodded. "He's very young, and-"

"A Cuban Wotan in the Vaterland." She shook her head. "Probably the only company where that might happen—and even there…"

"Exactly."

"Well, I still have a few friends in the imperial circle. I think I can make sure he's looked after."

"He's only singing the role and then returning to Paris."

"Probably wise. If I were his booking agent-"

"I'd keep him well away from Germany."

"Sad but true." She shook her head. "Still, for that short summer run, my friends will be more than happy to keep an eye on him."

"Thank you."

"None necessary. Good people pull together to make sure the right things happen."

"That they do."

We smiled together.

"Now, about the right things happening, my dear, you should get back to your house before anyone worries that you've absconded."

Another shared laugh.

"Of all the things that could never happen on this earth," I said, "that is probably at the top of the list."

"And good thing for both of you."

I doubt the sun really was shining any brighter as I turned back down my street, but I certainly felt a good bit brighter. Charlotte von Stade, I reflected, was definitely a fine friend to have—whatever her history.

Back at the house, Mack McTeer was in the parlor, nibbling divinity fudge and talking about books with Rosa.

"Mack!" I pulled her in for a hug. "How wonderful to see you!"

"Katie's visiting Andrew at the precinct house, and I thought I'd drop by."

"I'm so glad you did."

Mack, born and never called Mary Grace, is the intelligent and occasionally incorrigible younger sister of the detective's wife. She has the same dark hair as her sister and big gray eyes with a sparkle that suggests she's always up to something. At twelve, she was still very much a girl, with a simple pink calico dress and matching bows in her braids. But she was definitely not girly. Neither the pink, nor the bows were her choice; the dress a hand-me-down from her sister Kitty, the bows imposed by her mother.

"I know you don't have time for a library visit, but—"

My purse was still in my hand, and it was still a while until evening time. "We don't have time for the library, but we do have time for the bookshop on the corner. Your mama won't mind if I buy you a book as a memento for being a bridesmaid tomorrow, will she?"

Mack grinned. "Not a bit."

We trooped out to the shop, a few blocks away, and Mack quickly decided what she wanted: a wonderful, illustrated history of scientific discoveries. The clerk knows us, so Mack's choice was no surprise to her, though she was quite amused to learn it was a bridesmaid gift.

Katie was walking up as we returned, and she admired the book and wished me well. Inside, more gifts and flowers had arrived, boxes stacked in the entryway, with Rosa and Sophia standing there shaking their heads.

"Good heavens! It took me a month to write all of my thank-you notes!" Katie exclaimed. "And it was nothing like this. Would you like a bit of help, at least, organizing things so you can write when you have time?"

"Why yes, thank you." I motioned them in. "It's so kind of you to help."

She grinned. "Only fair to help a fellow bride!"

The flowers were easy enough; Mack checked the cards, and Katie wrote them down in my album, smiling because I'd bought exactly the same simple white-covered one for recording gifts and givers she had. The stationer had many fancier offerings for brides, but neither Katie nor I was fond of such overdone things.

She put the cards in a pocket of the album, and I put the flowers in the foyer to be sent on to the poor women at the lying-in hospital, except for two especially beautiful baskets to go home with Katie and Mack. I had more bouquets than I could enjoy on any given day, but flowers were a special treat at their homes, so, of course, I was pleased to share.

Most of the packages were from well-wishers I knew only slightly, matrons I served with on charity boards, and a few opera fanciers who'd read of the marriage, but not that Gil and I had no need or desire for gifts. I supposed it would be rude and presumptuous to urge people to give money to charity rather than send useless decorative items, but honestly, I wish one could.

The gifts were mostly various curios and large china pieces, most of which were nice enough, but not at all to my—or Gil's—very simple tastes. A few were rather adorable, like a settlement house board member's Limoges girl playing piano with a swain in knee breeches turning pages and clearly hoping for a kiss.

Most, though, were just heavy tureens and such, which might prove useful for large dinners at Leith Castle...if Leith Castle didn't already have a supply—and if we intended to host such things anyway.

Katie, Mack, and I couldn't hide our laughter when I opened the *third* soup tureen in a row.

After the tureen, though, came a small, thin crate from Colonel Vandergrift. A painting, of a man and woman in eighteenth-century garb, executed with the skill of a real master, not merely a traveling painter.

The note, in a bold and only slightly shaky hand:

Dear Miss Shane,

Please accept this piece from my personal collection and my best
wishes for you and your Duke.

The couple is my Great-great-uncle Nikolaas Van der Grift and his
second wife, Hulda. They were married for forty years, and their
happiness is a family legend.

May your marriage bring you the same.

With All Esteem,

Colonel Albert Vandergrift

"Oh, isn't that the sweetest thing ever?" Katie asked. "Do you know him?"

"We met him at the Lorimer funeral and had tea with him this week." I remembered the conversation, and what the Colonel had told us about the late magnate's plans for his home...and Mrs. Corbyn's likely reaction to it.

Katie, not for nothing a detective's wife, gave me a canny glance. "And..."

"He had many useful thoughts about Mr. Lorimer's finances." I returned the glance. "And Mrs. Corbyn's as well."

"Should Andrew perhaps ask around if he has time before the wedding?"

"He should."

"It's a bit late in the day on a summer Friday for finding an accountant or banker," reflected Katie.

"What do you need a banker for?" Mack asked, bouncing over with her arms full of wrapping paper. "Could I have this, Miss Ella?"

I blinked at her. Mack asking for pretty floral things? What was the world coming to?

Mack laughed. "It's nice stiff paper and all white on the back. I could make it into notebooks for my science studies."

"Take it all," I said with a laugh, "as much as you can carry."

"Thanks!"

"And I'll send any more white paper that comes in over to your house, all right? A lady scientist should have a place to record her findings."

Her eyes lit up, as pleased by my support for her interests as with her acquisition.

Katie grinned and looked to me. "I'm not sure we have a new Madame Curie...but I don't want to be the one standing in her way."

"If you have a gift, you should be able to follow it," I said as she smiled.

"As my husband made sure I could." Her face glowed, as it always did when she spoke of him. "You know, he sought out my new school on the West Side because it accepts married women teachers."

"I do. There's nothing better than a man who understands you—and stands with you."

"Yours, too, right?"

"I wouldn't be marrying him if he didn't."

Katie grinned. "And I can't wait to see you two at the altar."

"Well, first, there's the men's night out..."

"And the ladies' night in." Katie chuckled. "If I were you, I'd throw your aunt out of the house and drink a whiskey with your friend Marie."

I could feel my eyes widening. Katie and I weren't close enough to discuss private matters, but she'd been a properly brought-up Irish girl when her da presented her to Cousin Andrew at the altar and probably had a better idea than anyone what I'd been thinking in recent days.

"Well," she started as her chuckle bloomed into a full-out laugh. "For heaven's sake, don't listen to the aunties. They've forgotten everything they knew—if they ever did."

"I suspected that."

"Just enjoy." Katie grinned. "You're finally free to be alone together without the family snooping over your shoulder every second. That alone is worth it."

I nodded.

"And the rest is pretty nice, too." She patted my arm and nodded to Mack.

CHAPTER THIRTY-TWO

"Leave it at that and talk to your friend."

"An excellent plan."

Chapter Thirty-Three

Stags and Hens

On the night before a wedding,g one expects the gentlemen to go out to drink and misbehave a bit and the ladies to stay in and gossip over a genteel beverage of their own. Gil and I had no intention of missing out on any of these traditions, though he was not overly fond of the drink, and I was not overly fond of gossip.

But the forms must be obeyed.

Not, however, before we honored a far more important tradition, which we fully intended to observe together every week: the family candlelighting.

With one addition for this special week: a *yahrzeit* candle for my mother, a small extra votive normally lit on the anniversary of a death, though I often light one when I need to be closer to her.

I wanted to feel her memory in this joyful moment.

Anna, whose Hebrew is so much better than mine, flatly refused to take the matches when I offered them. "You're not that bad, and you'd best get used to saying the blessings in company now."

It felt like one more milestone, in what I knew would be a series of them. I put the small candles in Mama's holders, struck the match, and began.

I knew the blessings by heart, but my voice came out a little thin and tentative, and as I lit the first candle, I looked up to see Gil, watching me with love and admiration, his eyes perhaps a bit brighter than they should be, and I returned his smile. It steadied me, and I finished the ceremony with a strong voice, if not the most perfect pronunciation.

No one remarked on the extra candle, though I'm sure most of them knew what it meant.

As was now the family habit, thanks to the Countess's good offices, we ended with hugs all round.

"Do you do this every week, Belle Starr?" Jamie asked when it was his turn.

"We surely do. And you are welcome every time."

He gave me a contemplative nod, quickly followed by that bad-little-boy smile. "You and Pater may live to regret that."

"Doubtful." I grinned back as Hetty and Marie moved in to get their introductions and greetings with him.

Everyone seemed to take a little extra moment to hold and reassure me, and the same with Gil, and I supposed it was really the beginning of our special time as the wedding couple.

When we reached each other, he pulled me in and whispered, "Perfect, *mo chridhe.*"

"Thank you."

He nodded to the *yahrzeit.* "For your mother."

"Yes. She would be so happy for us."

Gil looked to the candles again and gave me a shy smile. "Next week as man and wife."

Our eyes held for a moment, and we both caught our breath.

Never mind, next week. Tomorrow night as man and wife.

"Come along, Barrister!" Preston called. "You can stare at her all the time after tomorrow."

Everyone laughed at that, and Gil squeezed my hand.

"You know we're just-"

I shook my head at him. "Even good boys need a night out."

Jamie grabbed his father's arm. "To the pub, Pater."

"Not with you—" the older Saint Aubyn began, a combination of exasperation and fear moving over his face.

I exchanged a wicked little smile with my soon-to-be stepson. "I'm sure

211

you'll keep your dear papa out of too much trouble."

Gil sighed. "I'm more likely to keep *him* out of trouble."

"Well, I'll be there to watch over you both," Tommy said firmly, carefully pointing them toward the door, "and the ladies have their own celebrations to enjoy."

"That's very true, *mo laochain*." The Countess appeared out of nowhere on one side of me and Aunt Ellen on the other, both looking quite amused. "Have a lovely night out."

Tommy and Preston herded the gents out, Gil looking more than a little bewildered, Jamie, Cabot, and Louis all grinning with anticipation.

"And we," Marie said, pulling the kitchen bell, "shall have a lovely evening in."

It quickly became clear that Miss O'Hanlon had been quite busy with the celebratory plans when she, Rosa, and Sophia appeared with trays of various small dainties and a generous pitcher of lemonade, tinted pink with raspberry juice. A very ladylike little celebration for my last night as a maiden lady.

Miss O'Hanlon had outdone herself with the refreshments, but even if she hadn't, Greta would not have said a word of criticism. The treats were rather beside the point, no matter how delicious.

We ate and laughed and talked of dresses and flowers and other inconsequential and amusing matters for perhaps an hour until Hetty checked the watch pinned to her bodice and noted that she had to return to the *Beacon* for a bit to double-check her upcoming article so she would not have to worry tomorrow evening. It might even have been true.

I walked her to the door.

"You don't have to leave, you know."

She shook her head. "Ells, the married ladies want to talk to you about married-lady things. They'll do better without me."

"But-"

"If—and I do mean *if*—I ever need to know such things, I expect you to give me a good honest talk. But right now, you need to get yours."

We hugged, and she swept off.

"All right, dear," said the Countess, taking my arm as I returned to the room where Aunt Ellen, Greta, Anna, and Marie were waiting.

Aunt Ellen gave me a topped-up glass of lemonade and a suspicious glance. "Did you talk to your doctor this week?"

She had not been especially in favor of this, since it struck her as far too modern, but from the way she looked over to the Countess, I suspected the senior ladies had discussed matters and come to some kind of truce.

Greta, mother of a nurse, and Marie, fellow patient of Dr. Silver, shared a wince.

"I did." I tried to keep down the blush. "It was most enlightening."

"Good." The Countess nodded. "Did she explain everything you need to know?"

I took a deep sip of lemonade and kept my eyes away from my friends, especially Marie, I could tell they were trying desperately not to giggle. Whatever questions I might have about private matters, I would never, under any circumstances, discuss them with these august ladies.

Actually, I dearly hoped I would never again have to think about private matters in the same room as them.

"Perhaps," Anna suggested, after a tiny cough that surely covered a laugh, "we might all do well to go to bed early tonight. I would like to get home to Morris, and it's going to be quite a busy day."

"Indeed it is," Marie agreed with the brisk tone that suggested she was hoping to move the ladies along.

"You know, I do need to work on the menu for a dinner next week." Greta gave a businesslike nod and rose. "You're not offended-"

"Not in the least," I assured her, knowing that she understood I would do almost anything to get out of this conversation. Or at least to make it a smaller one.

Aunt Ellen got the general drift. "I'd like to get home to Kat and Suze as well."

At the door, Anna gave me a hug and a grin. "I told you, you can handle the blessings on your own."

"You did, at that."

"Tell Miss Mary that I could not have done better with those raspberry meringues," Greta said after her hug. "And—to quote my dear spouse—don't look for trouble where there is none."

We shared a chuckle. "Exactly."

Aunt Ellen hugged me and looked down at me quite seriously. "You're quite sure about all of this with the doctor?"

"Yes."

"She told you to make sure you take care of your man's demands, didn't she?"

Dr. Silver would never have dreamed of putting it in such a way, but I would never escape this embarrassing moment if I didn't nod and smile. So that was exactly what I did.

Once the door closed behind Aunt Ellen, I turned to see the Countess and Marie.

Immediately, the Countess grinned. "I'm going upstairs. This is something for you two...and I wouldn't dream of interfering."

"Thank you," I said, the words coming out as a sigh of relief.

"Child, every married woman has been through this. You don't need to talk to your husband's mother right now."

Marie hugged the Countess and wished her a happy goodnight. And then she turned to me. "Whiskey. And plenty of it."

"I don't—"

"There are times," she said, turning over two of the nice crystal glasses Tommy and the other men used, "that even the most proper lady needs a bit of the creature."

"All right."

Marie poured two generous portions and handed me one. "To a happy wedding night."

"Your lips to God's ears."

She giggled and clinked her glass against mine. "Your lips aren't going to be on *God's* ears tomorrow night."

"Very funny."

"Sorry. I couldn't resist." Marie's eyes sharpened on my face. "Surely not nervous after all you two have been through and a frank talk with the Doc?"

"Not about me." I took a sip and almost choked as it burned down my throat. "About him. You know his first wife was a widow."

"Ah. *He's* afraid."

"I'm certain he is. He's been treating me like I'm made of glass since February, and it's only gotten worse the closer we get to the wedding."

She shook her head. "Poor dear. He's thinking and worrying it to death."

"Poor *him!*"

"So are you, Ells. You're both so busy worrying about making sure it's perfect that you're afraid to just jump in and get to it."

"Which means what?"

Marie smiled very wisely. "Sometimes you don't think. You just do."

"Just do."

"And leave it to Mother Nature, for goodness sakes. We're made to love each other, after all."

"In that way, too..."

"Especially in that way." She took a sip of her whiskey. "There's nothing wrong with either of you that won't be made right with a little time behind a closed bedroom door. Or a lot of time behind that door."

"Should I—"

"You'll know when you get there. Just make sure you take your pleasure, too."

I almost dropped my glass. "Meaning..."

"Meaning it will be just as much fun for you as it is for him if he's going about things the right way. And if he's not—tell him to slow down and make sure he is."

"I can do that?"

"You'd *better* do that. Nothing worse than letting a man think everything's all right when it's not. It's terrible for you—and worse for the marriage. And they always find out anyway. Grandma said so anyhow." She smiled at my stricken expression. "It's not the huge matter it sounds like. It's simply guiding him in the right direction. If he's a smart and loving man, and we know he is, he's waiting for you to do just that."

"He is?"

"Absolutely. Men want their women to tell them what they like. It makes it a lot easier on them."

"Ah." I took a drink. I needed it.

"You'll understand. Usually, it's just a matter of yes, please, more of this." She giggled. "Once you get over that initial moment of nerves and embarrassment, it's quite delightful discovering one's spouse."

"It is?"

"Oh yes." She gave me a sphinx-like smile and took another sip of whiskey. "Quite delightful indeed."

Chapter Thirty-Four

On the Wedding Morn

The whiskey ensured I slept well, though not late. The first thing I did when I woke was write a little note to Gil. I wasn't sure if I would send it to him now or closer to the ceremony, but we'd agreed to abide by the old wedding day tradition that the groom does not see the bride before the service, so I thought a sweet message might be a nice gesture. Just a few lines about meeting him at the altar and one of my favorite Donne quotes.

After I sealed the note, I put my wrapper on and headed downstairs. The sun was just rising, giving the whole house a golden glow. I took a few moments walking through the rooms, where the pocket doors had been opened and the furniture re-arranged for the ceremony in the drawing room. After the service, the chairs would be moved away to make room for the expected crowd at the open house. The other rooms were already set up. The flowers had not yet arrived, but all of the tablecloths had been laid down, and the ribbons and streamers were waiting.

I walked into the drawing-room, where a mahogany side table from the dining room had been moved in and draped to serve as the altar for the vows. The grandfather clock in the corner said seven o'clock. Twelve hours from now, we will be celebrating our marriage with the people we love most.

"Heller?" Tommy stood in the doorway, smiling. "Thinking about putting back in the promise to obey?"

"Not ever." I joined him in a laugh. "I couldn't just lie abed waiting for things to happen."

"Neither could I. We were home before midnight."

"I know. You almost passed Marie at the door."

He shook his head. "Some last night of carousing."

"You did your best."

Tommy laughed. "We ended up at the pub down the street drinking pints and discussing old cases with Alteiss."

"Really?"

"He won't say it, of course, but he has serious misgivings about Mrs. Corbyn."

"Don't we all."

"Yes, but he and the Barrister exchanged one of those, 'I can't tell you, but I'm telling you there's more' looks."

"Alteiss was close to Lorimer. He might have some interest in making the right thing happen."

"He can't ethically do much as long as he's representing Mrs. Corbyn."

"True." I toyed with a ribbon. "But I wonder if our lawyers are up to something."

"*Your* lawyer is up to getting married."

"You know the Barrister. If it's important, he'll be helping Alteiss right up until Louis plays the first notes of the processional."

"I'll drag him back here if I have to."

We shared a smile, and I shrugged. "Well, at least you learned something."

"Did you?"

I blushed. "What I need to know, yes."

"Good." His face turned serious. "You know you two will be all right. At the end of the day, all that really matters is that you love each other, and you'll figure it out."

It was at least as good as the advice Marie had given. And far less embarrassing.

"True." The moment was getting all too serious, and I was relieved to notice a little green wing on his jacket. "I see the maple trees are still dropping seeds."

I brushed it off, and as I did, seeing my hand on his shoulder, I had a sudden flash of Mrs. Corbyn at the Met reception, and I knew what I'd seen. And should have known that night.

Tommy caught my expression and stared at me. "What?"

"She did it. And we can prove it."

"What do you mean?"

"It's the way her gown was ripped. Not at the front, as it might have been if a man were grabbing at her, but from the shoulder toward the back…"

"I thought that was just how the fabric had given way."

"No. It had a rather fragile beaded front. If anyone had pulled on that, it would have ripped easily. But the rip came from the shoulder, like she grabbed it herself."

"To cover what had happened." He nodded grimly. "Now what?"

I sighed irritably. "Someone needs to talk to Alteiss—maybe Gil—and I can't do that. It's too early to do anything anyway."

"At least an hour until anyone's awake," he agreed.

"Well, then." I tapped my foot. Perhaps we should just get moving. Any kind of movement would do at this point. "Want to join me for a little fencing?"

"You know I'm not nearly as good as the Barrister…"

"Doesn't matter. Give us something to do."

"Sounds good to me. I'll do my best to hang onto the sword."

"Can I come too?"

Jamie was standing in the doorway, wearing a light-gray summer suit with a showy red tie that his father would never consider, a straw boater in one hand and an envelope in the other. "Pater made me his messenger boy, and I'm going to die of boredom before we get to the wedding."

"He's awake?" I asked.

"Gave it to me last night. I don't know. I just know *I'm* awake and bored."

"Good. I have a note for him as well—and a message," I said.

"Message?"

"He needs to explain to Alteiss that his client is guilty and decide how to

219

catch her."

Jamie grinned. "So we'll have more than family happiness to celebrate today."

"Quite possibly."

"But first, this." He handed me the envelope. "It's for you to read before the ceremony. I'm to take back anything you might like to send him."

A bit of the second sight from my half-Highlander? I grinned at Jamie. "I wrote him a note this morning. And, of course, now you'll have our message."

"Good. I'll take it over—but only after a nice breakfast."

"We didn't invite you yet," Tommy teased.

"Well, I'm hoping for Miss O'Hanlon's baked goods instead of the overcooked eggs and dry rolls at the hotel…"

"And you're very welcome, as long as you relay the information." I nodded to the stairs and plucked at my wrapper. "I'll meet you two in the studio once I change."

In my first, and easiest, costume change of the day, I scrambled into my favorite old breeches and washed-out shirt in record time and dashed up to the studio.

Montezuma greeted me with a surprising little arpeggio when I walked in. He was on the piano music stand, and Jamie was sitting at the bench, watching the bird with fascination.

"I see you two have met."

"He's a lot like my grandmother's bird, but Robert Burns isn't nearly as friendly."

"Neither is Montezuma," Tommy said, opening the foil cabinet, "unless he decides you are worthy. It's a major point in your favor."

"Good to know."

"So, how's your fencing?" I asked.

"I've had a few years of lessons. I doubt my instructor's as good as yours. Perhaps you can teach me a few things."

"Let's see how we go."

Tommy handed me my foil, then Jamie his, and sat down in the big old mulberry plush chair he uses during rehearsals—and I use when I hide out to read. He was clearly happy to be out of the fencing and glad to enjoy the show.

"*En garde*," I said, stepping into position.

"*En garde*, Belle Starr."

I laughed, which made me start at a bit of a disadvantage. I quickly got it back, though. Jamie did not seem as troubled by fencing a woman as many men I've dueled—particularly his father—but he wasn't nearly at Gil's level. Never mind mine.

Being a very perceptive and modest young man, he soon realized what a mismatch it was. "I'm sorry."

"Not at all." I slowed my pace to his.

"It's rather more of a lesson than a match."

"That's all right. I'm happy to work with you."

I caught Tommy's smile. Well, there are far worse ways to get to know one's stepson than a fencing lesson.

We were slowly making our way across the studio when there was a knock.

"Miss! It's-" Sophia skidded into the doorway.

"Sophia, please send James out."

Gil's voice from the landing was careful and a tiny bit exasperated.

"Pater?"

Tommy laughed.

I chuckled but said nothing.

"Excuse me, Belle Starr."

He bowed, and I returned the gesture, then he stepped outside.

Tommy and I shook our heads.

"The Barrister is taking this good luck thing very seriously," Tommy said.

"Well, after everything…" I narrowed my eyes at him. "You are not to tell Aunt Ellen about this until after the wedding."

"Not a word. None of us needs to have her crowing about how even sensible Britons follow the old ways."

"Old superstitions."

"If it's just superstition, go out there and give him a big kiss." Tommy laughed as I shook my head.

"I don't want him to feel uncomfortable."

"Right you don't. Heller, you two deserve all the good luck you can get. Any way you want to get it."

"We have to cause someone else a bit of bad luck first," I reminded him and walked to the door frame. "James, did you tell your father we have information for him?"

"No."

"Well, James, there's something you need to pass on," I pitched my voice loud enough that Gil could hear but addressed myself to Jamie. "I am reasonably sure that Mrs. Corbyn ripped her own gown that night. It gave way at the shoulder, not the front, and someone might be able to use that information against her."

"I will tell him."

A pause while Jamie and Gil probably stood on the landing staring at each other.

Then: "Thank you, James."

"Quite so, Pater. See you back at the hotel."

"Please give my compliments to Miss Shane and her cousin." His voice, too, pitched loudly enough for me.

"When do you start calling her by name?" Jamie asked in a cheeky, teasing tone.

"Never outside the family, son. We show respect to our women."

The response was a little stiff, but sweet in its way, and I smiled. So did Tommy.

"Of course, Pater."

Shaking his head a bit, Jamie walked back in and handed me a little box. "Pater forgot to include the charm."

"A charm?"

He shrugged. "No idea. Something special for the wedding, no doubt."

"No doubt. Am I allowed to open it now?"

"He didn't say. You're meant to have it before the ceremony, so..."

That was good enough for me. I opened the box. A simple oval charm, like the one he'd given me after our first misadventure. But this time, engraved with one simple word: **Bashert.** Of course. My mother's Hebrew word, something of her for this day she could never have imagined but would be so glad to see.

Not her daughter marrying a duke. Her daughter marrying the man who was meant—*bashert*—for her.

My eyes filled.

"Oh, Belle Starr, you're not supposed to cry!"

Tommy laughed and patted Jamie's arm. It was the first evidence we'd seen that my exceedingly poised and polished stepson-to-be was actually still very much a boy. "Jamie, friend, ladies cry when they're happy too."

"Oh."

"It's all right."

Jamie gave him a puzzled face, clearly trying to figure out what he was supposed to do.

Tommy grinned. "A little advice?"

"Please."

"If a woman's crying because she's happy, don't try to stop her. If a woman's crying because she's sad, comfort her. And if she's crying because she's mad at you..."

He waited.

"Run."

We all laughed. Hopefully, this would be a day of happy tears.

Chapter Thirty-Five

Bless the Bride

Most brides likely do not begin their nuptial day by fencing and plotting to trap a murderer. So, I surely should have expected that the rest of the day would be no more conventional.

Still, I hoped. I quickly changed into a simple pansy-print mull day dress, threaded the charm onto my bracelet and clasped it onto my wrist, then tucked the box in my jewel chest, and put the note in my pocket so I wouldn't lose it. Downstairs, I glanced toward the dining room, to see Tommy and Jamie happily devouring Miss O'Hanlon's offerings. No Countess in sight.

Good. I had a bit of time for a few last things I needed to do alone. While I could still slip away without having to answer to anyone or respond to their concern.

Mrs. Early was not in the park when I walked past, but I hoped she'd appear later. I could at least give her a generous handful of bills, enough to keep body and soul together until we returned and could look for a more permanent way to help.

Holy Innocents was quiet. I'd lit the *yahrzeit* candle for my mother the previous night at home, but for my father, it had to be in the church. I knelt at the feet of the Virgin for a few moments, thinking of how my parents had started full of world-defying love and hope and ended in such misery. A woman waiting her turn behind me cleared her throat, and I quickly scampered out of the way. Her tight, stricken face told me she was doing far more than paying tribute to the past, clearly needing the solace more than I.

Still, I wanted a little more of the enveloping quiet of the sanctuary and the Presence, and I stepped into a back pew. Father Michael gave me a wise nod from the altar, where he was making sure all was ready for the next Mass.

It was then, sitting in Holy Innocents, that I found Gil's note in my pocket. Just a few words, in his usual strong, legible hand, on the simple hotel paper rather than the thick, elegant personal stationery he'd used for the letters during our courtship. But this, perhaps, more precious because I was reading it on our wedding morn:

Mo chridhe,

> *I wonder, by my troth, what you and I did, til we loved.*
> *You will forgive my leaving it to Reverend Donne.*
> *Until we meet at the altar.*
> *G*

It was, of course, the exact same line I had sent him. And I too had apologized for using the poet's phrase instead of my own. Well matched indeed, in heart and soul and mind.

I put the note back in my skirt pocket and slipped into the aisle.

Father Michael was in the vestibule, opening a window. He smiled. "The happy bride."

I grinned back. "Just so."

His eyes lingered on mine. "As it should be. Rarely have I seen two people as well matched as you and your Duke."

"That's true."

"Once all the wedding fuss is over, you'll settle very nicely into marriage. Unlike many of the couples I see, you've already come through trouble and danger together...and know you can trust each other. It's a gift."

"I'd rather have earned it some other way."

"No doubt."

I put my hand in my pocket, touching Gil's note and the money for Mrs. Early, which reminded me. "Have you seen Mrs. Early? Do you think she'll be here today?"

Father Michael's face broke into a huge, boyish grin. "You two really are a match."

"How so?"

"Two days ago, he was here asking me what else we could do for her."

"Was he, now?"

"Indeed he was." The father beamed. "As it happened, my sister, the Sister, told me this week they needed a lay sister or helper at her convent's orphanage."

I chuckled at the way he referred to his big sister. The former Gracie Riley, now Sister Immaculata, had a year or two on him and never let him forget it. Of course, the Riley clan was impressively proud of both, since, in Irish families, it's a great honor to "give a child to God," and they'd given two.

The good sister belonged to a convent near the tenements, helping tend and educate children very much like she and her brother had once been.

"A lay sister?" I asked. "But don't convents still expect a bit of a dowry even from them?"

Some religious orders require sisters to bring a dowry, just as some families used to expect a bride to have one. I remembered Gracie working in a candy factory for a couple of years to save up her portion.

Father Michael shrugged. "I suspect they do, sometimes. But a rather generous donation was made to the convent, so there'll be no question."

His eyes sparkled, and I knew who must have made the generous donation. So much for the Anti-Papist aristocracy.

"I see," I said, reaching in my pocket. "Well, Mrs. Early may need a little something to outfit herself for her new life. I was going to give this to her today, but perhaps you can make sure she gets it and that it's put to good use?"

"Easily done." His smile turned wistful. "Mrs. Early's face absolutely lit up when I asked her if she'd like to help with the children. She asked if she might be allowed to hold the babies on occasion, and nearly cried when

Gracie—um, Sister Immaculata—told her she'd be expected to comfort them as she could."

I was ready to cry myself. "All of the love she never had a chance to give."

"Exactly."

"It feels like a miracle."

The priest smiled, and his eyes were a little damp, too. "A happy ending *is* a miracle, you know. And God uses us to bring joy to others—if we let Him."

"A very good thought for a wedding day," I said.

Father Michael patted my arm. "There are always things in the world that can destroy joy and love. It's our job to make sure they don't."

"So true."

"Now, Miss Bride, you need to start prettifying yourself for that ceremony. And I have my own responsibilities."

"See you this evening."

"Can't wait."

He held the door for me, and I stepped out into the bright sunlight. I took the long way home, walking around the edges of the park. The fresh air was exactly what I needed to calm myself. Not only that, I enjoyed a chuckle as I saw a rush of carriages heading uptown, no doubt for one of the other society weddings. I guessed Pearl Lally and her prince, they were planning a morning ceremony.

Amusing, if one considered it, that I, the first-time bride with every right to a society splash if I so desired, had chosen a small service at home while the remarrying widow plumped for the kind of festivities that many etiquette experts would suggest she had no right to enjoy. Not that I begrudged her the event. There isn't nearly enough love and joy in the world as it is; why shouldn't she have her day?

On the way back, I stopped for a moment at the empty bench where Mrs. Early usually sat, offering a little prayer that her new life would be better and easier. I hoped she'd find comfort with the babes at the orphanage. Perhaps even joy.

A bride surely has a right to wish joy on the world.

Chapter Thirty-Six

A Lovely Gown, and Un-Lovely Things

"Belle Starr! Grandmother was getting ready to send out a search party!" Jamie called to me from the stairs when I walked in. "She seems to think it's going to take you several hours to put on your dress."

I laughed. Jamie probably assumed that ladies simply *appear* fully dressed at the beginning of the day and snap their fingers to change into a nightgown at the end.

"Well, James, it is a rather time-consuming process."

He shook his head. "Good thing Mr. Dare has come over, then. We're hiding in Tom's office, and he's telling us about his last road trip with the Superbas."

"Coffee?" I asked with more optimism than expectation.

"With only a little whiskey, Belle Starr. We wouldn't do that to you and Pater."

"We surely would not." Preston appeared on the landing as I walked up, holding the promised coffee cup. "No one's going to ruin a moment of your day, kid."

"Good thing." We shared a smile.

Jamie nodded to us both and drifted back to Tommy's office.

"Nervous?" Preston asked.

"Only a little."

He chuckled and patted my arm. "He's more afraid than you are, kid."

"Why does everyone keep telling me that?"

"Because it's true." He shrugged. "A man's always expected to be in charge, know what he's doing, make everything all right. And what if he's not sure if he *can* make it all right?"

I stared at Preston.

"See here, all you're thinking about is that you've been a very good girl, and now you're going to be a very good wife, right?"

"I suppose."

"And you figure he'll tell you exactly how to do that."

"Well, he's surely got a better idea than I do."

Preston laughed. "Maybe not. He's terrified of meeting your expectations."

"I don't *have* any expectations. I've never been married—how could I?"

He shook his head. "You two are at a mess of cross-purposes yet again."

I sighed.

"Look. You love each other. All you have to do is be good to each other. Stop thinking about it and just live it."

"Just live it."

"Exactly."

I nodded, still nervous and confused.

"And if all else fails, get him good and drunk and start singing. A man with a hangover will do anything for quiet."

We shared a laugh. It wasn't the best marital advice I'd heard…but it might come in handy one day.

Upstairs, Rosa was preparing a bath, and the Countess was running in and out of the dressing room. "Dear! We only have a few hours!"

"I put on costumes for a living, remember? We have plenty of time."

"This," she said with a meaningful gaze, "is not a conventional performance night, my dear."

"True."

She turned to the occasional table and picked up a box. "Here. For later."

Even the box was lovely, pale pink with the words "Sainte Helene" lightly stenciled in gold. Inside, nested in tissue, a frothy mass of barely lavender silk, with thin cobwebs of creamy lace and ribbons a half-shade darker. A peignoir.

"Sewn with great care and devotion by an order of nuns who make their living providing lovely things for ladies. My mother gave me one for my wedding, and I did the same for Madeleine. Not only is it the prettiest you'll find, it's a good reminder that what happens between you and your husband is a holy and healthy thing."

"Oh." I couldn't help blushing. "It's so beautiful."

"Your favorite color."

"Yes."

"Later, you can order more…the sisters also make more everyday things just as beautifully. But this, of course, is special."

"It is."

She smiled and patted my arm. "Remember. You'll need to be brave and bold enough for both of you. You're up to it."

I nodded firmly. Nothing else would do.

"Right then. Your bath is waiting…and we have to start preparing our lovely bride."

"Miss! Miss!" Sophia burst in. "You'll never believe what happened at the Polish Royal Wedding!"

"What?" The question in three-part unison.

"Miss Hetty just called. She's running a bit late because there was a robbery at the wedding."

"A robbery?"

The Countess and I said it together.

"Apparently, a couple of men pulled guns on the bride at the end of the service and took all of her jewels. Even the engagement ring!"

"What was the groom doing?" I asked.

"Don't know, miss." She shook her head. "I'm sure Miss Hetty will tell us when she gets here…"

"How extraordinary!" exclaimed the Countess.

"Extraordinary indeed. I can't wait to find out what happened."

"Right now, dear, you have a great deal of preparation to do, and we need to get right to it." She took my arm and firmly steered me toward my room. I could not help feeling rather like a sheep being herded.

Marie and Anna, both glowing in the lovely lavender crepe de chine dresses Anna had designed for my attendants, had arrived by the time I was out of the bath, sitting in my wrapper with Rosa and the Countess trying out various configurations for my hair and the orange blossoms.

We were into the third attempt when Hetty blew in, face flushed and eyes alight with the sparkle that only a good story could bring. Fortunately, her bridesmaid dress was none the worse for wear, however exciting her day had been.

"So?" I asked as the countess shook her head, and Rosa started undoing the latest style.

"A society wedding we'll never forget, for sure." Hetty sat down on the bed with a grin. "They were walking back down the aisle after the ceremony, man and wife-"

"Prince and Princess," contributed the Countess with a chuckle.

"Precisely." Hetty joined the chuckle, too. "As they stepped out the door, three men appeared, whipped out guns, and demanded the jewels. Starting with the bride's!"

"And did the Prince jump to his beloved's aid?" Marie asked.

"Not hardly." Hetty shook her head. "He helped her get the jewels off."

"No!" Anna said it, but we all thought it.

"Yes, indeed. And then collapsed."

"So much for Prince Charming," I said.

"Oh, there's more," Hetty continued.

"What could there be, Miss?" Rosa asked, dropping a big chunk of my front hair over my face as she spoke.

I blew it away so I could see.

"Sorry, Miss." Rosa quickly picked up the hair.

"I don't mind," I said, laughing. "This is all quite exciting."

"Quite." Hetty nodded to me. "I like that style."

Another warm laugh, shared among us all.

"Come on, now, don't string us along," Marie urged.

"She's right, you know." Anna motioned to Hetty to keep talking.

"Well, here's the lead line: no one has seen the Prince since the wedding." A general buzz of shock.

"Do they think he was in on it?" asked the Countess.

"Perhaps. Or perhaps he's hiding out somewhere because his new wife saw him at such poor advantage. Either way, the search is on for him, too."

"Fascinating." Marie turned to me as Rosa settled the orange blossoms into place again. "I like that one."

"So do I, dear," agreed the Countess. "The cowardly prince will have to wait for another day. We have far more important matters now."

Aunt Ellen arrived soon after Hetty finished her story, with Kat and Suze, who looked quite adorable in their pale-lavender dresses with slightly darker sashes. Adorable and bored.

Fortunately, the other young maiden in the party, Mack McTeer, was already there, downstairs with a book, just waiting for potential partners in crime. Kat and Suze greeted everyone with the rigorous politeness Aunt Ellen enforced, then skipped off to the stairs to join Mack, watching the arrivals.

On their way out, they almost ran over Sophia and her tea tray.

"I suspect you haven't had much to eat today, dear, and we don't need you fainting at the altar," Aunt Ellen said. "I asked the girls to bring us all a little something."

Of course, she did.

"A delightful idea," the Countess agreed. "We all need a bit of sustenance before the festivities."

Soon enough, the tea was gone, and Rosa and Anna helped me into my dress, and pinned the veil carefully into my hair, leaving my face still uncovered, as I stood at the mirror. Being a mezzo, I'd never played a bride, and never dreamed of being one in real life.

It was a shock and a delight to see myself in white satin and orange blossoms, the beaded embroidery catching the evening light from the windows, and the silk tulle of the veil swirling around me. Who was this woman? No one I'd ever met.

CHAPTER THIRTY-SIX

Maybe she would be the woman to snap Gil out of his reserve.

A knock at the door.

"Let's go, Heller, it's time."

Chapter Thirty-Seven

Before God and This Company

Tommy, elegant in black tie with a lilac sprig on his lapel, grinned as Aunt Ellen opened the door. "I think you'll do."

"More than do, Tom." Aunt Ellen smacked his arm and then pulled him in for a hug and kiss. "She looks like an angel."

"Don't act like one tonight, hey?" Marie whispered as she leaned in, with the excuse of handing me my bouquet. Lilacs, of course, sent by Gil.

Marie winked, and I blushed.

Marie, Hetty, and Anna slipped out, leaving Aunt Ellen and the Countess to the final task, pulling the veil over my face, which was normally the mother's duty.

"Shall we?" asked the Countess, nodding to Aunt Ellen as she reached for one side of the veil.

"Yes. God bless you, child." Aunt Ellen kissed my cheek, and the Countess the other. Then, they settled the veil in place.

The tulle was so fine it did very little to obscure my vision, but hopefully, it did obscure the fact that my eyes were already damp. I reached for Tommy's arm, and he patted my hand.

"Why nervous?" he asked with a twinkly smile. "You don't even have to sing."

We shared a laugh and stepped out onto the landing.

The piano began, Louis playing an adagio elegantly as if he were accompanying me in a fine opera house. Mack, Kat, and Suze actually walked gracefully before us all instead of blasting out ahead. Anna, Hetty, and Marie were smiling and all aglow as they led the way.

Tommy and I reached the doors.

Louis struck the familiar chords of the *Lohengrin* wedding march, and there was a rustle as everyone stood.

And then…

I saw Gil.

I know Father Michael was standing behind the improvised altar, and I know Jamie and Preston were beside Gil. I'm sure my friends and family were watching me with all the love and joy I felt in that room.

But I don't remember any of it.

All I remember is Gil's eyes meeting mine, an instant of a stunned stare, and then a smile. An amazing, joyful grin, almost like Jamie's, but all his own.

Oh, my.

By the time Tommy and I had covered the short distance to the altar, I'd recovered myself, but I was still blushing when Father Michael asked, "Who gives this woman to be married?"

"I do." Tommy raised the veil, kissed me on the cheek, and gave me a grin and a light punch on the arm as he went to take his place beside Preston and Jamie. Gil had decided to go with the British tradition of supporters, instead of a best man, and good thing.

Gil leaned down. "Astonishing, *mo chridhe.*"

I smiled.

"I'm a lucky man."

"I'm a lucky woman."

Father Michael was busy for a moment, welcoming the company to the ceremony, and I realized I'd better use my presence of mind while I still had it. "Did you talk to Cousin Andrew?" I whispered.

"Yes, and Alteiss too." Gil's sparkly smile turned grim. "She's no longer his client."

"Good."

"But the dress may not be enough for the prosecutor."

I sighed. "Then what?"

"I wish I knew."

"We can't let her get away with it."

"We won't, *mo chridhe*." He squeezed my hand.

"Perhaps Cousin Andrew would…"

"I can look at the autopsy report-"

Father Michael cleared his throat.

Gil and I looked at each other, suddenly and horribly aware that we had probably missed our vows.

"We do!"

Everyone in the room laughed at our unintentional unison. Father Michael shook his head. "Well, we know for certain that you're a perfect match. But if you could perhaps pay attention to the ceremony for a few moments?"

Both of us drooped a bit like the bad children we truly were at that instant. Except that I saw Gil glancing toward me as I was glancing to him, and we both had to choke down another laugh.

Tommy caught the whole exchange and coughed, covering his own snicker. Father Michael gave us all the dirtiest look he could manage, even though he was clearly holding back a chuckle too.

"The rings, please?" The priest held out his hand.

Jamie handed Gil my band. Marie gave me his. We passed them on to the priest, who gave us an impish smile that told us he was having a hard time holding his holy demeanor.

After the blessing, Father Michael turned to me. "Gilbert has decided that he would like to wear a wedding band just as Ellen does. Ellen?"

I picked the band up from the Bible and took Gil's hand. The warmth of his skin on mine reminded me of the crackle of current between us the first time our fingers touched, now more than a year ago.

"Repeat after me: I, Ellen, give you, Gilbert, this ring as a symbol of our love and our vows…"

"I, Ellen…" I looked up at him and our eyes held as I slipped the ring in place, my fingers suddenly shaky, my voice wobbling a bit on the last few words.

"Now, Gilbert."

It was a relief to feel his fingers a little unsteady too and to hear his Northern burr, even a bit raspier with emotion. Once he settled the ring on my hand, he lifted it to his lips, kissing the band.

A murmur behind us, a glare from the Father and another suppressed chuckle from Tommy. That was definitely not part of the Catholic ceremony—or the Anglican as far as I knew. Gil had likely intended it as a reverent gesture, but at least to me, it felt entirely different.

I blushed.

Gil saw my expression and quickly let go of my hand, blushing himself as he realized how I—and quite possibly everyone else—had taken it. He leaned over to me as we turned to Father Michael.

"I meant no-"

"Sssh…he's blessing us!"

"Yes, right."

Father Michael clearly assumed it was a little love talk, and he gave in to his grin then, deciding to enjoy our obvious happiness. "Well, then, now that Ellen and Gilbert have exchanged vows and rings in the presence of God and this company, it is my pleasure to pronounce them man and wife. May God give you every happiness."

At long last, we belonged to each other finally, formally, and forever.

British aristocrats do not kiss their brides at the altar, of course, and until very recently, neither did most Americans. It's beginning to be fashionable for bride and groom to exchange a brief embrace—but Gil and I had decided to follow the more reserved tradition, reasoning that no one wishes to see public displays of affection. Of course, now, he had just made quite an impressive one.

Father Michael took a breath, giving the congregation a moment to understand that we would not be taking part in the overly showy new ways, then beamed at us. He shook Gil's hand, then turned to me and kissed my cheek.

"All blessings to you both."

Gil offered me his arm, and we turned to the congregation.

"Now, ladies and gentlemen, I present to you the Duke and Duchess of Leith!"

The room exploded in applause, and the Countess picked up the coronet from the sideboard and started walking toward me.

"I'll be taking that now, lady."

And yet another of Aunt Ellen's visions came true, with people rushing into the room—and not the happy crowd of well-wishers I'd hoped she'd seen.

No, it started with Jim, of "Jim and Tim" infamy. He rushed through the open pocket door and grabbed at the piece with one hand, reaching for a gun at his waist with the other.

That, of course, was the mistake. Never go into combat with a Highlander if you're not prepared.

"Indeed you will not!" the Countess snapped, planting one of her small but sharp Louis heels in his instep.

Jim let out a cry and fumbled his gun, dropping it to the floor. It went off, startling everyone and shattering the glass shade of my favorite lamp.

Wretch.

Never mind interrupting my wedding, he should pay for that!

"Ella, dear!" As the Countess shouted, she tossed the coronet to me, sending it sailing through the air in a perfect arc. I jumped for it and made the catch just as Tim barreled up the aisle—to find Gil grabbing for him.

A third miscreant whom I'd never seen before just materialized from the hall and started moving toward me. I climbed up on the small occasional table and looked around. I did not see any other guns, which was a good sign. Not that we had the upper hand. Tim was still trying to escape Gil and likely would have succeeded if Tommy hadn't gotten a good handful of the back of the creep's shirt. Preston had jumped into the Countess's tussle with Jim, even though it wasn't at all clear that she needed help. But the newest gentleman in the cast was nearby and not occupied.

"Jamie!" I slung the coronet at my stepson exactly as the Countess had thrown it to me.

"Nice work, Belle Star!" he crowed, catching it cleanly. "Hah!"

I turned back to my attacker. Marie was distracting him quite nicely by beating him with her bouquet, but even with their sturdy, woody stems, the lilacs would not last long. I grabbed the first weapon that came to hand, a book (what else in our house?), and thumped him on the top of the head. But he was moving, and I could only land a glancing blow.

Only a glancing blow on a moving target...you'd have to be terribly lucky to take someone down on the first try. At that—the worst possible moment to think of it—I remembered that Chester Lorimer had only one wound to his head. And right at the temple.

A good criminologist could probably tell if he'd been hit when he was down.

If the dress wasn't enough for the District Attorney, surely that would be.

That was for later, though. First, we had to win this battle.

I looked around the room, relieved to see Aunt Ellen and Cousin Andrew's wife, Katie, shepherding the three young ladies into a safe corner. All three, especially Mack, had mutinous scowls that strongly suggested they'd like to be in on the action.

I offered a small prayer of thanks that they weren't.

Aunt Ellen was not so completely focused on the safety of her charges that she didn't manage to shoot me a triumphant glance. I had no doubt an "I told you so" was coming.

"I'll just keep you till they give up the crown," a rough voice said as a hand closed around my ankle. I could feel his scratchy palm through my thin silk stocking, and when I looked down, I got a generous whiff of whatever sort of garlic wurst he'd had for lunch. Disgusting.

And quite enough. He was almost still, holding me and leering, and this time, all too easy to just slug with the book, which wasn't heavy enough to do much damage, but did at least discourage him. He let go and I kicked him away.

"Belle Starr!" Jamie called to me, and without even thinking, I put my hands up. He tossed the coronet back, then waded into what had turned into some kind of messy close combat between Gil, Tommy, Preston, Jim,

239

and Tim.

Yet again, I felt scrabbling fingers on my shoe and stepped on my attacker.

"That's enough already!" Hetty snapped, kicking him quite firmly in the backside. Marie whacked him with the back end of her bouquet, but it was clear that I was going to have to help them finish him off.

"Ella dear!" The Countess was now just a few feet away from me, with Father Michael beside her, clearly trying to provide some protection. "Toss it back now."

I lobbed the coronet back to her. She made the catch as cleanly as any baseball outfielder and picked up one of the little gilt chairs with her free hand, holding it the way a lion tamer does. Father Michael shook his head and took up a chair himself. I was not entirely sure how he planned to use it...or on whom.

"Stop this now!" I snapped at my still struggling attacker, this time managing to land a kick on his jaw. Hetty and Marie saw him fall back and stepped out of the way.

He hit the floor hard, but not so hard that he was unconscious, when Marie planted one of her tiny satin slippers on him. In a very important spot.

"If you want to learn to sing castrato roles, just try to get away." Our usually sweet and mild Marie was flashing fury, and she didn't need to press her heel down to let him know she meant business. But she did.

"I'd watch it, friend," Hetty said, pulling my old stiletto out of her bouquet, but leaving it sheathed. "That little lady's a killer."

"So's the redhead," Marie added, nodding to her companion. "Stabbed a man in the eye once because he looked at her funny."

The robber swallowed hard and closed *his* eyes, whether from the physical shoc, or the horror of being bested by two adorable ladies who knew. My maid and matron of honor grinned.

The men had finally gotten the upper hand with their criminals as well. I looked over just in time to see Preston, Tommy and now Rafe closing in on Jim. The robber looked between the three of them, and then Tommy grinned at Rafe. "You want him, he's yours."

Rafe, who'd probably been itching for just this opportunity since he saw Miss O'Hanlon's hand on the man's arm in the park last week, delivered the *coup de grace* in a right cross that might not have been as technically perfect as Tommy's, but was surely more strongly motivated.

Preston, who knew everything in play, laughed and stepped in as Jim went down, putting a foot on the robber's back. "No need for more, Coyne."

On the other side of the aisle, Gil and Jamie had backed up Tim, who was still casting about for a way to get to the door. Just then, Miss O'Hanlon appeared in the archway with a huge tray of silverware for the reception.

Tim turned, clearly hoping to push her aside and leave.

"Miss Mary!" shouted Rafe. "Run!"

Running was the last thing on Mary O'Hanlon's mind.

She didn't need anyone to tell her that very bad things were happening here. Her eyes flashed green fire, and suddenly, she wasn't a nice young lady cook, but an Irish warrior queen defending her castle. She hurled the tray at Tim. As forks and spoons rained down upon him, the criminal turned back into the room.

And right into the path of Jamie and Gil.

Father and son exchanged a glance, then punched him together, landing hard shots to opposite sides of his jaw.

Usually, at times like this, one says the person never knew what hit him. But I don't think there's much doubt that Tim knew exactly and precisely what hit him.

Mary O'Hanlon took a smart step out of Tim's path as he fell, and Rafe took her hands and pulled her the rest of the way, not that he really needed to. And not that she really minded.

As the robber made his not-very-gentle landing, Gil put a foot on his chest and shook his son's hand. "Well done, James."

"Yourself as well, Pater."

A few feet away, Rafe was still very carefully holding Miss O'Hanlon's hands and staring at her with an expression that would not have been out of place on a baby duck. She was smiling back, more than a little bemused herself.

Perhaps more than one happy ending in the offing.

"What the hell is going on here? Sorry, Ellen."

Connor Coughlan stood in the doorway, a pistol in one hand and—of all impossible things—Prince Mrzawzy in the other.

Just when you thought our wedding couldn't get more interesting.

Chapter Thirty-Eight

Unkind Hearts and Coronets

Connor strode into the room, dragging the alleged prince by the collar. He gave Gil a wry grin. "Quite a donnybrook, Saint Audrey. We Irish only *dance* at weddings."

Gil laughed. "Well, it looks as though you've found our last unwanted guest."

"Didn't I, though?" He chuckled as he nudged the alleged prince with his pistol. "We're done here, Mr. Prince."

"How dare you, you ruffian—"

Connor responded with a wicked little scowl. "I dare pretty well. I was in the street just now when those ugly friends of yours handed you those other jewels before coming in here to get some more cake."

Prince Mrzawzy wilted a bit.

"What's going on here?" Cousin Andrew ran in and took in the scene, his eyes widening as he tried to figure out what it all meant. "Coughlan!"

"No problem here, Riley. I'm on your side this time." Connor gave the copper a friendly nod and put his pistol back in his waistband. "I came by to kiss the bride and just happened into a bit of excitement."

"Yes?"

"The wedding party took care of those three numbskulls...and I happened along to take out the rest of the trash." Connor gave the Prince a shove toward the detective, who reflexively took his arm.

The henchmen were moving a little, and Jim let out a groan, which got him just a bit more pressure from Preston's foot on his back. Tim just looked up at Gil with a resigned expression.

Marie and Hetty's catch, whose name we did not learn that day, opened his eyes, assessed his situation, sighed, and closed them again.

I had such a good view of course, because I was still standing on the table. Tommy was closest, and he offered me a hand down.

Cousin Andrew looked around the room again, catching a small glare from his wife, who was still in the far corner with Mack, Aunt Ellen and the cousins. "I just stepped out for a second during the last blessing to call my captain about the Lorimer matter..."

"Well, obviously, dear boy, our miscreants waited for their opportunity." The Countess sighed, holding up the coronet as she nodded to the purple velvet cube on the shelf behind Tommy. "Give me the box for the moment. The coronet is quite fragile."

He chuckled as he handed it over. "Not that fragile."

"Indeed not." She grinned and settled the piece in its satin nest. "But I want it to be safe until we put it on, dear Ella."

"Can we sort this out first?" Cousin Andrew asked wearily.

"Simple enough," Gil began, pointing to his miscreant. "These three charming fellows decided they wanted to add the Leith coronet to the collection of jewels they'd already stolen at the Polish wedding this morning."

"And we discouraged them." Preston gave in to a wicked grin. Out of the corner of my eye, I saw Greta shake her head and stifle a laugh. It was no more than I wanted to do.

"Quite strongly." Marie smiled at Hetty and moved her heel a fraction. Her suspect let out a squeak.

"Perhaps too strongly." Tommy glanced to Marie, and she backed up a touch.

"Definitively, at least," Jamie said, turning to his father and sharing the exact same bad-child grin.

"Which is when Mr. Coughlan walked in, bringing Prince Mrzawzy," Gil continued, attempting some semblance of a serious tone.

"Unless I'm mistaken, Saint Audrey, he's no Polish Prince."

Connor and Gil held each other's gaze for a second, and I was reminded that they had had a confluence of interests before. One never knew.

Then they nodded together, sharing a much different, and scary smile. A pair of extremely bad boys.

"Sadly, not even a Pole." Gil agreed, his eyes turning almost as cold as Connor's. "Meet just plain Jerry Moore of Pittsburgh. Went West looking for gold and got there too late for that, but just in time for any number of confidence games. But the American authorities will be happy to get their hands on him. Which he might well prefer to the Tsar's justice."

Prince Mrzawzy—Jerry Moore—was suddenly very pale.

"Penalties for theft are rather more severe in the Eastern Empire, Your—er—Serene Highness," Gil offered.

"Not too serene now." Connor chuckled.

"With cause." Gil nodded. "The District Attorney will likely prefer to leave that to the various consulates to sort out. In the meantime, Detective, you have your three suspects in the Polish Wedding robbery, who will be more than happy to implicate their mastermind."

"It's a good deal for me." Cousin Andrew agreed, then quickly glanced suspiciously around the room. "What do you get out of it, Coughlan?"

Connor's jovial grin returned then. "Why, simply the pleasure of knowing that everyone ends up where they belong, Detective Riley."

Cousin Andrew watched him with a gimlet glare as he crossed to me. Connor still had that cheerfully wicked expression when he took my hands and turned to the detective.

"And I get to kiss the bride and wish her well."

His face changed as he looked down at me, taking on that gentle expression he gave no one else. Once he had asked me if I had read medieval romances in which a man who cannot have the woman he admires makes sure she's safe and happy with an appropriate husband.

I knew then what it meant. And I saw it now, as he held my gaze, all of the things that would never, could never, be said hanging between us. We both knew Gil was the only man for me, but we still had that shared bond of brutal childhoods, and the knowledge that if we had not taken opposite turns off Orchard Street, life might have been far different.

Not better.

I could never explain that to Gil.

"Be happy." Connor bent and kissed me on the forehead, just a gentle, innocent gesture like a brother would do.

"Thank you." My voice came out a little raspy with emotion. "For everything."

"No, Ellen." The name I was born with, as always an endearment in his mouth. "I owe you my life. I never forget that."

He squeezed my hands and pulled back. "All happiness to the bride."

I nodded.

Connor turned and walked toward the door, stopping at Gil. They shook hands and held for a moment longer than expected.

"Be good to her, Saint Audrey."

"Impossible to be anything else."

"What I like to hear." He didn't need to say anything more. We all knew what that meant, too.

Connor resolutely turned from Gil and stalked out, walking right past the uniformed officers running in to scoop up the robbers.

It would not surprise you, or anyone who knows many gangsters start their careers as pickpockets, to learn when the officers searched our alleged Prince Mrzawzy, all they found was that splashy engagement ring he'd given Mrs. Lally. It was engraved and damning enough evidence, of course, but not—since it turned out to be actually tourmaline and white zircon — anywhere near as valuable as the bride's diamond necklace and bracelets. Those, interestingly, would never be seen again.

It may surprise you a bit more that Pearl Lally married a Hungarian Grand Duke three months later, and the two were happy as the proverbial clams until his untimely death from a dyspeptic attack a few years after that—by which time he'd also made her a Papal Countess, a very rare and coveted title in some circles.

That was neither here nor there at the moment. As the coppers dragged our robbers away, I turned to Gil. Whatever I was going to say flew right out of my mind when our eyes met.

"A moment, my lady wife?" he asked, his voice low and warm, as he glanced about to be sure all eyes were on the apprehension—and not us.

I nodded.

He took my hands and pulled me into the little alcove under the stairs, drawing me into a kiss that had all the wonderful intensity of the night he returned. The reserve was gone, and my Wicked Duke was back, and mine, all mine.

The small part of my mind capable of producing rational thoughts wondered if Dr. Silver had been right about giving him a chance to play the hero.

Or perhaps he was reminding me to whom I belonged after that moment with Connor. Not that *I* had ever had any question.

Never mind. I had other things to occupy my concentration. In the best possible way. Gil pulled me closer, his hands around my waist, his mouth hot on mine...

"Children!"

The voice was annoyed and very far away.

We ignored it.

It had nothing to do with us, and we had much better things to do.

Much, much better.

"Children, really!"

This time, we realized it might indeed have something to do with us.

We pulled apart a fraction, but did not break the embrace, my hands still on Gil's chest, his arms firmly around me.

The Countess was standing in the archway slapping at Gil with her handkerchief, a mix of amusement and annoyance in her face. "Surely you can behave yourselves for a couple of hours."

I took a breath. So did Gil.

"Mother, we—"

"Have guests to greet. And good heavens, what are we going to do with poor Ella's hair?"

Gil and I started laughing. So did the Countess.

"Ah, well, if anyone deserves to sneak off for a few minutes at the reception, it's you two." Her smile turned a little rueful. "I did the same with your father."

Gil's eyes widened, and if the Countess had hoped to supply a dash of cold water, her comment surely accomplished the purpose.

"All right, then, Gilbert. Let me get Ella straightened up and into this coronet."

As he pulled back from me, he kissed my cheek and whispered one word: "Later."

I blushed. There was hope yet.

One might say I gave it away, but I had fair cause. I suppose I had so much else on my mind I did not remember to maintain my proper face as I exchanged a formal greeting embrace with Mrs. Corbyn.

So, we shall blame it on the coronet. The little corner of my mind that should have been devoted to dissembling was instead devoted to the worry that the quite literally hard-won sign and symbol of my new status would fall right off my head and bash her in the nose.

Which is when I remembered my thoughts about the criminology in her case.

How hard it would be to land a significant blow on a moving target. How much easier to brain someone once they were down. She was a fairly sturdy woman, and Lorimer was unsteady enough on his feet to need a cane.

All it would have taken was a healthy shove.

And the rock.

I caught Cousin Andrew's eye as I pulled back. I meant only to have a word with him before we left on the honeymoon, to make sure he knew all that Gil and I did about the Lorimer matter.

But Aline Corbyn was guilty, and the guilty flee where no man pursueth. Not to mention that I'm a horrible dissembler at my best, and with so much else on my mind at that moment...

It is not, I admit, much of an excuse, but it will do for an explanation.

As we released the formal embrace, she took a hard glance at my face, and saw something.

"You know, don't you."

"That it was very kind of you to come to—"

"Oh, do shut up. Of course, I removed him. We were not going to let him turn that lovely house into a home for a bunch of dirty old soldiers."

In addition to being sharp-eyed, Cousin Andrew has excellent hearing. Especially when walking over to greet the bride and killer. He nodded grimly.

"They'll never convict me. He was-"

"He wasn't because he couldn't." I met her stunned gaze coolly. "And the way your dress was ripped, not to mention the angle of the death blow would demolish your story even if the other facts in evidence would not. It is not my place to advise, Mrs. Corbyn, but I suggest you consult your lawyer. Mr. Alteiss has no doubt found you appropriate counsel."

Her face tightened, and her small eyes glowed with poison. "How dare you, you jumped-up Jewish foundling—"

It was of course intended as an insult. But I had no intention of taking delivery. "That's exactly what I am, and proud of it."

"And," Gil said, stepping up and taking my hand, "I am very fortunate that she has done me the honor of becoming my wife."

"Disgusting!" Mrs. Corbyn snapped. "What is the world coming to? Nobody knows their place anymore."

"I know yours." Cousin Andrew said calmly behind her. "Jail."

She wheeled on him.

"Mrs. Aline Corbyn, on the strength of your own confession, I am placing you under arrest for the murder of Chester Lorimer."

And so came the second untoward incident of our wedding, though thankfully, this one was shorter and much less disruptive. Cousin Andrew offered an apologetic shrug to his wife, and guided Mrs. Corbyn out.

Gil raised my hand to his lips. "Well done, wife."

"Say that again."

"Well done?"

"No."

"Wife."

"That's the one."

Chapter Thirty-Nine

In Which the Countess and Jamie Stun All

"Ella dear, you're looking a bit peaky."

I was fluffing the lace on my shirtwaist after putting on the jacket of my going-away suit when the Countess spoke. I didn't catch quite what she'd said, because I was a bit distracted.

Aunt Ellen had just given me a hug and kiss—and of course, that "I told you so"—then swept out, leaving me, as she said, to my new family. Well, she wasn't able to resist one last whispered reminder to not be too shocked by my husband's "demands."

I couldn't very well shock *her* by saying I might well have demands of my own, so I'd mumbled something dutiful and given her what I hoped was a brave smile.

And promptly returned to thinking about the various demands that might await me at the hotel. Not with trepidation, either. Not after that kiss in the alcove...

I realized the Countess was waiting for me to respond.

"I'm sorry—Mother?"

It was the first time I'd called her that, and we shared a joyful smile.

"Ah, very nice, darling." The grin widened. "But really, you're looking a little tired, and I do think you might need a wee sweet. So do I." She reached for the point of the coronet and broke off the top pearl, then popped it in her mouth.

My jaw dropped.

"Gilbert is not the only one with friends in the Foreign Office." Her eyes had a wicked sparkle. "Barley sugar would never be a believable simulation for diamonds, but of course, we are a border clan and have a magnificent collection of ancient Scottish pearls."

"We do?"

"Well, of course we do. But I was not going to deliver them into the hands of that nasty Prince Mrzawzy and his jewel thief friends. Don't worry, dear. When there is a Coronation, hopefully, quite a while from now, God save our Queen, the coronet will come out of its very safe vault."

"I thought as much, Mother."

At some point during that amazing soliloquy, Gil had walked in, as was, after all the husband's prerogative. He gave her a dry smile.

"Pater?"

His son, a step behind, observing the whole scene. Father and son exchanged significant glances, nodded, then each snapped off a pearl from the top row.

"Tasty," Jamie observed.

"A bit bland. I might have suggested a touch more rosewater. But well done, Mother."

The countess met their wicked grins with her own.

I have just joined a clan of highland bandits, I thought.

Then Gil turned to Jamie, who handed him a tiny blue velvet box. "Ah, thank you, *a bhobain*."

"My pleasure." His son gazed back at him with the exact same smile. "I was glad to have a wedding errand to do in addition to talking to your friend at the Russian embassy."

The Countess and I gave them a puzzled glance.

"Count Soloviev had heard of our pretend prince?" Gil asked.

"Indeed he had." Jamie nodded. "Seems Mr. Jerry Moore charmed a minor Princess in Petersburg out of some rather nice pieces a few years ago. Same idea, though that time he posed as an American timber magnate."

Gil chuckled. "Of course he did."

252

"He would have been caught if he tried to be a Polish prince at the Romanov court," Jamie pointed out. "No one there knew any more about American businessmen than people here do about Polish Princes."

"Just so, son." Gil's face shone with fatherly pride. "Good work."

The Countess and I shared a tiny smile, and once again, I hoped I'd someday get to see Gil look at our own wee one with such joy.

"But what put you on this?" asked the Countess. "It's not as if there aren't plenty of imposter princes running about."

Gil colored and narrowed his eyes at his mother. "Pearl Lally's sister is Charlotte—er, Landgravine von Stade's—sister-in-law, and the family was concerned that Mrzawzy might be a bounder."

"So you followed him on to the *Atlantic Star.*" I could not stop the tiny wobble in my voice at the name of the ship that had almost been his grave.

Gil took my hand. "I did, *mo chridhe.* It was the right thing to do, and-"

I took a breath and nodded. "No question about that. When you know that someone could be harmed, you have a duty to stop them. You had no way to know…"

He squeezed my fingers. "And I came back to you."

"Only after giving us all a truly dreadful scare, Gilbert." His mother narrowed her eyes a bit at him, exactly as he'd just done to her. "I am still quite angry with you about those three days of waiting for word."

He blushed and looked to me. "I have apologized to you both, and my Foreign Office friends owe me what I believe Mr. Coughlan would call a rather large marker after all this."

"They should." She glanced to me, but I did not want to join this wrangle. I would be just as happy to forget those days.

"Well, I plan to use that debt to smooth my wife's path."

"Really?" I asked in surprise.

"Well, yes. When Ellen, Duchess of Leith, makes her debut-"

"Ellen?" I had assumed I would go by Ella. That he would not want me to use the name I was born with in the tenements.

"There's nothing wrong with your real name, Shane."

"Indeed not. Such a pretty name, and a family one at that." The Countess smiled. "My father's aunt was named Ellen. It's quite appropriate for you to use it."

"All right, then."

She put her hand on my arm with a gentle smile. "I will not, however, be able to change now, since I think of you as my dear Ella," she added decidedly.

"That's quite all right...Mother."

I patted her arm, too, as we shared a smile. Truly family now.

"At any rate," Gil said, reclaiming the conversation, "you shall have an absolutely rapturous welcome, because my friends will insist that their wives give you one."

Rapturous was perhaps a poor—and telling—choice of words, in view of what remained on the agenda for the evening. And I doubted the society ladies of London would be especially amenable to sharing tea with a woman most considered one very small step removed from a streetwalker.

That, however, was another fight for another day.

"Thank you for the other errand as well, James." Gil patted his son's shoulder and turned to me with the little box.

Jamie winked at his grandmother, and she grinned back.

"Shane, I know why you only accepted my mother's tiny ring for our engagement and insisted on the plain wedding band, but I think my duchess needs something a bit fancier when she's not on the stage."

Only when he handed me the box did I recognize the distinctive deep purplish-blue shade of the velvet as that used by a very good London jeweler. *Oh my.*

Far more than that when I opened it. Inside was a ring, a thin pavé band with one sizable square-cut stone at the center, lilac-colored, the light striking a hectic sparkle that told me it wasn't an amethyst. "What?"

"A lavender fancy diamond," Gil said with a small, deliberately modest shrug. "I thought you might be willing to wear a jewel if it were your favorite color."

Not to mention exceedingly rare and insanely expensive, however simply set, I knew. "It's lovely."

254

"Unique and beautiful, just like you." Gil took my left hand for the second time that day and carefully settled the diamond in place over my wedding ring. "I know you cannot wear it on the stage…"

"But at all other times, I can…and it will be in your waistcoat pocket when I perform."

We shared our first smile of perfect marital understanding. I turned to Jamie. "Thank you for bringing it safely here."

"Always a pleasure, Belle Starr."

Gil's eyes narrowed a tinge, and the Countess gave him a light slap on the arm. "You should be more respectful, grandson."

I shared the family bandit grin with Jamie, then cut my eyes to my husband. "He says it in a completely respectful tone. And what's a grown man to do when he acquires a stepmother anyhow?"

The senior Saint Aubyns shrugged.

"Dear Ella does have a point," the Countess allowed.

Gil decided to walk past the entire dispute. "Well done with the ring and the rest, James."

His son blushed a bit and bowed, then turned to me. "Well, Belle Starr, you and Pater have a honeymoon to start…"

The Countess took a moment to admire my hand, then smoothed the lapels of my jacket. She picked up the little ribboned lilac corsage from the vanity and pinned it on. "Lovely."

"And you gave us a lovely ceremony, Mother."

"Thank you, *mo laochain*."

"Heller! Stop dilly-dallying!" Tommy yelled as he knocked.

We all laughed.

Jamie opened the door, and Gil took my hand. On the landing, Tommy and Preston were waiting.

The Countess took Jamie's arm and guided him to the stairs, leaving us to our moment.

"I'm not ever going to call you 'Your Grace,' kid," Preston said, leaning in and kissing me on the cheek. "Just be happy. That's all."

I nodded. "Thank you."

"And you, Barrister, don't think things to death, all right?"

Gil gave him a puzzled glance as they shook hands but left it. Preston headed down the stairs to join Greta near the door, near a beaming Dr. Silver. I noticed that Alteiss had arrived, too, standing beside Hetty. They were a good pair.

Whether anything would come of it, who knew, but if Gil and I could agree on a marriage, surely they had a chance.

"All set for the trip?" Tommy asked. "The luggage was sent on, and the cab's waiting."

"That's it, then."

For a full stanza, we stood there, just watching each other, knowing that life was changing around us, even if the bond between us could never be broken.

"Enjoy the Falls," he said, his voice a bit raspy with emotion, pulling me in for a quick hug.

"Back for the Fourth of July." There was a tiny wobble in my voice.

"You never miss the fireworks." He grinned. "And this year, Cabot is reading Lincoln's Second Inaugural at the ceremony."

"Good. You two can cheer on the Giants while we're gone."

"We can only hope. At least they're not the Spiders."

And once more, the wretched Cleveland Spiders supplied a much-needed laugh for us all. God love them.

"Come along, dear!" called the Countess, adding in her best practical tone: "You don't want to pay the driver for just sitting there!"

Tommy went down the stairs first, and then, as Gil and I took the first steps, started the applause. We didn't have rice, of course, being inside, and my bouquet was a casualty of the battle with the jewel thieves.

But as we reached the foyer floor, I realized there was one thing I could do. I unpinned the corsage from my lapel and tossed it right at Hetty.

She glared for an instant.

"It's not a bouquet, silly. It's just a start. Something that might *become* a bouquet if you give it some love and care...and don't crush it before you give it a chance."

CHAPTER THIRTY-NINE

Rowan grinned. "I like that idea."

Hetty smiled. "Fair enough."

"Get out of here, already!" Preston called.

The applause began again, and Gil took my hand.

"Now?" he asked.

"Now."

Epilogue

...And Think of England

When we arrived in our suite, Gil kissed my hand and muttered something about having brought a good book, so I should feel free to take as much time as I liked to change. I suspected I'd best not leave him with that book for long, lest his nerves return.

Mine certainly had.

The cab ride had been short, but not so short I didn't have time to think about the night ahead. And what it would mean for our marriage if it didn't go well.

In any case, the first task was a familiar one: a costume change.

I'd chosen that simple going-away suit, elegantly styled by Anna in light-violet cashmere, with the specific intent of something easy to put on and take off so that I would not require Rosa's help on this particular night. Probably, as the wife of a British aristocrat and a lady who attends the occasional evening event, never mind performing, I would eventually have to accept the idea of being undressed and handed over to my husband like some kind of offering at night, but it was definitely not something I wanted this first time.

So that at least was no more difficult than any other change I've made, whatever the stakes.

Once done, I took a last look at myself in the mirror. Hair down and brushed, a little lip salve, a dab of Marie's seductive tuberose perfume, and, of course, the frothy lace and silk peignoir from the Countess. I supposed I would do.

Time to stop thinking and worrying and wondering. *Just live it*, Preston had said.

Gil was in the sitting room, his jacket off, tie and waistcoat loose, leaning on the mantel with a whiskey in his hand, watching the empty fireplace. The book needless to say, was nowhere in evidence. Even though the shine of his new ring warmed my heart, I could see the tension in his fingers around the glass and the tightness in his jaw.

I would never have suspected it after our embrace at the wedding, but just as I'd returned to my worries, so had he. And he was at least as nervous as I was.

Nothing for it now.

You will have to be brave and bold enough for both of you, the Countess had said. *Sweep him off his feet and let nature take its course.*

I walked over to him and very carefully took the whiskey glass out of his hand.

Gil stared at me for a second. "Do you want—"

"I want you."

His eyes widened.

I took the last of the whiskey as a shot and set the glass on the mantelpiece with a firm click. "Close your eyes and think of England if you have to."

He laughed, then, and pulled me into his arms. "Well played, Shane."

I got on tiptoe and kissed him, and that was all it took.

After all that.

One simple kiss.

The nerves and the tension and the worry vanished as if they'd never been real at all, and they hadn't. What *was* real—the love and attraction between us—rushed back, blotting out everything else. All that mattered was we were there, and together, and alone.

In the wrong room and wearing far too many clothes, but that was easily remedied.

Gil scooped me up, without breaking the kiss, and carried me to the

259

bedroom, kicking the door closed behind us. Probably overplaying, the swashbuckling hero a little, but I had no complaints.

No complaints on the other side of the door, either.

And yes, Marie was right. About everything.

It *was* quite delightful to discover one's spouse.

I told him so, much later, when we were lying twined together and watching the moonlight filter through the blinds.

He smiled and pulled me a bit closer, and his fingers brushed the healing scar on my ribs. The smile faded immediately. "You nearly died for me. I was afraid I could not live up to you."

"I was afraid of disappointing *you*." I snuggled closer to him, still amazed at the feeling of his skin on mine. Just a few months ago, we'd been shocked at the electricity when our fingers touched.

"Never, *mo chridhe*. But I'd never been with a woman who was—innocent, and even with all the good advice of Dr. Silver and Madame Marie, a maiden is still a maiden."

"No more."

"No, no more." He buried his face in my loose hair, kissing the neck beneath. "I know it's supposed to be the treasure of all—but *you're* my treasure, Shane, and I would not have minded if you'd come with a little experience…well, as long as the bounder was safely dead."

"Really?" I turned to him to get a better look at his face.

"Absolutely." He smiled a bit sheepishly as he twined a stray curl around his free hand. "It's quite challenging for a man, you know. All you had to do was arrive pure and untouched, and the rest was up to me."

"You managed rather nicely." I kissed him lightly. "And I really was worried about pleasing *you*, you know."

Gil did laugh at that. "Men are easy to please. A willing, loving woman is all we want. And all I want is you."

Dr. Silver, I thought, was entirely right about men and their fragile feelings.

"All I want is you." I ran my hand down his bare shoulder, enjoying the feel of his skin and the way he smiled in response.

"A waste of time, waiting and worrying. At the very least, I should have taken you up on your kind offer at my rooms."

"Kind offer?"

"I am attempting to be delicate."

"Ah. I think we are well past delicacy."

"Too true." His hand moved away from my scar to a much more pleasant place. "You were right."

"Get used to saying that."

"After this rather hard lesson, yes."

"Hard lesson indeed."

He chuckled. "A smart man knows when to obey his woman."

"And you are a very smart man."

"Smart enough to know when to stop talking, for certain." He pulled me closer.

"When there are so many better things to do…"

I do not need to tell you we never did find out if Eggs Benedict was on offer for breakfast. Or that many further misadventures followed our marriage…not all of them involving our feisty progeny.

Acknowledgements

First, thanks to my agent, Eric Myers, and editor, Verena Rose, for giving me a chance to continue Ella's story.

Deep appreciation to my Sisters in Crime sibs, on the National Social Media Team, NY/SinC Board, and SinC-CT for their support.More gratitude to Kevin Tipple, Short Mystery Fiction Society President...I'm the Vice President, so I'm supposed to be his backup, but it's turned out the other way around!

Finally, to my families of work, blood, and choice. I don't have the words to thank you or the space to tell each of you what you've meant to me over the last few rough years. Just know that I appreciate you every single day.

With love and gratitude,

Kathleen Marple Kalb

About the Author

Kathleen Marple Kalb describes herself as an Author/Anchor/Mom…not in that order. An award-winning weekend anchor at New York's 1010 WINS Radio, she writes short stories and novels including the Ella Shane and Old Stuff series, both from Level Best Books. Her stories, under her own name, and as Nikki Knight, have been in *Alfred Hitchcock's Mystery Magazine, Black Cat Weekly, Mystery Magazine*, and others, and short-listed for Derringer and Black Orchid Novella Awards. Active in writer's groups, she's served as Vice President of the Short Mystery Fiction Society and Co-VP of the New York/Tri-State Sisters in Crime Chapter. She, her husband, and son live in a Connecticut house owned by their cat.

SOCIAL MEDIA HANDLES:
   Facebook:https://www.facebook.com/Kathleen-Marple-Kalb-1082949845220373/
   Twitter: https://twitter.com/KalbMarple Instagram: https://www.instagram.com/kathleenmarplekalb/
   Threads: @kathleenmarplekalb
   Bluesky: @mysterymarple.bsky.social

AUTHOR WEBSITE: **https://kathleenmarplekalb.com/**

Also by Kathleen Marple Kalb

Ella Shane Mysteries (Kensington)
A Fatal Finale (2020)
A Fatal First Night (2021)
A Fatal Overture (2022)

Old Stuff Mysteries:
The Stuff of Murder (2023)

Vermont Radio Mysteries – As Nikki Knight
Live, Local and Dead (2022) Crooked Lane
Live, Local, and LONG Dead – Fall 2024 from Wild Rose Press

Grace the Hit Mom Mysteries – As Nikki Knight (Keylight Books)
Wrong Poison (2023)
Hound of the Bonnevilles (forthcoming May 2025)

Short Stories in Magazines, Anthologies, and online, including:
"A Fatal Saint Patrick's Day" (Ella Shane Mystery) in Luck of the Irish Anthology, March 2024
"No Angels Here," *Black Cat Weekly*, December 2023
"The New York Goodbye," *Black Cat Weekly*, September 2023
"The Telltale Request," *Mystery Magazine*, September 2023
"Second Chances are…Murder," *Malice, Matrimony, and Murder Anthology*, November 2023
"Pie a La Poison," in *The Perp Wore Pumpkin*, Misti Media, November 2023
"The Custodian of the Body," (Old Stuff Mystery), *Black Cat Weekly*, May 2023
"This Never Happened to Wolfman Jack," M2D4 Podcast August 2023, season anthology, November 2023
"Don't Mess with the Boss Cat," CatsCast Podcast by Escape Artists, June

2023

"The Annual Mud Season Homicide," *Alfred Hitchcock's Mystery Magazine*, May/June 2023

"Owl Be Damned," Mysteryrat's Maze Podcast, January 2023

"Blame it on the Blizzard," Deadly Nightshade: Best New England Crime Stories 2022

www.ingramcontent.com/pod-product-compliance
Lightning Source LLC
Chambersburg PA
CBHW050152120726
47903CB00002B/586